SILENCE IS GOLDEN

Presented by

the Exxon Foundation

PACIFIC
GROVE
PUBLIC
LIBRARY

SILENCE IS GOLDEN

A HILDA JOHANSSON MYSTERY

Jeanne M. Dams

Walker & Company ✹ *New York*

First published in the United States of America in 2002 by
Walker Publishing Company, Inc.

Published simultaneously in Canada by Fitzhenry and Whiteside,
Markham, Ontario L3R 4T8

For information about permission to reproduce selections from
this book, write to Permissions, Walker & Company, 435 Hudson
Street, New York, New York 10014

Library of Congress Cataloging-in-Publication Data

Dams, Jeanne M.
    Silence is golden : a Hilda Johansson mystery / Jeanne M. Dams.
       p.   cm.
    ISBN 0-8027-3373-5
    1. Johansson, Hilda (Fictitious character)—Fiction.   2. South Bend
(Ind.)—Fiction.   3. Women domestics—Fiction.   I. Title.

PS3554.A498 S55   2002
813'.54—dc21   2002016780

Visit Walker & Company's Web site at www.walkerbooks.com

Series design by M. J. DiMassi

Printed in the United States of America

2 4 6 8 10 9 7 5 3 1

To Barbara D'Amato, whose talent is awesome,
whose kindness and generosity are limitless,
and whose friendship I hold dear.

Preface

Dorothy L. Sayers called her *Busman's Honeymoon* "a love story with detective interruptions." This book might fairly be so characterized. Both family love and romantic love play such a large part in the story that I felt I owed readers a warning. In my own defense, I may say that I never had the least idea of allowing the relationship between Hilda and Patrick to become so complicated, but characters often seem to make their own decisions about such things. An author must either be ruthless in dictating actions and emotions, or else let the characters work out their own destinies. Some time ago, I chose the latter course.

Those interested in such things might like to know that I looked up the word "kid," meaning "child," to make sure it wasn't too recent a usage for a book set in 1903. The first such usage cited in the *Oxford English Dictionary* is dated 1599. And I had thought the word might be too modern!

The headache powders Hilda took might have been aspirin. This miracle drug was developed by the Bayer people early in the century, but I have been unable to determine when it became widely available in America. However, preparations of willow bark had been marketed for some time, and willow bark contains acetylsalicylic acid, the active property of aspirin.

The core of this story reflects an event that did happen in South Bend in 1903, the beating and sexual abuse by a trapeze artist of a little girl. Presumably the child was raped, but since such things could not be reported in the newspapers of the day, the *Tribune* leaves one to read between the lines.

I have interpolated other real events with fictional ones. The Ringling Brothers circus did visit South Bend on April 27, 1903. There really was a Chapin Street gang. The orphan train was real, though I can find no evidence that it stopped in South Bend that year. The entire background of the story, the gritty world of child abuse and abandonment, the diseases running rampant, the overflowing orphans' home—all really existed. It was not a good time and place to be a child.

SILENCE IS GOLDEN

1

BIG CROWD AT THE CIRCUS
Record Breaking Day For Ringling Brothers Shows
—SOUTH BEND *TRIBUNE*, APRIL 28, 1903

MUCH later, after it was all over, after the fear and the anguish and the horror were past, Hilda was to wonder when and how it began. Had it been when the other boy disappeared, a year ago and more? Perhaps even farther back, when a twisted mind first conceived a dreadful plan?

For her and those she loved, it really began that day in the park . . .

"And I'll treat you both! Now, how's that for a handsome offer?" Patrick gave Hilda his most winning smile, twisting one end of his luxuriant mustache.

Hilda pushed with her toe and set her swing into gentle motion. "I would like that, Patrick," she said mildly, "but Erik—"

"I want to go!" Erik jumped from his swing. "Oh, please! I'll be good, I promise. All my *life* I've wanted to go to the circus!"

His face was full of passionate longing, and Hilda smiled. It was certainly true that her little brother wasn't getting a lot of fun out of life. But as Erik's life compassed only a little more than twelve years, and he had never heard of a circus until his arrival in America five months ago, she was not overly concerned. "I do not mind. You may come if you wish. Only—Mama will not like it."

Erik's face fell. He dug one toe into the ground and scowled. "Mama never lets me do *anything*. Or anybody else, either. I bet she won't even let *you* go. Not with Mr. Cavanaugh."

"I will do as I think best," Hilda said, raising her chin. "I am a grown woman, not a naughty little boy. You have given Mama much worry, Erik. You know you have."

"And so have you!" Erik shot back. "She doesn't like you goin' around with a Catholic. It's wicked, she says. She says—"

"That," said Patrick, "is enough out of you, me boy! Now run off and play, and let your sister and me have some peace."

"But I want—"

The combined glares of Hilda and Patrick silenced him. Scuffing the grass defiantly with his Sunday shoes, he set off to find more congenial company. He found it almost immediately in a boy Hilda knew slightly, a friend of Erik's who lived near the Johansson family. The two of them capered away, shouting and turning cartwheels. Patrick watched them with amusement.

"He's a pretty good acrobat, that one. Look at that! Flipped right over and landed on his feet. Who is he?"

"His name is Fritz, I think. I cannot remember his last name. He is German. They live just around the corner from my family, on Robertson Street."

"Lookit me! Watch me!" The timeless boy-cries came faintly from a far corner of the park, where Fritz (if that was his name) was walking along the narrow railing at the park's edge, as surefooted as if it were the grass.

Hilda frowned. "He should not do that. The river is just on the other side. If he should fall—or if Erik should decide to try—"

But Fritz did not fall, nor did he entice Erik to dangerous

feats. He jumped down and led Erik on a wild chase through the trees.

Hilda sighed and prodded her swing into motion once more. The grass was damp. Beneath the swings it was sparse, turning to mud in places. April had not been a kind month thus far. With Easter a week past, the weather was still wet and cold. Though the clouds that hovered overhead were not actually producing rain, they obviously intended to do so any minute.

It wasn't the best sort of afternoon for the park, but Hilda and Patrick nearly always went there when they walked out together, and she wasn't free to pick and choose her times of leisure. As live-in housemaid for the Studebaker family at their mansion, Tippecanoe Place, she worked hard from dawn till far past dusk every day except Wednesday, when she had most of the afternoon off, and Sunday, when she was given, at least nominally, the whole day. Church attendance, however, was mandatory. And after church she was expected to eat Sunday dinner with her large family in their small house.

That little ritual had been a pleasure in times past. It was Hilda's one chance in the week to see her family, to speak Swedish, to eat Swedish food, to revive fading memories of her roots. Her older sister, Gudrun, was a good cook, which made it easier to tolerate her tendency to boss Hilda around. And brother Sven and younger sister Freya were both dears, in their very different ways.

But now that Mama and the three youngest siblings had come to live in America . . .

"It is good for Erik to run in the park, to have space," said Hilda. "It is too crowded at home now. There are too many of us. On the farm there was one big room, kitchen and parlor combined. We were not pushed together as we are now. The house was old, and it was not—not—" She gestured, hunting for the right word.

"Fancy?" Patrick suggested. "Well built?"

Hilda frowned and shook her head. "I do not know the

right word. It was built well. My grandfather built it. But it was not a city kind of house. Not an American house. For us it was better. The house was cold in winter, anyway up in the loft where we slept, but there was plenty of wood to burn in the stove, so the kitchen was always warm. And when my father was alive, there was good food. We were happy until he died. Then . . ." Her voice trailed off.

Patrick could see in her eyes memories of hard times, times perhaps like those he could remember, just, back in Ireland. They were not happy memories.

"But we're here now, darlin' girl. We're in America, where we have good jobs. We don't have to go hungry anymore."

There had been a time when Hilda would have reproved Patrick for his term of affection. Now that they had admitted their feelings for each other, she let him say what he wanted. She even let him kiss her on rare occasions. This was not such an occasion.

"We are not hungry, no, but there is more in life than food."

"Not when you're starvin', there isn't. It's all you can think about, all you want. I can still remember the pain in my belly, small though I was then."

Hilda touched his hand in sympathy. Never, she knew, never when things were at their worst, had her family suffered as the Irish had. There had always been something for the Johanssons to eat. True, it had never been quite enough, not after her father's death. Tending the farm had been hard without him, and the weather had been bad for several years in a row. But food of a sort there had always been, and if Hilda had grown very tired of potatoes and beets day in and day out, she had tried not to complain. Mama had worked so hard to keep her seven children healthy. It had seemed ungrateful to complain.

Then the four eldest had left the farm and come to America, and after six long years of toil and scrimping, they had finally been able to bring the rest of the family to South Bend.

"I thought it would be better," she burst out resentfully. "I thought it would be wonderful to have Mama here again, and the little ones. But even with me living at Tippecanoe Place, there are too many in Sven's house, and Mama does not like you, and she tries to tell me what to do, and she is too strict with Eric, and I do not *like* it!"

Another woman might have wept, but Hilda stamped her foot. The swing bucked wildly.

Patrick didn't laugh. He knew his Hilda and her temper, and in truth, the situation was not a laughing matter. He shook his head. "Erik needs a firm hand. He ought to be goin' to school."

"His English is not yet good enough."

"Hah! It's better than yours," said Patrick bluntly. "Kids that age, they pick it up like breathin'."

"He speaks well, yes. Like an American, almost. But he cannot read English well yet, or write it—only a little."

"I still say he needs school, or *somethin'* to keep him up to snuff. He's a nice enough kid, but he's spoilin' for trouble, that boy."

"Patrick! He is my favorite. Of all my brothers and sisters, he is the one most like me. He is smart—"

"And stubborn," Patrick put in.

"Yes, when he thinks he is right! Like me. And loving. Like me." She gave Patrick a sidelong look. He grinned and aimed a peck at her cheek.

"Anyway," she pursued, dodging away, "Erik maybe needs a little more discipline. Sven works so hard, he does not have time to talk so much to Erik and tell him what is right and what is not. But he does not need to be scolded all the time and treated like a baby. Mama keeps him tied to her apron strings. He is twelve, Patrick, but he has less freedom than when he was five. On the farm he could do as he liked, once his chores were done. Here—" She threw up her hands in an exasperated gesture, lost her balance, and nearly fell out of the swing.

Patrick took both her hands and pulled her up. "Here, me

girl. That swing's no safe place for you in such a mood. Anyway, it's going to rain. We'd best be heading home. Where's Erik?"

Hilda looked around. Her brother and his friend were nowhere to be seen. She shrugged. "I do not know. He can find his way home. Mama will not like it that I left him, but he must have some freedom."

"Next week when I take him to the circus, he'll have all the freedom he wants," Patrick promised.

"If Mama lets him go," said Hilda darkly.

A week and a day later Hilda and Patrick sat, enthralled, as spectacle succeeded spectacle in the huge Ringling Brothers tent. They sat alone, however. True to Hilda's predictions, Mama had refused to allow Erik to accompany them. "Anyway, Mr. Williams let *you* come," Patrick remarked, seeing a shadow cross Hilda's face as she watched a young boy perform on the trapeze.

"Almost he did not. He said I could not expect to take time off whenever I wanted it. He said it was not allowed that I leave the house after dark. I told him I had never asked before, and I would give notice if he did not let me go. Ooh! The boy will fall! No, he is all right."

"All part of the act," said Patrick as nonchalantly as if his own heart weren't pounding. "What would you've done if he'd taken you up on it?"

"I knew he would not. Good maids are hard to find, and I am very, very good. Oh, Patrick, look at the baby elephant!"

There were lots of elephants, and performing seals, and horses. One act had fifty-one horses performing together in one ring. "They dance," said Hilda in awe. "They are as good as the—what did you call it? The people dancing, in that act before?"

"The ballet," said Patrick, pronouncing it more or less like "bullet," "or at least that's what it says here in the program. Meself, I think the horses are better."

Hilda loved it all. Each act was better than the last. The lions and tigers in their cages both terrified and delighted her. "Look," she said, laughing. "It's washing its face, just like the kitchen cat. And the tamer is so handsome, and so brave." The latter remark, an attempt to arouse Patrick's jealousy, fell flat. His attention was on the new antics of the trapeze artists.

After the show, they lingered to watch the performers pack up their wagons. "Stand away, folks," cried the lion tamer. "These boys are hungry, and you look like dinner!" Hilda squealed, and the handler cocked his head in her direction. "Hmm. You look pretty appetizing to me, too, little lady."

Hilda clutched Patrick's arm. He scowled and pulled her away from the lion wagon. "Impudent masher," he muttered, looking back with blood in his eye. "And you thought he was handsome. I ought to—"

"Patrick! He is a horrid man." She tossed her head. "Do not fight with him; I want to go away from here. Look, there are the trapeze artists. At least that is what their wagon says, but they do not look the same in ordinary clothes."

The wagon, gaily painted with circus scenes and emblazoned with the words "The Stupendous Shaws" in fancy lettering, was as gaudy as one would expect. But the performers, bereft of their tights and spangles, their faces washed clean of paint, were barely recognizable as the high fliers of an hour before. Hilda could see a family resemblance among some of them, evidently mother, father, and children. All looked weary as they packed up their costumes and equipment, paying scant attention to the dawdling onlookers. The father dropped a large, gaily-striped hoop. It rolled to Hilda's feet; she picked it up and handed it back.

"Thank you, young lady," he said with a smile and a bow, and twirled the hoop around his finger for a moment before stowing it away in the wagon.

"Now *he*," she said approvingly, "is a gentleman."

"With a wife and family, I'll remind you." Patrick was tired and on the verge of becoming cross.

They watched the clowns, looking sad and weary without their costumes and face paint. Hilda had found them rather frightening in performance, with their grotesquely exaggerated features, but now they seemed just ordinary. One of them swore loudly when his horse took a playful nip of his shoulder. Again Patrick pulled Hilda away.

The crowd had thinned out. The roustabouts scarcely bothered to be polite to those who were left, and who were very much in the way. It was time to go home.

It was well after eleven o'clock before Hilda finally fell into bed, sated with both sensation and indigestible food. She nearly choked on trapped yawns at the servants' breakfast table the next morning. Mr. Williams, the butler, was watching her like a hawk, ready to swoop down with reproof if she showed the least sign of an inability to carry out her duties. To spite him, she drove herself and the maids under her supervision at a frenzied pace all day, exhausting herself and them, but unwilling to give the butler any excuse for a lecture. By the end of the day, she was ready to fall into her bed the moment her duties were done. She didn't even take time to read the evening papers.

By Wednesday morning, however, she had fully recovered. She rose at her usual hour of five o'clock and went about her morning chores at an unhurried pace. She was not to have the afternoon off, having traded it for the unheard-of privilege of her evening out. So there was no point in rushing through her work.

She could spare the time for a search through the wastepaper bin. Yesterday's newspapers would be there, and she wanted to read about the circus.

Hilda and Mr. Williams waged a quiet, ongoing war about the newspapers. They were, the butler contended, the sole property of the Studebaker family, to be read first by them and, only later, when they were about to be discarded, by Mr.

Williams himself. The female servants were not to read them at all. He did not hold with females getting ideas above their station.

Hilda, of course, ignored the prohibition, but she had to be devious about it. If she could, she read them when they first arrived, about four in the afternoon. She was always careful to refold them exactly as they had been, and to make sure the ink was unsmudged. If the butler was vigilant and brought in the papers as soon as they were delivered, Hilda would make a discreet foray to the trash bin just before she went to bed, taking them upstairs with her to read by the single gaslight in her bedroom.

So now she removed them from the bin in the semi-basement and took them up to the main floor to read at her leisure. Colonel George's office would be the best place. Hidden away in a corner of the house, with four or five broad steps leading up to it, it was as private a room as any in the vast mansion.

The accounts of the circus were most satisfactory. Reading about it was, Hilda thought dreamily, almost as good as being there again. Having satisfied herself, she went on to a quick scan of the main front-page stories. Mr. Williams would be making his appearance soon. After he had swept his critical eye over her work, he would give her any special orders for the day. She had time for only a brief perusal. But one of the stories caught her eye. She let out a small gasp and snatched up the paper.

"BOY DISAPPEARS," the *Tribune* headline read. And underneath, in smaller type, "Parents Say He Went to Circus and Vanished."

2

Newspapers always excite curiosity.
—CHARLES LAMB, 1833

M R. Williams's tread sounded on the steps leading up to the office. With one swift movement Hilda slipped the newspapers under a pile of large books on the desk. When Mr. Williams came through the door, she was straightening the books.

"Don't move anything!" he said sharply. "Colonel George does not like his things disturbed. You ought to know that by now."

Hilda rolled her eyes. She was, of course, familiar with the eccentricities of all the family members. Mrs. George was forever changing the arrangement of various ornaments, forgetting she had done so, and accusing the servants of breaking them. Mrs. Clem, widow of the man who had built the house (and the fame of the Studebaker Manufacturing Company), preferred her rooms to be left as they had always been and was usually gentle with the servants, though firm in her expectations of superior work. Each liked a particular brand of soap, a particular type of towel—different, of course, for the two women, and heaven help anyone who mixed them up. The exact height to which windows were to be raised, which doors were to be left open and which shut, the style of napkin folding—oh, there were hundreds of details to be remembered and taught to new servants, and Hilda knew them all.

There was no point in going over all that with the fussy butler. "Yes," Hilda replied briefly. "But I must move them to dust under them. I will put them back."

She did so with precision as she spoke, careful not to let the newspapers show. Mr. Williams, annoyed, ran a gloved finger along the mantel. Finding no dirt, he pursed his lips in near disappointment. He enjoyed scolding his underlings. "I trust you will not forget the windowsills."

"No, Mr. Williams." As if she ever did!

"There will be a new daily in today. That stupid Alice didn't work out. The new one has some outlandish Hungarian name, or Polish, or something. We will call her Joan."

Hilda had to bite her tongue. Mr. Williams might call the new maid anything he liked. She, Hilda, would call the poor girl by her proper name, or as near to it as a Swedish tongue could manage.

"You will teach her her duties, of course, and make sure she understands that the work must be done properly."

"Yes, sir," said Hilda with ill-disguised impatience. "Is there anything else, sir?"

"Not at the moment. Don't take all day in here. The new girl will be here at nine sharp, and the work will go more slowly what with the training to be done."

The butler departed at last, and Hilda, with a deep breath, pulled the *Tribune* from its place of concealment and read the article as quickly as she could.

It was worse, far worse than she had feared. A twelve-year-old boy, Fritz Schlager, was reported missing by his parents, Mr. and Mrs. Albert Schlager of 720 West Robertson Street. "But that is Erik's friend!" Hilda exclaimed under her breath, and read on. Fritz, according to his parents, had pleaded with them to be allowed to go to the circus. They had refused to allow him to do so, on the various grounds that he was too young to go alone, the tickets for two people would be expensive, the expense was unnecessary, and the entertainment would be unsuitable. No, neither of them had ever attended a circus. Fritz had gone out of the house after he had eaten his supper, having pled his case one more time and been once more refused. He had been sullen, said his mother, and the family was annoyed, but not particularly surprised, when he failed to come in at nightfall. When he had not returned by bedtime, however, they became alarmed. Mr. Schlager and Fritz's brothers took lanterns and searched the neighborhood, to no avail. When morning came, the frantic family questioned Fritz's friends. It was from them that they learned of the boy's determination to go to the circus whether or not he was permitted.

The circus, the *Tribune* concluded, was next performing in Fort Wayne. In case Fritz had run away with them, police in that city had been notified to be on the watch for a boy of his description, which was printed.

Hilda gave it scant attention. She knew what Fritz looked like. Small for his age and slender, with the very fair hair and high cheekbones that young Germans often had. He looked delicate, but Hilda knew he must be strong to perform the acrobatic feats he was so good at.

No, she didn't need to read his description. She could almost see him in front of her, and her heart went cold. She could also, in her mind's eye, see another boy, a boy she had never met.

It had been about a year ago. Yes, almost exactly a year ago, the last time the circus had come to town. It had been a small circus that time, neither Ringling Brothers nor Barnum and Bailey, but it had attracted a large crowd, including, of course, many children.

One of them, a boy of eleven, had disappeared. His father was dead, but his mother, thinking he had run away and would come home when he got hungry, had waited for two or three days before notifying anyone that he was gone.

Hilda had noticed the news item particularly because the boy was just Erik's age. She had shaken her head over the mother's attitude, thinking her no fit parent, and had eagerly read the papers for news, day after day. The stories grew smaller and less frequent as time passed, however, and all said the same thing: no trace of the child.

He had never been found.

Hilda turned back to the *Tribune*. Yes, the story about Fritz went on to mention the old case and concluded with those very words: "Tom Brady has never been found."

Hilda stood very still until sounds from the kitchen below reminded her of her duties.

Mechanically she ate her breakfast. Mechanically she went about her daily chores. She knew them so well after nearly seven years that she often thought she could have done them in her sleep. The new maid, whose name turned out to be Janecska (which almost defeated Hilda's good intentions), was bright enough, and willing enough. Teaching her was not especially arduous. There was nothing during the whole long morning that required enough of Hilda's attention to take her mind off Fritz Schlager.

Fritz and Erik. Had anyone thought to question Erik about Fritz's disappearance? Would Erik know anything about it?

Was Erik, unhappy with his new life in America, maybe planning to run away himself?

After lunch she plodded up the steep, narrow back stairs with Norah, the household waitress and Hilda's best friend. Hilda was headed for the brief rest she was allowed in the middle of her day's work. Norah was going upstairs only to change clothes before taking her afternoon out with her current beau.

Hilda took a deep breath as they reached the top of the stairs.

"You out of breath? Used to be able to climb those stairs at a dead run. Not gettin' sick, are you?"

Hilda shook her head, not in the mood for backchat. "No, it is not that. It is—I have something I want you to do for me, and you will not like to do it, and I do not know how to ask."

"An' when did that ever stop you? But move. I want to get to my room and out o' this dress."

Norah moved past Hilda to the tiny bedroom next door. Hilda followed her inside and helped her undo the back buttons on her black shirtwaist.

"So what d'you want me to do, that I'm not going to like?" Norah's voice came, muffled inside the folds of heavy black serge.

"I want you to go and see my brother."

"Sven? What for? Drat, that button's caught in my hair."

"No, Erik." Hilda freed the button and Norah finished pulling off the garment.

"Whatever do you want with Erik? Doesn't he plague your life enough when you *have* to be with him? Hand me my white waist, will you?"

"He is not a bad boy," said Hilda, finding the garment in question in a drawer and giving it to Norah. "Mischievous, like every boy his age. He would behave much better if Mama were not so strict with him. But I want you only to give him a message for me."

Norah sighed acceptance. "It's not for everybody I'd go gallivantin' around on me day off, I hope you know. He'll be at home, will he?"

"No, of course not. I would not ask you to go so far!" Hilda sounded shocked. "He is working now for Mr. Hibberd at the printing company. It is on Michigan Street, next to—"

"I know. That's easy, almost on the way to the park. How long's he been workin' there? I thought he was deliverin' groceries for the Bon Ton."

"He was, but that last snow we had—remember?"

"An' could I be forgettin' it snowed on the day before Palm Sunday?"

"Well, some boys started a snowball fight just in front of a house where Erik was delivering groceries. A snowball went right down his neck, so of course he put the box down and paid the other boys back, and somehow—"

"You don't have to tell me." Norah grinned. "Knowin' Erik, I reckon he stepped in the box without meanin' to."

"Fell in it." Worried though she was, Hilda couldn't help smiling, too. "One of the boys pushed him, and the sidewalk was slippery, and whoosh! Right into the tin of cocoa!" Her shoulders began to shake. "He looked like a little black boy when he came home, Freya said. And he was very angry, not because he lost his job, but because he had tried to lick the chocolate off his face, and it hadn't tasted sweet. He said there should have been *some* good come to him out of such a catastrophe."

Norah chuckled. "He's a caution, and no mistake. That's how many jobs he's lost, now?"

"Many. I do not remember. He is a printer's devil now, and maybe he will do well there. It will be better, though, when autumn comes and he can go to school."

"Well, he's a bright kid, from what you tell me. Likely he'll do well enough in school, but meanwhile you've all got the summer to get through with him." Norah fastened the hooks on her skirt, adjusted the waist, and reached for her hat. "And what did you want me to tell him?"

"Only to stop and see me on his way home. There is something I want to ask him."

She turned on Norah the same look of guileless innocence that she was accustomed to using with Mr. Williams, but Norah knew Hilda better.

"Here! What're you up to?"

Norah didn't often read the papers, and Hilda didn't want to explain right then. "I need to talk to him for a little, that is all, and I cannot leave the grounds here until Sunday. That is a long time. You will be late meeting Sean if you do not hurry. It is Sean today?"

Norah took the bait. "Ah, him! He's taken to seein' Eileen Monahan." Hilda looked blank. "That cousin of Patrick's, the little one with red hair, you know? I'll show him! I'm walkin' out with Lee Riley, an' we'll see how Mr. Sean O'Neill likes that!"

She swept out of the room and down the stairs.

Erik knocked on the basement door at about five-thirty. Hilda, on the lookout for him, glanced around to see if Mr. Williams was watching and then slipped out the door and up the outside steps with her brother.

He stumbled up the stairs ahead of her and threw himself down on the grass at the top. Hilda studied him with concern.

"You look very tired, little one," she said in Swedish.

"I'm all right," he said in English. "They're heavy, the things they make me carry. And everybody is always in a hurry."

He sounded discouraged. Hilda knelt on the grass and stroked the hair back from his face. "What is it, Erik?"

"I don't—it was better on the farm." His voice cracked. Hilda wasn't sure whether he was about to cry, or just that his voice was changing. She knew she dared not ask, nor should she sympathize. He was prickly these days and needed careful handling.

She stood up. "Erik, I am sorry to rush you, but I, too, am in a hurry. Mr. Williams will be cross if he sees me out here. But I had to ask you about your friend Fritz."

"What about him?"

"Then you do not know?"

"Know what?"

"Fritz is missing."

He uttered a startled sound. Hilda studied his face carefully, but he seemed genuinely surprised. "His parents think he went to the circus when it was in town on Monday. Did he ever talk to you about that?"

But Erik's face had shut down. He shook his head and stood up. "No. I don't know. I have to go now. Mama doesn't like it if I'm late."

And before Hilda could say another word, he was running down the drive as fast as if he hadn't been carrying heavy trays of type all day.

"He knows something." Hilda sat on Norah's bed and yawned. It was bedtime, and she had told Norah the story of the boy's disappearance.

Norah yawned, too. They were both tired, but Hilda wanted to talk. "He'd better tell the police, then," Norah said.

"It may be nothing important, but I would swear he knows something about it, and I worry."

"Can you make him tell you?"

"How? I cannot see him until Sunday. I could, I think, make him talk if I had enough time with him. I am his favorite sister. But I work, he works . . ." She held up her hands in a gesture of futility.

"Get a headache tomorrow and sneak out. You haven't had one for a while. The old geezer won't suspect."

Hilda considered. She was, in all sober truth, subject to debilitating headaches from time to time. Mr. Williams knew that, had seen her ashen-faced and sick from the pain. He knew she had to go to bed with a cold cloth on her head until she was better. He was always annoyed, but he had never actually objected, in so many words.

"It is an idea. Yes, it is a good idea, Norah. I will leave when we begin our rest tomorrow, and if I have not returned when it is time to begin work again, you will tell Mr. Williams I am ill. I will pretend I do not feel well and eat only a little, at lunch. That will make him believe you."

"I hope so, for both our sakes." Norah sounded dubious. Now that Hilda had taken her up on it, her idea began to sound not quite so attractive, after all. "It's really all that important?"

"He is my little brother, Norah," said Hilda simply. "And he could be in trouble. Yes, it is important."

Hilda had once helped Norah's brother escape a trial for murder. Norah said no more.

3

*Smith . . . ran away from home and for thirteen
years worked with circuses of little or no reputation.*
—SOUTH BEND *TRIBUNE*, APRIL 28, 1903

HILDA drooped artistically all the next morning as she
went about her work. It was not as hard as it might have
been. Her concern over her brother made a sober coun-
tenance perfectly natural. Mr. Williams watched, lips pursed,
as she picked at her breakfast. Even Mrs. George, downstairs
for her daily conference with the cook, noticed Hilda's debil-
ity. "Are you not feeling well, Hilda?"

Hilda curtsied, careful to keep her face set in a mask of
pain. "It is one of my headaches, madam. It is not bad."

"Hmm. It's going to be a hot day, and with guests coming
for dinner, it will be a busy one for you." Over a year had
elapsed since the death of Mr. Clement Studebaker, Colonel
George's father, and the family had begun to entertain again
on a small scale. "If your head gets any worse, come up to my
room. I have some powders that might help."

"Thank you, madam." Another curtsy. This was a piece of
good fortune. She would certainly avail herself of the offer. It
would make her story much more convincing, and she would

have the powder for the next genuine headache. She was careful not to look pleased.

By the time the family lunch was imminent, her determined pretense had produced an unexpected effect. She had the beginnings of a real headache. She slipped upstairs, tapped on Mrs. George's sitting room door, and went in. Mrs. George, who was sitting at her writing desk finishing a letter, took one look at her, said, "Oh, dear," and got up to fetch the headache powders. She was quick about it, too. She knew the unpleasant side effects of Hilda's worst headaches, and if Hilda was to be sick anywhere, Mrs. George didn't want it to be on her Persian carpet.

Hilda didn't take the powder. The pain wasn't unbearable, not yet. She did feel sick enough that skipping most of lunch came easily, and it was Mr. Williams himself who said, "Hilda, you'd best go up to bed now. Don't bother with cleaning up after luncheon. I can see you'll be no earthly use until you feel better, and there's extra work to be done, with dinner guests coming."

Coming from the butler, that was almost an expression of sympathy. "Thank you, sir," she said faintly, and slipped up the back stairs.

She did go to her room. It was uncomfortably warm. If most of April had been unseasonably wintry, this last day of the month was almost summerlike. When the sun shone, the rooms at the top of the house heated up quickly, especially now when the great oak trees were barely beginning to bud and had no leaves to provide shade.

Hilda would have liked to lie down, but there was no time. She bathed her head with the water remaining in the pitcher on her washstand, took off her cap and apron, put on her hat, and tiptoed back down the stairs as far as the main floor.

Hilda had the matter of sneaking out of the house down to a fine art. It wasn't difficult, really. The house was so big and rambling, with so many doors, that there was always some exit no one was observing. She'd used windows, in a pinch, but today it was so simple as to be dull. The servants were all downstairs finishing their lunch; the family were all upstairs digesting theirs. Hilda slipped out the porte cochere door, hugged the wall of the house to avoid being seen from upper windows as she edged toward the back, and then melted down the back drive.

If she'd felt better it would have been a pleasant walk. Spring was taking full advantage of the first real warmth. Daffodils turned their bright yellow faces to the sun, crocuses almost quivered with the strength of their multicolored blooms. The trees were all enveloped in a pink or green mist; some of the maples had leaves already. Even at this hour, just past midday, the robins and sparrows and finches and cardinals and jays and starlings sounded a symphony of joy.

It made Hilda's head hurt.

There was a public fountain at the corner of Washington and Lafayette. Designed for horses as well as people, it had a low trough on one side and a waist-high basin on the other. Hilda took the headache cachet out of her pocket, unwrapped the paper and tipped the powder into her mouth, and then took a long drink from the gentle jet of water in the middle of the basin. She made a face. The powder tasted terrible, salty and somewhat sweet at the same time. That, however, was a good sign. Everyone knew medicine had to taste bad to do any good.

It didn't help immediately. When Hilda reached a bench in the shade of a building, she dropped onto it. She was only a few minutes away from Erik, and she hadn't thought about what she would say to him. If only her head would stop hurting!

Then, to her amazement, it did. Not all at once, but gradually the pain diminished. The sun, creeping toward her toes as the shade gradually removed itself, began to feel pleasant. The birds were really singing beautifully, weren't they? Why, it was a lovely day!

And she had at most an hour to coax Erik's boss into letting him take some time off and then to make Erik talk.

She felt in her pockets. Had she any money? No, not a penny. She hadn't been thinking clearly when she left the house. If she had—ah, but there! One thin dime hid in the seam of her pocket, almost ready to slip through the tiny hole she had intended to mend. It wasn't much, but it was enough.

She stood cautiously. No, the pain did not return. Oh, she must ask Mrs. George what those wonderful powders were!

She set off briskly for the Hibberd Printing Company.

Hilda had to manufacture a family emergency to get past the man at the desk in the anteroom. When she walked into the room where the actual printing was being done, Erik was loading a stack of very large pieces of paper onto a rolling cart of some sort. She watched as he trundled the cart over to a press which was, for the moment, idle, and began to put the paper on the press.

"No, not that way!" An angry man in a grimy brown apron took the paper from Erik and rearranged it. His voice was raised, partly in annoyance, partly to be heard over the noise of the other presses. "It has to be *straight*, don't you see? Oh, for Pete's sake, go and eat your dinner and maybe you'll be some use when you come back!" Muttering to himself, the man expertly jogged the paper into place. Erik looked up and saw Hilda, who beckoned to him.

"Get your dinner pail," she whispered, "and come with me. Don't say anything until we are outside."

They were barely on the sidewalk when he exploded into questions. "What's happening? Why are you here? Has something happened to Mama?"

"No, nothing. I am here to take you for some ice cream, but first come around the corner where we can sit down. What did Mama give you for lunch?"

He rooted in the pail. "Bread, cheese, ham. Beets. I hate beets! An apple."

"If you will share, I will buy you ice cream at the Philadelphia."

Erik handed her a slice of bread and some meat and cheese.

"You can have all the beets," he said with a grin. "But didn't they give you any dinner? And why did they let you leave in the middle of the day?"

Hilda chose to answer the first question. "They call it luncheon, and I did not want it, but I am hungry now." She tore the slice of bread in half, assembled a sandwich, stuffed in a couple of slices of pickled beet for flavor, and munched happily, taking care not to spill beet juice on her skirt.

"But how did you get them to let you leave?" Erik was not going to let his curiosity remain unsatisfied.

"This is my rest time."

Erik looked at her skeptically and then giggled, a pure little-boy sound that reminded Hilda of when he was much younger. "You snuck out, didn't you?"

Hilda sighed. The last thing Erik needed was a bad example . . . and then she grinned, and her dimples matched his. "That is not good English, but yes, I sneaked out. And I must go back before Mr. Williams catches me, so are you ready for that ice cream?"

The Philadelphia, South Bend's fine new ice-cream parlor, was just across the street from Hibberd's. Hilda worried that someone from the print shop might see Erik there, but the only other customers were women. She and Erik seated themselves at the long counter and traded her dime for two ice creams, vanilla for Hilda, strawberry for Erik.

Erik finished his first, licked his spoon, and turned his dark blue eyes toward his sister. "You want something, don't you?"

Hilda put down her spoon. This might be harder than she had thought. This Erik was very different from the small boy she remembered from Sweden. Then they had been the best of friends, and he had believed every word she had spoken. Every fairy story, every tale of trolls under bridges and tomtes that lurked in forests had been accepted with shivers of horror, turned to glad delight when the ogres were vanquished. This clear-eyed Erik was new to her. Caught between childhood and manhood, now one, now the other, he had a keen perception she had not anticipated. If she was to keep his trust, she must tread carefully.

"Yes," she said, returning his gaze. "I want you to do something. You will maybe not want to do it, but you know I would not ask if it were not important."

"Important for you?" All traces of the little boy were gone from his voice, though a pink smear of strawberry ice cream still adorned his chin.

"Yes, for me, but mostly for you. Erik, you *must* tell me what you know about Fritz Schlager."

The steady eyes that had been meeting hers looked away. She gently took hold of his chin, turned his face toward hers, and said again, "You must, Erik. He could be in great danger, and so could you."

"Well, I'm not!" He pulled his head away, once more a petulant child.

"Be more quiet. Erik, what do you know of crime and criminals?"

He looked up at her, one quick, resentful glance, and then down again.

"You know little of them, *ja?* I know, not much, but something of them. There is more crime here than at home in Sweden, and you know that I have been touched by it. I hope that you are in no danger, and probably it is true, but even if you are not, Fritz may be, and you must tell me what you know."

The resentful glance again. "I promised not to tell."

Hilda was careful to suppress her sigh of relief. "I promised not to . . ." was more than halfway to ". . . but I will, anyway."

"Promised Fritz? About—about what, exactly?"

"About him wanting to join the circus." He was still looking at his lap, but his tone had become almost resigned.

"Yes? Why did he want to do that?"

"Because he's so tired of living at home and going to school and doing his chores and never having any fun!" It came as a cry from the heart.

Hilda tucked away a reminder that Erik must, somehow, be given some fun now and again, and pursued her inquiries. She also noted that Erik had known all the time about Fritz being gone. His surprise and dismay must have been upon learning that *Hilda* knew.

She didn't mention it; there was no point in making Erik even more defensive. Better to find out what she could. "What did he plan to do in the circus? Look after the animals?"

"No! He doesn't know anything about animals." This with the scorn of one who knew a great deal about them. "He wants to be a trapeze artist. You saw how good he is, there in the park, and that wasn't even half what he can do. He's been practicing, out in the shed. And sometimes he'll walk on the clothesline, when his mother isn't watching. I saw him do that once. He's really good. I wish I could do that stuff."

"So." Hilda leaned closer, intent on the story. "So Fritz went to the circus—"

Erik shook his head. "He didn't have money. He said he was going to go late, sneak in, maybe, and try to get the trapeze artists to let him show them how good he was. Then he was sure he could get a job with them." Erik kicked the rungs of his stool. "And I promised him I wouldn't tell anybody."

"But you didn't know—" Hilda began, and then stopped. Should she tell him about the other missing boy?

Maybe better not. It would frighten Erik. He might even go off to try to find Fritz. Yes, he was enough like her to do that, maybe. No, she would not tell him. Better to soothe him. "This is important, what you have told me, Erik. It makes me feel very much better. I was afraid that something very bad might have happened to Fritz, and that something bad might happen to you, too, if you knew about it. But it is very different, now that I know he went away on purpose. Has anyone told the police this, do you know?"

"His parents don't know, and his brothers promised not to

tell, just like me. They didn't even want to say he'd gone to the circus at all, but their father made them. What did you start to say I didn't know?"

Hilda had to think fast. "You didn't know how worried his parents would be."

Erik sighed and ran his spoon around the dish once more in search of a few stray drops of melted ice cream. "I think he's lucky. I wish I could run away."

"That is enough of that," said Hilda firmly. "You will not do any such thing, or think of it."

"But I hate being a printer's devil! I liked the name and I thought it would be fun, but it's just hard work. And they don't like me. They think I'm stupid. I'm not stupid! I will, too, run away with the circus! But I'll do it right, I'll be famous, I'll—"

"Erik, listen to me! You must not do such a thing! I will help you find a job you will like, and I will take you to the circus, I promise, when it comes again."

"That won't be for a whole year."

"No, my little one, you are wrong. The other big circus, Barnum and Bailey, it comes to town later. In June or July, I think. And you will go, I promise you."

"But Mama—"

"I am old enough that I do not always have to do what Mama says, Erik. You, you must still obey, but if Patrick and I force you to go with us, Mama cannot blame you, *ja*? And if she scolds me, I will tell her that you have helped me and I wished to reward you!"

She smiled dazzlingly at him, and he almost smiled himself. Then he frowned, puzzled. "How have I helped you?"

"You have helped me tell the police how to find Fritz. Now run back to work."

"But he doesn't want to be found."

"Erik, his parents are worried about him. If they find him and he is all right, maybe he won't have to leave the circus right away, but if he is in trouble, then it is good if he is found. Do you understand?"

"I guess." Reluctantly he got down from the stool. "You won't forget, though? About finding another place for me to work, I mean?"

"I will not forget. Hurry, now!"

4

*The board [of public safety] expressed itself today as
having no little difficulty in maintaining the high
standard the force should be kept at when the
present salaries are so low.*
SOUTH BEND *TRIBUNE*, APRIL 30, 1903

HILDA had, she felt nervously, been away from Tippecanoe Place for a long time. As she left the Philadelphia,
she heard the clock on the old courthouse strike the
hour of two. Oh, how she wished the police station were still
in its old location! That would have been on her way home.
Instead she had to go a long block out of her way to the new
city hall, find her way through its impressive marble corri-
dors, and try to get someone to listen to her.

Calling on the police had never been one of Hilda's favorite occupations. The old station had been cramped, inconvenient, and dirty. The new facilities would doubtless be more
attractive, but Hilda doubted she would be treated with any
more courtesy than in the past.

There was only one policeman she knew well and trusted,
Patrolman Lefkowicz, and when, cross and breathless, she arrived at the police offices and asked for him, she was told he
was not on duty.

"Then I wish to speak to the policeman in charge of finding the little boy."

"And what little boy might that be?" said the man at the desk. "Lost one, have you?"

Hilda felt her temper rising, as it always did in the police station. She frowned. "Fritz Schlager, of course! How many little boys are missing, Patrolman?"

"You can keep a civil tongue in your head, miss. If you know something about that disappearance, it's your duty to give us the information. Anything you have to say, you can say to me. Sergeant Wright is busy." He sounded pompous and condescending.

Hilda's frown became more pronounced. "I wish to speak to Sergeant Wright. It is important!"

"Then you can just sit right down and wait."

"I cannot wait! I have only a few minutes, and it is important—"

"You said that before, but Sergeant Wright is still busy. Wait or not, just as you like—"

"Did someone want to see me, Eddie? I thought I heard my name." A tall, soft-spoken man appeared in the doorway of an inner office. He was dressed in a neat suit, not a uniform, and smelled pleasantly of toilet water or hair tonic.

The man at the desk started to say something. Hilda interrupted him. "You are Sergeant Wright?"

"Yes, Miss—"

"Johansson. Sir, I must hurry, but I think I know how you can find Fritz Schlager quickly."

The sergeant's attention sharpened. "You're in a hurry, you say?"

"Yes, I must go back to my work. I have been out too long, and I will be in trouble. But please, sir—"

"Then, if you will allow me, I will walk with you, and you can talk as we go." He nodded to the disgruntled patrolman, picked up his hat, and bowed to Hilda as he held the door open for her.

Her story was soon told. "And that is what my brother told me, and it is the truth, I think. So you see, sir, if you can find the family of trapeze artists, I think you will find Fritz."

"And you say you spoke with these trapeze people at the circus? Did you see Fritz at all?"

Hilda shook her head. "No," she said regretfully, "but he would, I think, take care to stay out of sight until they were well away from town. He maybe even hid somewhere else and talked to the trapeze artists only later. But I am sure that, if you send a telegram, the trapeze family will help you. The father, he was a very nice, polite man."

"Well, Miss Johansson, it was good of you to talk to us. Not many people would have taken so much trouble."

"It is because of my brother, you see. Little Erik, he is only twelve, and Fritz's friend, and I—I worry, Sergeant Wright. That little Brady boy, last year, he has never been found, and I think maybe it is not so safe for boys in South Bend."

"But Fritz seems to have run away of his own accord. He's probably fine. I wouldn't fret too much, Miss Johansson. Now, wait a minute—Johansson. Haven't I heard Patrolman Lefkowicz speak of you?"

"I know him a little," Hilda admitted.

"And wasn't he saying you'd been of some help to the police before?"

"I maybe have done some things to help learn the truth." Hilda lowered her head modestly, hoping the sergeant would say that she had done much more than that. It would sound better, coming from him.

He said nothing, however, but looked at her narrowly. "Didn't he say you worked as a maid? At Tippecanoe Place?"

"Yes," she said, somewhat provoked. "I am the head housemaid."

"So your half day is Wednesday, like everybody else's?"

Now she was annoyed. What business was it of his when she had time off? "Yes," she said shortly.

"So you're out without leave, aren't you?"

"I had to talk to my brother! If Fritz had been kidnapped, and Erik knew something about it, it would maybe have been bad for him! And when I learned what he knew, I had to come and tell you! And if that stupid patrolman had not been so rude to me, I would not now be so late!"

"I didn't mean to pry, Miss Johansson. I think you're very courageous to do what you did, and I hope you can avoid getting into trouble for it. I think maybe I shouldn't take you all the way to the door. Someone might see and wonder why you were with a policeman. Good luck to you, and thanks again."

Somewhat mollified, she stood a moment before turning up the back drive. "You will tell me if you find him?"

"I'll tell you, I promise." Sergeant Wright tipped his hat and walked away quickly, and Hilda walked toward the house, keeping an eagle eye out for Mr. Williams or anyone else who might observe her flagrant violation of the rules.

She was out of luck. Mr. Williams was just coming up the back steps from the semibasement door, the servants' and tradesmen's entrance. There was no escape.

"And where, may I ask, have you been? At a time when you are badly needed, and when I presumed you to be in your room, recovering from a doubtless spurious headache? Or is it too much trouble for you to explain the meaning of this? You have violated my trust, young woman, and let me tell you, there will be serious consequences, serious indeed." His face was red; the loose flesh of his throat quivered. He shook his finger in Hilda's face and went on with his tirade for some time, long enough for her to recover her wits.

"Well?" he said at last. "Are you going to answer me, or not?"

"I did not want to interrupt you," she said demurely.

"You are mocking me!"

"No, sir. I would not dare. I went, sir, to Mr. Cimmerman's drugstore."

"*In* the middle of a working day, *without* asking permission—"

"Yes, sir. I was gone only for a few minutes, and I did not like to disturb your rest." Her fingers were crossed behind her back and a prayer was wafting heavenward, a prayer that her absence from her room had not been noted and that Mr. Williams had only just awakened from his nap.

"Hmph. You know quite well that it is forbidden for you to be away without my express permission."

"Yes, sir. I went only to the drugstore. It is not far. Mrs. George had given me a headache powder from Cimmerman's, and it made me feel so much better, I thought I would go and see if he had any more."

"And did he?"

"No, sir. He makes them up himself and he had used up his supply. He said he will have more later in the week, but of course I will have no time to go and see until next Wednesday. If that is all, sir, I must hurry. Norah will need help in the dining room for the dinner party tonight."

"It's high time you thought about your duties, young woman! I've half a mind to discharge you, for all your fine story. How do I know you're telling the truth?"

"You can ask Mrs. George, sir, about the headache powder," said Hilda, thanking her stars that part of her story, at least, could be verified. "I *must* go!"

She slipped past him and hurried down the stairs.

Once she had resumed her cap and apron, she joined Norah in the dining room. Norah's eyes were full of questions she dared not ask in front of the daily servants, but when they were alone in the butler's pantry for a moment, Norah whispered, "I heard him rakin' you over the coals. Are you all right?"

"Yes. I have much to tell you, but later." She handed Norah a stack of damask napkins and began herself to place heavy crystal water goblets on two trays. Only fourteen guests were expected, but with Mrs. Clem and Colonel and Mrs. George, that made seventeen glasses, far too many to risk to a single tray.

The servants were so busy they had no chance to snatch

their own bite of supper before serving the dinner. Hilda, whose appetite had returned in full force, thought she might perish of starvation before everything was cleared away and the live-in servants were able to sit down to a belated meal of leftovers from the party.

The leftovers were copious, of course, and delicious. Mrs. Sullivan had an uncertain temper, but she was a treasure of a cook. Hilda helped herself to a little salmon, some lamb, creamed potatoes, and asparagus as the various dishes were passed around the servants' table. She refused the beets. Her mother made them better.

Norah, in an agony of curiosity, forced herself to hold her tongue until all the dishes and pots had been washed, dried, and put away, the kitchen scrubbed clean, the tablecloth and napkins put to soak for the laundress, and all the hundred other chores accomplished. Finally the two women were able to climb, wearily, the fifty-one steps to their rooms. Norah walked with Hilda into her room, shut the door and the transom as a precaution against eavesdroppers, sat down on the bed with a creak of springs, and said, "Tell."

Hilda yawned and tried to think of the quickest way to tell a long story. She was very tired, but she owed Norah at least a summary. "It is well that I went out," she said at last, unhooking her skirt. "I think that Erik was in no danger, after all, but he told me some things that will help the police to find the little boy. He has run away with the circus to become a trapeze artist. I went to the police station after I talked to Erik and told them."

"You talked to that patrolman you know?"

"No, he was not on duty. I talked to the man in charge of the matter, Sergeant Wright."

"Hmph. Hope he was nicer to you than most of them are to the likes of us."

"He was very polite." Hilda yawned again.

"You're just lucky old Williams didn't catch you out of your room earlier. How did you keep out of trouble this time?"

"I told him I went to the drugstore to get some headache powders, and next week, on my afternoon out, I really will do so. Or maybe earlier, if I can get away from here for a little while. Mrs. George gave me one of hers, thinking I was ill, and Norah, do you know, I really did get a headache after pretending all morning! So I took the powder and it was wonderful, better than coffee or anything else I have ever tried."

"Mmm." Norah wasn't particularly interested in Hilda's headaches. "Hilda, are you goin' to work here all your life? Havin' to sneak out an' make up lies about where you've been, an' put up with that old—buzzard?"

"I do not know." Hilda sat down in the one hard chair her employers provided for her, and began to unbutton her boots. "There is Patrick—but our families—"

Norah understood completely. Patrick had wanted for some time to marry Hilda, but a union between an Irish Catholic and a Swedish Lutheran was so irregular as to be almost scandalous, and both families had forbidden the match. Patrick and Hilda were old enough, according to law, to make their own decisions, but defying family traditions was hard. And if Hilda married, she would be out of a job. A married woman obviously couldn't keep a live-in position unless her husband was a servant in the same household, and Patrick had not the slightest wish to give up his good job as a fireman.

"You don't like it here as much as you used to," Norah pursued.

"No. It is not the same, now that Mr. Clem is gone. Mr. Williams, he grows more cross every day. He does not like me."

"He doesn't like you thinkin' you're not a black slave to be bossed around by the likes of him." Norah crossed her arms and tapped one foot on the floor. Her voice rose. "I don't know where he thinks he gets off, tellin' us what we can do an' where we can go an' when we can breathe—"

"Ssh! He will hear!"

"Fat chance. He's in bed an' snorin' by now, an' anyway, his room's too far away." Mr. Williams, of course, occupied the best room of any servant in the house, a large room on the east side of the house, much cooler in the afternoons than Norah's and Hilda's west rooms. There was, indeed, small chance he could hear anything they said. But Norah lowered her voice again, anyway.

"Hilda, I'm thinkin' of leavin', meself."

"Norah!" Hilda's weariness was forgotten. "Why?"

"Sean's asked me to marry him."

5

THE SCARCITY OF ANTHRACITE
STILL CONTINUES
Factories Running Short
SOUTH BEND *TRIBUNE*, JANUARY 9, 1903

HILDA was flabbergasted, and suddenly wide awake. She had so many questions she hardly knew where to begin. "But—but I thought you went out with someone else yesterday. Lee something."

"I did. But Sean followed us, an' I don't know quite how it happened, but I ended up comin' home with Sean instead of Lee. An' before he left, he—well—"

"He proposed to you! And you never told me!"

"I didn't know what I was goin' to say, you see. I still don't know for sure. I'd like to kiss the back of me hand to His Nibs, but in a way I'd miss this place. It's a fine house, Hilda, and no mistake."

Hilda nodded. It was the finest house in town, almost a palace, really. Living there, even as a servant, represented more luxury than Hilda had ever imagined before she'd come to America. Here she spent her days walking on soft carpets, surrounded by beautiful things. She ate good food, and plenty of

36

it. Indeed, she watched food being thrown away, enough food, some days, to have fed her whole family in Sweden for a week.

But—

"But it is not *our* house."

Norah barked a short laugh. "Not likely! The likes of us don't get mansions, not in this world."

Another time Hilda might have pointed out that the Studebakers had been poor, once, that they had come to South Bend fifty-odd years ago with nothing, and look what had become of them. Tonight she was too tired. She sighed and turned practical. "Does Sean have enough money to marry?"

"Not yet. He's savin' up, though. They've promoted him, at Birdsell's. He's a foreman now. The money's not bad, not bad at all."

"But you never know when there might be a coal strike again, or something worse."

The coal strike of 1902 had been devastating, not only for those directly connected with the mines, but for the economy of the entire country. The railroads and the huge factories had set aside sufficient coal reserves to keep them operating, but smaller plants like Birdsell Manufacturing, which did a big business in clover hullers, had been forced to slow down production, sometimes putting workers on short hours or laying them off altogether. In October, President Theodore Roosevelt had finally intervened, and strikers quickly went back to work, but even now, more than six months later, repercussions were still being felt.

From what Hilda had been able to glean from her stolen moments with the newspapers, the stock market was unstable, creating what Hilda thought of as a "rich man's panic." She, Hilda, didn't care two hoots whether stocks went up or down. With no money to invest and precious little even to set aside for emergencies, she felt far removed from any turmoil on Wall Street. But coal shortages, factory troubles, those things affected her directly. She had come to America to seek security, with a firm conviction that America was a land of infinite prosperity. That conviction had been shaken, had been replaced by the bitter knowledge that here, as everywhere else, times could be hard.

Hilda had grown up a little.

"No," said Norah, getting to her feet. "I don't know when there might be a strike, an' I don't know when there might be a flood, an' I don't know when the smallpox might come and kill us all. There's no knowin' aught in this life, but I know you got to take your chances when they come to you, because they may not come again."

"So you will marry Sean?" Against her will, Hilda sounded forlorn. Norah was her only close friend.

Norah suddenly grinned. "I don't know yet. If I do, it won't be for a good long time, anyway. You'll be married to Patrick long since. Good night, me dear. It's late. Sleep fast."

Even with all her worries, Hilda was too tired to stay awake for long, but she woke at the shrill summons of the alarm clock with the sense that something undefined was wrong, the world somehow out of kilter. She remembered as soon as she heard Norah stirring next door.

Norah was maybe going to be married. No, not maybe. She *would* be married, if not to Sean, then to someone. Hilda suddenly saw the inevitability of the thing. Norah would, sooner or later, go away and leave Hilda friendless in this great house. There would be no one to share complaints about the tyrannical Mr. Williams, no one to help Hilda with her frequent escapades.

Hilda had never before thought about how much Norah meant to her. She thought about it now, as she went about her early-morning chores. She was very silent at the breakfast table.

"You thinkin' about—what I told you last night?" whispered Norah as they cleared the servants' table together.

Hilda nodded.

"You don't need to look so downhearted about it! Anybody'd think I told you I was dyin'."

"It is almost the same, for me," Hilda muttered. "You will go away, and when will I see you? And things will change here. I do not like change."

"We'll always be friends."

"How?" said Hilda, plunking her tray of dishes down by the kitchen sink. "We never see each other away from here, and you would always be away from here. We do not go to the same church, we do not have the same friends—"

"But if you marry Patrick—"

"If I should marry Patrick, which I can never do, it would be even worse. Your people would hate my people more than they do now."

Norah could offer no counterargument. She removed the dishes from the tray and put them in the sink for Elsie to wash up. "I thought you'd be happy for me," she whispered, a catch in her voice.

"I am happy for you, Norah, if this is what you want. It is for me that I am not happy. Be quiet, now; Mr. Williams is coming."

Whatever befell them, the first rule was always: Don't let Mr. Williams find out.

The day dragged along. Spring was warming rapidly. The great furnace in the house was allowed to grow cold; windows were opened. Hilda went about her duties listlessly in her hot uniform. In summer she was permitted a lighter weight of wool, but it was not yet summer, not according to the calendar, so, perforce, she wore her winter clothing. Her neck itched. She hoped the heat wouldn't bring on another headache until she had a chance to buy some of those wonderful powders.

So preoccupied was she with her discomfort and her gloomy view of the future that she nearly forgot about little Fritz Schlager. When, therefore, a visitor presented himself at the back door a little after five o'clock and asked to see Miss Johansson, she answered the summons of the curious footman just as mystified as he.

"Oh, Sergeant Wright! I did not expect to see you here."

"I hope I won't get you in trouble by coming," he said hastily.

"Well—" She glanced about for Mr. Williams. He was not in sight, but he had the unpleasant habit of appearing out of nowhere. "This is not a bad time. I sometimes go outside for a few minutes at five o'clock." She often met Patrick then to exchange a few stolen words, but she wasn't going to tell the police that. She slipped out the door and gestured for Sergeant Wright to follow her up the stairs. "But we must be quick. I am working, really."

"I won't keep you. I simply wanted you to know that we have followed up on the information you gave us, and it is as well that you were so quick to find out all you could."

"Have you found Fritz, then?"

"We have not. But we have learned some disquieting news about the troupe of trapeze artists."

"Oh, yes?"

"Yes. Shaw, their name is. A husband and wife and two children, a boy and a girl. The others in the troupe aren't family, but they all go by the name of the Stupendous Shaws."

"Yes," said Hilda with a sharp little nod. "Now I remember the name."

"Well, at any rate, they've left the circus, according to the management. When we got the wire telling us that, late last night, we sent a man to Fort Wayne to scout around. We've had a report from him, and it isn't good."

"Tell me, please, and quickly! The butler . . ."

"Yes. But—well—it isn't pleasant, Miss Johansson."

Hilda made an impatient gesture and the sergeant capitulated.

"It seems some of the other performers in the circus have mistrusted the Shaws for some time. Nothing definite, just a vague idea that something was wrong. But two nights after the circus left South Bend, when they were close to Fort

Wayne, there were screams coming from the trapeze wagon. Screams and shouts, and other sounds of an altercation."

"Oh! And Fritz?"

"The Shaw family—wagon, apparatus, and all—have vanished. And the boy apparently with them."

Hilda walked back to the house in a whirl of emotions. Fritz was not, after all, simply a runaway. He was now truly missing. And Erik—what of Erik?

She wanted to make sure he was safe, make sure he would do nothing foolish like set out to look for Fritz. She wanted to do something herself, anything, to find Fritz and bring him home safely.

She could do nothing. She had no freedom, no time even to go visit her family. She might have risked Mr. Williams's wrath by making a flying trip down the block to see Freya at the house where she worked, but Freya was a daily and had now gone home for the day—and home was much too far away for a stolen trip.

Hilda nearly wept with frustration.

She pursued her duties that evening with a savagery that concerned Norah. At the first private moment together, Norah whispered, "Are you mad at me, then? Or what's got into you?" She stacked a few more dirty plates onto her tray.

"No, I am not angry at you. Move your feet." Hilda, on hands and knees, brushed crumbs from the carpet with such vigor that most of them missed the crumb pan. Muttering an imprecation in Swedish, Hilda crawled backward and retrieved the strays.

"What then?" Norah stayed where she was.

"Move your feet! You are grinding crumbs into the carpet. It is Erik, and this job, and—and everything!" Hilda turned a stormy face to Norah for a moment and then doggedly went on with her task, crawling halfway under the table. "I am very,

very worried about Erik and I cannot even leave for an hour to make sure he is safe!"

"You could—look, is this a coffee stain?" Norah pointed with her toe at the carpet. Hilda looked and could see nothing, but Norah's toe waggled furiously. Peering the length of the underside of the table, Hilda saw two impeccably polished black shoes and the bottoms of a pair of gray striped pants.

"No," said Hilda, "it is only a shadow, I think."

"Let me see," said Mr. Williams.

When he had satisfied himself that nothing was wrong with the carpet, and that Hilda and Norah were doing their work properly, he sailed out again.

"Does your sister Freya work all day tomorrow, or only in the morning?" Norah continued.

"Only in the morning, on a Saturday, unless there is a party."

"If it's really all that important, whatever it is about Erik, and can't wait until Sunday, you could send Anton to Freya with a note. He's quick and he's in and out on errands all day long. The old buzzard'd never know."

Hilda stood up and brushed her apron into place. She nodded wearily. "Yes, I will do that. Thank you, Norah. But—" She lifted a hand and dropped it again.

"I know," said Norah, and gave Hilda a quick hug.

Before they went to bed, Hilda gave Norah a quick summary of the situation, which she had not felt free to do earlier. "I did not want anyone else to hear," she explained.

Norah nodded. "Especially not His Nibs."

"It is the other boy, the one last year, that makes me so worried. The circus comes to town, he disappears. Now, the circus comes to town, Fritz disappears. If these circus people are—"

Norah nodded again, very soberly. "Not respectable, circus people aren't. You can't trust 'em, my mother says."

"And oh, Norah, I am so afraid Erik will run off with them!"

"Well, there's nothin' you can do about it tonight, so say

your prayers an' hope for the best. Try to sleep. Likely the kid'll be all right."

Hilda slept a little. Her dreams were troubled, but when morning came, all too soon, she could remember only the sense of dread that had pursued her through the night. She felt a little better after her urgent note had brought Freya for a brief visit early in the afternoon. Erik was fine, a bit downhearted, maybe, because his best friend was no longer available to play with. Yes, Freya would keep a close eye on him.

Hilda hoped she would. Freya could be flighty, and Erik was very good at evading supervision. But Hilda had done all she could, and tomorrow was Sunday.

On Sunday afternoon, after dinner with the family, Hilda took Erik into the back garden. As they weeded the rows of young cabbage plants, she questioned him about the Schlager family. Getting Erik to talk was uphill work, but Hilda finally gathered that her brother didn't know the latest frightening development. Had the police not told the parents, or had the parents not told the other children? At any rate, all Erik knew, apparently, was that the Schlagers had heard nothing of their missing son. Hilda had no intention of telling him anything else. The less he knew, the safer he was, in Hilda's opinion.

"Kurt and Joe," Erik went on, "say all their mother does is cry, all the time. She thinks Fritz will never come home again. And Mr. Schlager, he drinks too much and then he swears and breaks things."

"Erik! You should not gossip about your neighbors!"

"It's true, though. Mr. Schlager's a nice man, most of the time. He lets us play in the shed sometimes, and he says we can have apples from his tree when they get ripe."

"Who is 'we'?"

"Me and Kurt and Joe, and sometimes Art and Andy and Greg."

"And who are they?"

Erik became very interested in a caterpillar that was work-ing its way up the stake that marked the end of the row. "Just some boys I know."

A suspicion formed in Hilda's mind. "They are not from the Chapin Street gang, are they? You know Mama has said you are not to play with those boys. Erik, Mama is right this time. They are very bad boys. Even the newspaper says so!"

Erik tugged at a stubborn dandelion. "Art and Andy and Greg are all right. They're fun. Hilda, I don't s'pose you've found me a new job yet, have you?"

She was not blind to the change of subject, but she knew her Erik. She would get no more out of him at the moment, and it was important that he keep his confidence in her. "No, my little chick, I have had no time. On Wednesday, I will see what I can do. I have promised, remember."

6

*A story far too revolting in all its details to appear
in any decent newspaper was told in Justice J. N.
Calvert's court yesterday afternoon by . . . a twelve-
year-old girl. . . .*
—SOUTH BEND *TRIBUNE*, OCTOBER 30, 1903

NEITHER Erik nor anyone else was to remain in ignorance of Fritz's situation for long. The news broke in all
its horrifying detail in the South Bend *Tribune* Monday
afternoon. Hilda, taking in the papers as usual, scanned the
front page, caught the name of Fritz Schlager, and stood
rooted to the spot. The boy had been found hiding in a barn
near Ligonier. He was in pitiful condition, having been severely beaten. The *Tribune* hinted at even worse abuses. "Revolting details . . . not fit to print . . . ," the paper gravely
pronounced.

Nearly faint with horror, Hilda read on. Surely they couldn't
mean that the boy—*a boy!*—had been—well, abused—but
what else would be so bad they couldn't even talk about it?
Hilda had heard of such things, dimly, but she had scarcely
believed the stories. If they were true . . . she stood in the
backstairs hall, so absorbed in what she read that she failed to
hear Mr. Williams descending the stairs.

"I'll have that, *if* you please, Hilda. You know quite well you are not allowed to read the newspapers."

"Look, Mr. Williams!" Hilda pointed out the story with a shaking finger.

The butler adjusted his spectacles with maddening slowness, held the paper at arm's length, and read a sentence or two before uttering a shocked exclamation and thrusting the paper down. "You've no business reading such things, no business at all! That is precisely why I have forbidden newspaper reading, and I hope you've learned your lesson! I will not have my orders disobeyed in this—"

"He is a friend of my brother Erik," said Hilda, who hadn't heard a word. "The boy, he lives around the corner from my family. Erik knows him and his brothers. This is a terrible t'ing." Only rarely, now, and only under strong emotion, did Hilda's Swedish accent break through her practiced, fluent English.

Mr. Williams didn't notice, or didn't care. He tucked both papers under his arm. "It is none of your concern, Hilda. It is no concern of any decent woman, and I'll hear no more of it. There, now!" The clock in the servants' room struck the half hour. "Four-thirty, and you with half your work yet to do, most likely. Go on, girl, don't dilly-dally!"

He swept away, and Hilda was left standing there, shaking with anger and fear.

Sergeant Wright came to call again that afternoon around five. This time Hilda was out behind the carriage house, collecting tea towels that had been hung out to dry on the clothesline. The policeman approached around the corner of the carriage house and cleared his throat. "May I speak to you for a few minutes, Miss Johansson?"

"Yes! I had hoped you would come. Tell me everything! I saw what the paper said, but that old—the butler would not allow me to finish reading. It is terrible, Sergeant Wright!"

"Yes, it is," he agreed gravely. "The little boy may not be telling the truth, of course, but he has been brought home and his doctor says he has certainly been beaten. He has— er—other injuries as well."

Hilda blushed at the mention of such a forbidden topic, but she had to know. If Erik could be in danger, she would talk even of such matters. "It is true, then, what the papers hinted? I could not believe it. A twelve-year-old boy, and that man with a wife and children! I did not know there were any men in the world so wicked! And I thought he was a *nice* man when I talked to him, after the circus."

"I'm sorry you spoke to Mr. Shaw, Miss Johansson. I don't like to think . . . well. What did he say to you?"

"Only a few words. He dropped one of the hoops they use, and I gave it back to him, and he thanked me. That was all. He was polite." A note of doubt had crept into her voice. "Are the police *sure* he was the man who—mistreated Fritz? The lion tamer, he was *not* polite to me. He was very rude!" She colored a little with the memory. "And the clowns, well, one of them, he was not nice to his horse. And the—the laborers, the—"

"Roustabouts?"

"Yes, I think that is the word. I do not know what it means, exactly, but I think that is what they are called. They are very rough men, Sergeant, not polite at all, and maybe even violent, I think. They all are much more the kind of man, I think, who might do such a thing."

"We know very little as yet, Miss Johansson, but young Fritz quite definitely says it was Mr. Shaw. I *wish* you hadn't spoken to him. I wouldn't want you to be in any kind of danger."

Something in his tone penetrated Hilda's perturbation. She looked at him again. He smiled nervously.

"I thought—that is, I wondered—I mean, you have time off this Wednesday, and if you have no other plans, and the weather is nice, it might be pleasant to take a boat out on the river. If you have no other plans," he repeated, looking into her eyes and smiling again with a little more self-confidence.

Hilda blushed and looked down.

It was unfortunate that Patrick chose that very moment to appear around the corner of the carriage house. His hand up-raised in greeting, he had begun talking before he saw the sergeant. He got as far as, "Say, Hilda, I—" before he stopped.

"Oh, Patrick!" Hilda looked as guilty as though the situation were her fault. "I did not expect you this afternoon."

"I guess not," Patrick growled.

Hilda swallowed. "Sergeant Wright, this is my friend Patrick Cavanaugh."

"We've met," the sergeant growled in very nearly the same tone of voice as Patrick's.

A silence fell.

"I guess I interrupted you," said Patrick, finally.

"Oh, no, we were only—the sergeant came to tell me about Fritz Schlager. It is a terrible thing, Patrick!"

"It is that. Not at all the sort of thing to talk about with a decent woman, I'd've thought."

"But I—"

"But she—"

Hilda and Sergeant Wright spoke at the same moment, stopped, apologized.

"I am interested, Patrick," said Hilda with dignity, "be-cause, you know, the Schlager boys are friends with Erik. I worry that he will learn too much."

"Seems to me you've maybe learned too much, yourself. Sounds as if you know all about it, an' there wasn't all that much in the papers."

"I am not stupid, Patrick! And I am not a child. Of course there were things that the papers could not print, but I can—can read inside the lines—"

"Read between the lines, I suppose you mean. That's one thing, but to talk about it to someone you don't even know, and a man, too—that's somethin' else again!"

"Patrick, you will not tell me what to do!" Hilda stamped her foot, and Sergeant Wright chimed in.

"Look here, Cavanaugh, you have no right to talk to Miss Johansson that way! She's done nothing she ought not to have done."

"Oh, no? I suppose you an' her was havin' tea when I come up? Well, I'll go, seein' as I'm not appreciated around here. I *had* come to tell you about a job Erik might want, Hilda, but I guess you're too busy to think about him right now." He strode back around the corner of the carriage house.

"Oh, but—excuse me, Sergeant Wright—Patrick, *wait*, I want—"

Hilda hurried after him, tea towels clutched to her breast, but he was halfway down the drive and did not turn his head.

"Hilda! *Hilda!* Where are those towels, girl? Are you dilly-dallying again?"

"No, sir," she said demurely. "Here they are. One blew away and I had to go and fetch it."

"There is no wind," observed the butler.

"A sudden gust," said Hilda firmly, and marched down the stairs to the basement door. For perhaps the first time in her life, she was glad of a summons from the peremptory Mr. Williams.

It meant she didn't have to think up a reply to Sergeant Wright's invitation.

After her evening's duties were done and she had climbed the many stairs to her room, she cast aside her cap and apron. Then she sat down on the bed, unbuttoned her boots, massaged her swollen feet, and gave serious thought to the day's problems.

Fritz—and Erik. Erik would know, of course, that Fritz was home, and that he had been hurt. He almost certainly wouldn't read the papers. He couldn't read English very well yet. And Hilda was sure that no one would tell him the most horrible parts of Fritz's story. She certainly hoped they wouldn't, because if he knew—she shuddered.

Her mind turned to what Patrick had said. What he had *really* said, leaving out the jealous posturings. He wasn't so concerned that she knew what had happened to poor little Fritz as that she had discussed it with another man. He knew Hilda wasn't a pampered, protected lady. She was a working woman, albeit a respectable one, and she knew something about the seamier side of life. Patrick just didn't like the idea of her talking about it.

Hilda didn't like to talk about it, or even to think about it. She was horrified and sickened. That any man could take advantage of a little *boy*, a boy, moreover, who had sought his approval and protection—no, it was not to be thought of. Hilda toyed briefly with the idea that it was all a lie, that Fritz had made it up. Mr. Shaw had *seemed* such a pleasant man. But there was the report of the doctor. Fritz had undoubtedly been beaten and interfered with, if not by Mr. Shaw, then by some other man. Hilda shivered, though her room was very warm.

No, poor Fritz was almost certainly telling the truth, and Hilda hoped fiercely that the Shaws would be found and punished, for Mrs. Shaw must surely bear some of the blame as well. How she could let her husband do such a thing . . . Hilda felt sick at the very thought. But her most pressing concern was Erik.

Hilda was profoundly sorry she had ever told him anything about her own involvement in the investigation of crime. Would he think it a brave, exciting thing to try to find the man who had hurt his friend?

She shivered again; shut up in this house day and night, she could do nothing to protect him. Mama and the rest would do what they could, but they, too, were away from him all day. Was there nothing to be done?

Well, there was maybe one thing. Hilda had made a promise to find Erik a better job. If he had a job he liked, he would be less likely to do foolish things.

That brought her back to what Patrick had said. Patrick knew of a job. The situation was serious. Something had to be done about it as soon as possible.

And she couldn't see Patrick again, legitimately, for two days.

She made up her mind. She would go to the firehouse. She had been there several times before, even once in the dark of night. If Patrick was on duty, well and good. If not, most of the other firemen knew her. She would leave a message.

She stood up and resumed her boots, not without wincing. She really was going to have to get a new pair. The small, pretty feet she had been proud of when she was younger had certainly grown a bit under the stress of being on them all day long. Besides that, the boots were nearly worn out. She had put new soles on twice, new heels once, and had the buttonholes reinforced. Besides, no one except small children wore buttoned shoes anymore. That was one mercy. Laces allowed for a little ease on a hot day.

The old boots were quiet, at least. Hilda stole down the back stairs. The evening was really far too young for such flagrant disregard of the rules. Usually when Hilda decided to defy Mr. Williams, she took reasonable precautions. Midnight, when he had been asleep and snoring for at least an hour, was much safer. Tonight she was too tired. Midnight would find her sound asleep, too, and she dared not set her alarm. It would waken Norah, and maybe even the cook across the hall.

No, tonight she would take her chances. Mr. Williams had gone to bed early and had no reason to wake. And now that the back door had a Yale lock, getting out was easy; she need have no recourse to the kitchen window, her favorite escape route of old. It meant, of course, leaving the door on the latch, and that meant the house would remain unlocked for a time. Hilda's conscience bothered her a little about that. Such a wealthy household had always to be on guard against burglars.

Well, then, she'd leave a booby trap. A stack of cooking

pots placed where an incautious entry would knock them over would be as good as an alarm. She found what she wanted in the kitchen and arranged them in uneasy balance a couple of feet inside the door. Her heart was in her mouth the whole time lest she, herself, touch off pandemonium, but at last the unsteady tower satisfied her. Easing the door open, she slipped through and ran lightly up the outside steps.

It was a pity that the central fire station had been moved. Its old location, on Jefferson Street, right downtown, had been very convenient. The new one was two blocks farther away, in a residential area. Not very far, perhaps, on a summer afternoon. At eleven o'clock of a dark, moonless night, it was something else again. There weren't many streetlights in that part of town, and the darkness between them was thick enough to remind her of every dire Swedish folk legend she had ever known.

And when she arrived at last at the haven of the firehouse, with bright electric lights inside and out, her journey was for nothing. She knocked and introduced herself to the fireman who answered the door, a man she had never seen before. Patrick was not on duty that night, she was informed. The man's curiosity was veiled by only the thinnest overlay of courtesy.

"Tell him . . ." She paused. She must think this out carefully. "Tell him I wish to talk to him as soon as possible. Tell him I am sorry I was unable to meet with him for very long today, but that I was very interested in everything he had to say, and that I agree with him. Shall I write it down?"

"No, miss, I'll remember. Anything else?"

"That is all, thank you. When will he be here?"

"Not till afternoon. Are you all right, miss? You're not in any trouble, are you? We have an extra man tonight; he could walk you home if you like. It's late for a lady to be out, miss."

Hilda secretly concurred. She would have given a good deal for an escort through the dark. But an escort might ask questions, and she didn't want to talk about her errand. Particularly she didn't want to talk about her encounter with Patrick. So she shook her head. "No, I am all right. But thank you. Tell Pat—tell Mr. Cavanaugh I will be able to see him at five o'clock or around then."

"Yes, miss. Be careful, miss."

Hilda hated to leave the friendly circle of light, but she made herself plunge into the dark. The faster she walked, the sooner she would be safe at home. Stubbing her toe now and then on an unevenly laid brick or a tree root that had pushed out of the sidewalk, she walked as fast as her sore feet would allow. She was almost running when she arrived at the back drive of Tippecanoe Place, also dark, but blessedly familiar. Here she could find her way blindfolded. She reached the steps, scampered down them, and opened the back door with a sob of relief.

She stepped straight into her tower of pots and pans, which cascaded to the floor with a clatter loud enough to wake the dead.

7

After all, what is a lie? 'Tis but the truth in masquerade.

—BYRON, DON JUAN, 1823

MRS. George, who had the shortest distance to come from her bedroom two stories above, was the first on the scene.

"Hilda! What on earth? I thought there was a burglar!"

"I thought so, too, madam. I could not sleep—the night is so hot—and I was on my way down to the kitchen for a cool drink when I heard the noise. And here is the back door, wide open—but I saw no one, only these pots on the floor."

It wasn't at all a good story, but it was the best she had been able to think of in the two minutes she had been allowed.

"But you're still dressed."

"Yes, madam. I dressed to come down. I did not want to wander about the house in my nightdress."

Mrs. George was sleepy and upset. There was something about Hilda's demeanor that didn't seem quite right, but she had more pressing problems on her mind. Her husband, in nightshirt and hastily tied bathrobe, appeared at her side.

"What's happened?"

Mrs. George turned to him. "Oh, George, we don't know!

Hilda heard the crash and came down to find the door open and all these pots on the floor. Do you think you'd better call the police?"

Hilda's heart sank. Above all things she wanted the police to stay away. "Perhaps Colonel George and I should see if anything is missing, madam? It could be that Mr. Williams did not lock the door properly and the wind blew it open."

"That," said Mrs. George tartly, "would not explain those pots. I think it best to call in the police."

"As you wish, madam. But I will begin to look, anyway. We ought to be able to tell them what is missing."

"That's good sense, Ada," said Colonel George with a huge yawn. "Ah, Williams, here you are. We're having a little excitement, as you see."

Hilda had hoped that the butler would sleep through the upheaval. He did sleep heavily. Now she saw that he had taken the time to dress before coming down. How like him to think more of his appearance than his duties in a possible crisis!

There was no doubt, however, that his impeccable attire gave him a psychological advantage over the others. He cast his somewhat protuberant eyes over the scene with disapproval. The disapproval sharpened when his glance lit on Hilda.

"What are you doing, girl, downstairs without your cap and apron?"

Hilda explained again, an explanation that was growing thinner by the moment. Mr. Williams looked highly skeptical and opened his mouth to speak, but Colonel George intervened.

"This isn't the time for talk, Williams. I want you to go outside with a lantern and see if this fellow is still hanging around the grounds, while Hilda and I see what's missing. And hurry, man! He's not likely to wait to be caught."

It did poor Hilda's heart some good to see the haughty butler being ordered around like an errand boy, but it was the last good thing that happened that night. Dutifully she followed Colonel George around the big house, searching perfectly orderly rooms for any signs that their treasure had been plundered, and entangling herself deeper in the web of deception with every step. She was tired and cross, and wanted nothing more than to tell Colonel George that there had been no intruder, but she dared not.

Eventually, after Williams found no felon lurking in the lilacs of Tippecanoe Place, and neither Colonel George nor Hilda—amazingly—could find any evidence of burglary, the call to the police was deemed not to be necessary.

"Well, I'm sure I don't know what to think," said Mrs. George. "I'm thankful it's no worse, but I can't imagine what those pots were doing there. Maybe Mrs. Sullivan knows. I'd ask her, but I suppose it's a shame to wake her. I'm surprised she isn't down, with her room just by the stairs. You'd think she'd have heard the commotion."

"She has grown a little deaf, I think," murmured Hilda, thanking her lucky stars for the fact. Maybe by morning she'd be able to think of some story that would account for those pots, and meanwhile she hadn't had to contend with an angry cook on top of everything else.

"I'm thankful Mother didn't hear," said Colonel George. "She's not as young as she was, and she needs her rest. Very well, Williams, lock up, and make sure this time the door catches. You'd better bolt it, as well."

"Yes, sir," said the butler through stiff lips. He was perfectly sure the door had been properly locked. He was perfectly sure that Hilda, somehow, was at the bottom of this. Tomorrow he'd have the truth out of her. "Hilda, put those pots away at once."

"Never mind, Hilda," said Colonel George, further enraging the butler. "Morning will do. We don't need any more clanging around tonight."

For her part, all Hilda wanted to do was fall into bed and sleep as hard as she could for what remained of the night. It was not to be. She had stripped off her clothes, folded them neatly by sheer force of training, and put on her nightdress when the door opened softly and Norah entered, her finger to her lips.

"Hilda, what's happened?"

Hilda sighed and collapsed onto the bed. "It is a very long story."

"Are you in trouble again?"

"Yes, and this time it is bad. I do not know how I will get out."

The defeat in Hilda's voice caught Norah's sympathy. "Tell me, then, quick. I can see you're tired, but maybe I can think of something by mornin'."

"You heard the noise?"

Norah rolled her eyes. "An' how could I not hear it? I'm not deaf, like Mrs. Sullivan. I didn't come down 'cause I was scared you was in the middle of it all, an' I didn't want to say the wrong thing."

Hilda yawned, almost cracking her jaw, and condensed the tale into the fewest possible words. "I went to talk to Patrick. I worried about leaving the house unlocked, so I stacked pots by the door to catch a burglar, but I forgot and they caught me. And it was all for nothing. Patrick was not on duty."

Norah was bursting with questions, but she confined herself to one. "What did you tell them? I have to know, Hilda, so I can try to think up the rest of the story."

Hilda told her hastily-concocted tale once again. Shorn of facial expression and gestures, it sounded even balder.

Norah shook her head. "Not good enough by half. Don't worry, I'll come up with somethin' by mornin'. Sleep in a little; I'll do your chores for you and wake you in time for breakfast."

Hilda's attempt at thanks was interrupted by another huge yawn. Norah tiptoed back to her own room; Hilda was asleep by the time Norah climbed into bed.

Norah was not usually as adept at prevarication as Hilda. With Hilda around to think up ruses, excuses, and downright lies, Norah didn't get a lot of practice. But under the threat of disaster for her best friend, her Irish love of the tall tale surfaced and she came through nobly. She couldn't wait to tell Hilda about it.

"Get up, quick," she said, shaking Hilda's shoulders. "Breakfast's almost ready, and you'd better be on time. His Nibs slept late this morning, too, but he's up and about now and he'd better not see you in your room."

Hilda groaned. "I do not want to get up. I could sleep all day. And I do not want to see Mr. Williams at all!"

"I told you not to worry about that," said Norah with fine nonchalance. "But for the love of heaven, hurry! It'll all be to do over again if you make him mad. Here."

Norah tossed a wet sponge at Hilda's face. Sputtering, Hilda got out of bed, performed a sketchy toilet, and started to dress. "But what do you mean, I do not need to worry? Of course I need to! He will make me tell the truth, and then—"

"Use your fingers, girl, not your tongue! Here, I'll do up the back buttons. I told him I left the pots there because they weren't clean. No, don't interrupt, there's not time. Here's your skirt. I thought it all out, and when I got up this morning I went down and dirtied the pots a bit and stacked them up by the back door again. Mrs. Sullivan like to had a fit when she come down and saw them, but I said they were dirty when I went to put 'em away, and I left 'em stacked there so Elsie couldn't help seein' 'em when she come in. I pretended, o' course, that I didn't know nothin' about the disturbance last night, and I couldn't understand why they were all tossed about like that."

Hilda's eyes opened wide. Her hands dropped the braid she was pinning to the top of her head. "But that is brilliant, Norah! That is wonderful! Only—the door—"

"It blew open, didn't it? His Nibs'll have to be more careful next time, won't he? Oh, for the love o' Mike, let me pin up your hair, and get a move on!"

It helped a good deal that Norah spoke to Mrs. George

before Mr. Williams had the chance. The butler, still sleepy, cross, and behind in his work, got to the family dining room just a few seconds too late, but in time to hear Norah apologizing to Mrs. George for the disturbance in the night, and taking the full blame.

"And it's sorry I am, madam, that your sleep was spoiled. I had me pillow over me head and never heard nothin', or I'd've been down explainin' at the time."

"Goodness, Norah, what an extraordinary thing to do! Next time do leave the pots in some less vulnerable spot. You meant well, I suppose, and it's a mercy it wasn't a real burglar. But I am still displeased about the door. Williams should be more careful. There are a great many items of value in this house, and I shall lose sleep at night if I think anyone might come in."

Mr. Williams cleared his throat for a dignified rebuttal, but once more Norah got in first. "Oh, madam, that might have been my fault, too. I recollect I bumped up against the door, trying to get the pots straight. I might have touched the lock somehow."

"Yes, well, it's over and done with," said Colonel George, looking bored and rattling his newspaper. "I trust it will never happen again. More coffee, please, Norah, and would you tell Mrs. Sullivan I'd like another fried egg or two?"

"So that's all right," Norah said comfortably to Hilda when the two were clearing the dishes away later. "I've taken my scolding, such as it was. Mrs. George was more relieved than anything, and I put a spoke in old Williams's wheel by taking blame for the door, too. I hope you're grateful!"

"I am very grateful," said Hilda, with as much humility as she was ever able to muster. "I was very foolish to go out last night, and this time I could not think fast enough. You have saved my ham, Norah."

Norah giggled. "You mean bacon, silly. And you never told me why you wanted so bad to talk to Patrick, anyway."

So Hilda, snatching moments of privacy over the course

of the morning, told Norah about Patrick's unfortunate visit. "And it is very important, to find a job for Erik. I thought it could not wait until Wednesday. And now it will have to, because I will not dare to go out and meet Patrick today. Mr. Williams, he watches me every minute. He is still suspicious."

"As well he should be, me girl. As well he should be!" The two giggled their way into the servants' lunch, Hilda claiming they had been talking about Norah's beau.

When they went up for their rest after lunch, Norah stopped in Hilda's room for a moment. "Hilda, if you want, I'll talk to Patrick for a minute before supper."

"Oh, will you? If I do not go out, he will be more angry than ever, because I think he will have to take time off duty to come. If you could explain that I do not like Sergeant Wright at all—well, I *like* him, he is a nice man, but—and tell him I will see him tomorrow, and—"

"I know well enough what you want me to say, don't worry. And I'll find out about that job for your rapscallion brother, too. Now put your feet up. The Lord knows we can both do with a little rest."

Hilda set her alarm for an hour and fell asleep with the contented feeling that another set of life's shoals had been successfully navigated.

8

The boy,—oh! where was he?
—FELICIA HEMANS, "CASABIANCA"

ILDA's feeling of contentment lasted only through the afternoon. After watching Norah slip out the basement door at five-thirty, she busied herself with her chores, which took her to the top floor of the house. Thus she did not see Norah reenter the house wearing a discouraged look.

The servants' supper that evening came before the family dinner. Hilda and Norah had no privacy to talk, but Norah stole a brief, unobserved moment to shake her head in Hilda's direction and raise her eyebrows meaningfully. Hilda's heart sank. Whatever Norah's news was, it wasn't good.

They kept busy the rest of the evening. Both were anxious to give Mr. Williams no excuse to scold. So it wasn't until bedtime that Norah had a chance to slip into Hilda's room and tell her the worst.

"I did me best, but it's no good, Hilda. He's mad at you. He says you're making a fool of him, one way and another."

"But I could not help it that Sergeant Wright came to call on me! I talked to him because I wanted to know about Fritz, and then he became foolish, but that was not my fault!"

"Patrick says you must've encouraged him. And he didn't like it that you came callin' at the firehouse, so late at night. He says the other firemen twit him about it, and besides, it's dangerous."

"Oh, I know now I should not have gone, but I was worried about Erik, and still I worry. Norah, I will talk to Patrick tomorrow and make him understand, but what about Erik's job? It is important, Norah."

Norah sighed. "That's the worst of it, Hilda. Patrick says the firehouse needs a new stable boy, and he thought Erik would be good at it because of workin' on a farm and lovin' horses an' all. But now he says Erik'd likely be undependable, an' he'll tell the chief to look for somebody else."

Hilda plied her buttonhook with such furious vigor that one shoe button popped off and went flying across the room. "He is unfair! It was *not* my fault about the sergeant, and Erik is *not* undependable! He needs only to find the kind of job he can do well. He will be a very fine stableboy. Oh, I will have much to say to Patrick tomorrow!"

"No, you won't, then," said Norah with another sigh.

"I will! What do you mean?"

"He's not comin' tomorrow. He said he's on duty, an' he's not takin' off two days in a row. An' you're not to come 'round to the station, neither, he says."

Hilda sat on the bed, boot in hand. Norah eyed her nervously. Hilda had been known to throw her boots while in a temper, and Norah had no wish to become a target.

But Hilda sat very still, showing no inclination to throw anything. "Very well," she said at last in a voice with no expression at all. She bent over to place her boot on the floor at a precise angle to the bed. "Thank you, Norah." She stood up and stepped out of her skirt.

"What're you goin' to do, then?"

"I do not know. Good night."

When Norah closed the door behind her, she discovered she had been holding her breath.

Hilda slept not at all that night, but she rose at her usual time in the morning and went about her duties with brisk efficiency. When she encountered Norah they chatted as usual, but something about Hilda's set face kept Norah from uttering even one of the questions she burned to ask. And when Norah was ready for her afternoon out, she couldn't find Hilda to ask her plans.

Hilda had, in fact, changed her clothes with lightning speed and was already on her way to Hibberd's print shop to talk to Erik.

If Patrick wouldn't help Erik, she thought as she hurried, then she, Hilda, would. She would tell him about the job at the firehouse and take him there herself. If the fire department had already found a boy, there were other stables where a good boy might be needed. She ought to have thought of it herself, knowing Erik's love of horses, but now that the idea had entered her head, she didn't intend to let it go.

Ten minutes later she was out on the street again, trying not to worry. Erik had not come to work that day. It didn't, she told herself, have to mean anything except that Erik was being naughty. He was in no trouble. Of course not. He would be playing with his friends, or mooning about the house. The energy of Hilda's walk, the expression on her face as she headed purposefully for Sven's house boded no good for Erik when she found him.

But he was not at the house. No one was at the house, which was locked up tight. Hilda had a key, of course, and let herself in, but no trace of a twelve-year-old was there to be seen.

Her wrath mixing with growing anxiety, she locked the house again and went around the corner to the Schlager place. She knew she ought not intrude on their trouble, but if Erik was playing with the Schlager boys . . .

He was not. Josef and Kurt, who were playing a dispirited game of mumblety-peg with an old jackknife that looked good for little else, said they hadn't seen him all day. "He'd be at work, though," said Kurt shyly.

"He is not at work," said Hilda. "If you see him, tell him he is to go home at once. At once, do you understand?"

"Yes, ma'am," the boys chorused. When Hilda had stalked away, the boys looked at each other. Erik had said this sister of his was nice. What a story!

It was only a few steps to the corner of Chapin and Sample Streets. Sure enough, a group of boys loitered there, boys inclined to cast rude looks and ruder words at Hilda. She did not react as they had anticipated. Instead of shying away, she strode up to them and stood, hands on hips.

"Which of you knows my brother Erik Johansson?"

"That little kid?" jeered one.

"Shut up, Zig," said another, taller boy. "I know him, miss. Why?"

"Do you know where he is?"

"Baby gotta go home?" inquired Zig.

"Shut *up*, I said!" The tall boy aimed a kick at Zig, who dodged easily and sauntered away. "My name's Andy, miss. I'm a friend of Erik's. Don't mind these others. They're good-for-nothings, most of 'em. I haven't seen Erik since Monday. I reckon he's at work. Are you his sister Hilda?"

"Yes, and he is not at work. He is not at home. I have word for him of a better job, and I must find him. Do you know where I should look?"

"Not unless he's down at the river, fishing. He likes to do that sometimes. I'll ask the others if you want."

"Yes, please, Andy. I will go and look for him on the river. Where does he like to fish?"

"Mostly Howard Park. I dunno, though. He might not be there. It's a mite sunny and hot to catch anything today."

"I will try the park, anyway. And will you send word to me if you learn anything? Or send Erik if you find him?" She fished in her pocket and found a nickel. "Here, this is for you."

Andy brightened. "Yes, *ma'am*. Thank you, ma'am."

Wearily Hilda turned to retrace her steps. Her boots were too tight and she was too warm, and both worry and anger are tiring.

She winced as one of her blisters bit sharply. This business of looking after Erik's interests was getting expensive. She'd never have enough for new boots if she kept spending dimes here and handing out nickels there as if she were rich.

She thought hard about her boots, trying to crowd other thoughts out of her head.

Howard Park was a long, tiresome walk away. By the time Hilda got there, she had allowed anger to dominate her thoughts. She was furious with Erik, with Patrick, and with herself. This was her afternoon off! If Patrick hadn't behaved so annoyingly, Erik would have his new job by now, and she and Patrick would be enjoying a leisurely talk, sitting on the grass or perhaps floating down the river. There were boats for rent at Leeper Park, a little way downstream.

Or, of course, she could at this moment be lolling in a boat rowed by Sergeant Wright.

She banished that thought and, reaching the park, looked around her. It was not a large park, and the trees were spaced far apart. She could see easily that Erik was not fishing from the low bank. No one was. Andy must be right about the weather being wrong for good fishing. Nor was Erik to be found anywhere else in the park.

Where was he? Fear clutched at her.

He had talked of running off with the circus, but there had been no circus nearby since Ringling Brothers had left town. He had no money to go anywhere, anyway.

Or did he? What did he do with the money he earned at the print shop? Gave it to Mama, probably, but . . .

And a boy could go off with only a few belongings and some bread in his pocket. Boys had done it before.

No, surely he had done no such thing. He was not stupid,

and he trusted her. She had promised she would find him a job. He would not have run away so soon after she'd made that promise, would he?

But what if he knew something about Fritz? What if . . .

She would not allow herself to finish that thought. There was no point, she told herself firmly, in letting her imagination run away with her. Erik was quite safe, somewhere. She must think what to do next.

She couldn't go to Patrick, that was sure. She sat down heavily on a park bench, wishing she could take her boots off, and thought dark thoughts of Patrick.

Making a fool of him, indeed! She had done nothing, absolutely nothing, to make him angry. He knew that she loved him. Well, if he didn't, he had no sense. She had never exactly said so, but neither had he ever said he loved her. It was understood.

Just as it was understood that there were far too many obstacles in the way of their marriage. If the differences of nationality and religion weren't enough, there was the question of money. He could not support them, not yet, anyway, and marriage would cost her her job.

He has been saving money as fast as he can. The thought came unbidden. Hilda tossed her head. Well, she'd never said she would not wait, had she?

You never said you would.

He ought to know without being told.

Even when he sees you with another man, blushing like a schoolgirl?

It was *not* my fault!

But whether it was or not, Hilda had to admit to herself, the appearance had been deceiving. She hadn't helped, either, by losing her temper. If only she could learn to take things calmly. She was not the only one at fault, though. Patrick had no *right* to be so upset, and she meant to take the very first opportunity to tell him so.

Oh, and that is taking things calmly, is it?

"Miss Johansson! Miss Johansson!"

She looked up to see Andy pelting across the grass.

He stopped before her, out of breath. "Miss Johansson, I talked to some of the boys, and one of them said Erik said he was gonna go down to the train station today, 'cause the orphan train was comin' through and he thought it might be fun to watch, and it's s'posed to be in just about now, and I thought you'd maybe want to go and see."

Completely out of breath, he paused, panting. Hilda stood up, greatly relieved by both the news of Erik and the distraction from her unpleasant reveries.

"Thank you, Andy. It is the Chicago and South Bend station, yes?"

"Yes, miss," he managed to gasp out. "I'll come with you if you want, miss."

"Yes, but I must hurry."

Wincing with each step, she marched back south and west, Andy following as fast as his wind would allow.

The orphan train was in the station as Hilda approached. She could tell by the pandemonium. Groups of frightened-looking children stood on the platform being herded by weary adults. As Hilda cast her eyes over the groups, trying to spot Erik, the orphans were organized into lines and marched out of the station. They were, Hilda knew, headed for a nearby church where they could be sized up and perhaps chosen for a new home.

Hilda had seen many sorry things in her twenty-two years, but she thought she had never seen anything sadder than those little faces. Some bore the traces of tears, some were angry, some still looked hopeful, some—the saddest of all—wore only the blank look of despair.

Hilda knew all about the orphan trains and their pitiful cargo. She had read about them in the newspapers. They had come all the way from New York, these children, stopping at heaven only knew how many towns along the way. Many of their friends had found homes, for better or for worse. But no one had wanted these waifs. Some, Hilda knew, had one or even two parents yet living, but the parents either could not or would not care for their children. So they had sent them off in search of a home. A happy home, with people to love and care for them? Or a place of misery, slaving, between beatings, for a crust of bread and a blanket in the hayloft? They had no way of knowing, these helpless ones, and virtually nothing to say about their fate.

The children were gone. Hilda wiped away a tear and turned to Andy, who had arrived belatedly. "Help me look for him."

The train station was small, with few places for concealment. Erik wasn't there. Andy checked the waiting room and ticket office. Hilda surveyed the platform and the surrounding bushes. No Erik, nothing but the orphan train, which stood puffing impatiently, waiting for the return of those who were, yet again, left unchosen.

"Can you stay here for a little, Andy? In case he comes when the children return? I'll go to his house; maybe he is there now."

But the house was still deserted.

Hilda fell into Sven's big chair in the parlor. She couldn't think what to do. She was too tired. If Erik had been at the train station, maybe he had hidden somewhere nearby. He was all right. He had to be all right! He would come home soon, and she would scold him thoroughly when she saw him, and then broach the idea of his working as a stable boy. Meanwhile, she would go to the pump in the backyard and pump herself a dipperful of good, cold water. She would find the buttonhook and ease her painful feet. In a moment . . .

Her doze was interrupted by a knock on the back door. Muttering some highly improper Swedish, she answered the summons.

"Miss, I know where Erik is," said Andy. He sounded scared.

"Where? What is the matter?"

"He's on the orphan train. He was hiding somewhere, in the building next door, I guess, and I saw him jump on the train just before it pulled out. He's gone, miss."

9

Of all the animals, the boy is the most unmanageable.
—PLATO, *THE REPUBLIC*, FOURTH CENTURY B.C.

FOR a moment Hilda's mind held only one thought: Patrick! Tell Patrick what had happened! This was a crisis of the first order, but Patrick would help. He would know what to do.

Then she remembered. "Don't go to the firehouse . . . he doesn't want to see you . . . the other firemen tease him . . ."

She gave Andy such a fierce look that he took a step back, but her anger was not for him. "Andy, you must go to the police."

"The police, miss?" He took two more steps back. "The police, they don't think much of the likes of us. I don't want—"

"But you must! You can run much faster than I. You must go to the main station—you know where it is, in City Hall?"

Andy nodded unhappily.

"You must go and ask for Sergeant Wright. He knows me. If they do not want to let you speak to him, tell them Miss Johansson sent you and it is very urgent."

"Please, miss!" Andy was nearly in tears. "I can't go there!

They won't believe me, and if my ma ever found out I was in the police station, she'd skin me alive."

"But, Andy! We must do something, and quick! Erik is going away, we do not know where, we do not know how to stop the train . . ." Hilda, too, was near tears, but she pulled herself together and tried to think. "Sven, then. We must tell my brother Sven. Do you know where he works?"

"Oh, yes, miss! Erik told me he's the best painter at Studebaker's. And I know where the paint shop is, too. And, miss, he would know where there's a telephone, and maybe he could call that policeman you know."

"Andy, you are one smart boy! Go, run!"

It would be, Hilda knew, at least half an hour before any help could come. She also knew that there was nothing useful she could do in that half hour. Nevertheless, it took all her strength simply to wait.

Patience had never been one of Hilda's virtues. She wanted to run to the train station and ask the stationmaster to send a telegram to the next stop on the orphan train's route. He would certainly pay no attention to her, but she wanted to try. She wanted to go out on the street and accost the first policeman she saw, begging him to do something. That would do no good, either. By the time she could make him understand, better help would be at hand.

Most of all she wanted to fly to Patrick, berate him, weep, seek his aid and comfort.

She gritted her teeth and set out for the nearby Wilson Shirt Factory where Mama and Elsa worked. They had to be told, and better that Hilda bring the bad news than a policeman. She could, she hoped, minimize the threat of real danger. Mama would fuss, and scold Hilda as though it were her fault, but that was better than seeing Mama's face filled with terror. And anything, anything was better than sitting doing nothing.

The people at Wilson's weren't eager to let Hilda in. "It is our rule not to distract the women at their work," said the hard-faced woman who sat, dragonlike, at the front of the room full of sewing machines. She had to raise her voice over the clack-whirr, clack-whirr of dozens of foot pedals moving up and down, dozens of balance wheels turning busily, dozens of needles tirelessly punching hundreds of tiny holes in fabric as dozens of seams were joined. In one corner sat the younger employees, some (like Elsa) barely out of their childhood, doing the hand work, making buttonholes and sewing on buttons. They talked but little at their work. Hilda knew that socializing was frowned upon as another distraction.

However . . .

"This is an emergency," she said fiercely to the dragon lady. "I must see my mother. It is a matter of life and death!"

The dragon lady had heard it before. "Hmph. And who's died?"

"It is my little brother, and he is not yet dead, and he needs his mother!" With that Hilda set off across the room to where her mother sat, back turned to the door, hard at work on a shirt of some striped material.

Mama's shriek when Hilda spoke a few words was satisfactory from one point of view. The dragon lady, convinced at last that something really was seriously wrong, consented with bad grace to Mama's departure, and with even more reluctance to Elsa's accompanying her. "I suppose she'd be no use anyway, with her mind on other things." Her tone said quite clearly that nothing other than work was of much importance, but girls being what they were, one sometimes had to give in. "Mind you're both here bright and early tomorrow."

"If all is well with my son, we will be here," Mama said with a steely glare.

"Hmph!" said the dragon lady.

"Now," said Mama when they were out the door, "tell me." Both her voice and the clutch of her hand on Hilda's arm were dry and hard.

Hilda took a deep breath and began, in rapid-fire Swedish, to tell what she knew of the situation, picking her way between truth and expediency. "Erik has run away,

Mama. I said he was hurt so that terrible woman in there would let you go. I am sorry I had to say it and worry you. He is not hurt, anyway, I do not know that he is, but he has gone on the orphan train. And we must hurry home, because the police will soon be there to help find him."

Mama paled. "And why would he do such a thing?" she whispered. "Why would my little boy leave his good home?"

Maybe because he's not a little boy anymore, and you treat him like one, Hilda thought. It was, she hoped, the real explanation, but she didn't say it out loud. She offered palliatives. "He is confused, Mama. America is not like Sweden. The city is not like the farm. He loves you, Mama, he loves us all, but he has not found a way to fit in, here in South Bend. It was a very foolish and naughty thing to do, but he is young."

"He has always liked you the best, of all the family," Mama said after an interval of silence. The comment seemed irrelevant, but Hilda understood. She patted Mama's hand.

"And this friend of yours, the policeman," said Mama, walking faster, her chin lifted. "He will help us? You trust him?"

"He is the man who found Fritz Schlager, Mama." She glanced at Elsa, and Mama shook her head fractionally. Elsa mustn't know the details of Fritz's harrowing experience.

"He is a good man, Sergeant Wright," Hilda continued, "and I think a good policeman. And I am sure that he will help us." She almost succeeded in convincing herself.

When they arrived at the house, Mama, who could sit still no more easily than Hilda could, busied herself making coffee while awaiting the police. Elsa scurried to the pantry and found a tin of *spritsar*, the rich butter cookies Mama made to perfection. They were set out on one of Mama's best plates. Even in the midst of crisis, even when callers were the police come to do their duty, the rules of Swedish hospitality were to be observed.

Hilda, with nothing to do, paced.

They had to wait for only a few minutes. Sergeant Wright,

with a clatter of hooves on the new brick pavement, pulled up in one of the police buggies, a Studebaker Izzer. Sven was with him. Andy, shy and fearful of the police, was not.

"Quickly, Hilda," Sven commanded, and Hilda responded with all she knew of what had happened. She left out what she feared, but an exchange of glances told her the policeman understood the gravity of the situation.

He wasted no time. Without so much as a sip of coffee or a bite of cookie, he was off again in the direction of the train station. Once more the family had to wait, and now Mama's tongue was loosed—and her temper, as well.

"You should have stopped him," she said fiercely to Hilda. "It was foolish to come back here when you knew he was there. You should have found him and brought him home."

Hilda knew it was in vain to protest that she had not known where Erik was, that she had come back to the house to look for him, that she had been tired and confused and was not, in any case, her brother's keeper. But the first crisis was past, and her feelings had to be vented, so she said all those things anyway, and added more. Sven tried to intervene, Elsa wept, and the altercation was growing bitter when Sergeant Wright returned.

He walked into the parlor. "Ahem," he said. "I did knock, but no one heard."

Mama, Hilda, and Sven fell silent; Elsa sobbed quietly.

Sergeant Wright cleared his throat again. "I'm sorry you folks have been worried so, but it's all right. I wired New Carlisle to have 'em stop the train when it came through. I was afraid I might have missed the train there, so I wired Michigan City, too. But I got a reply from New Carlisle right away, and they have Erik. The authorities on the train spotted him and put him off, first chance they got."

Mama turned so white Hilda thought she was going to faint, but she reached for the top of a chair and steadied herself. She took a deep breath. "Sir," she said in English, "we are grateful to you. Will you take coffee and *spritsar* with us?"

When everyone was provided with refreshment, and not until then, she asked the next question. "When will my Erik come home?"

"Soon, ma'am. I hope you don't mind, but I told the C and SB folks to put him on the next eastbound train and we'd pay for his ticket when he got here. I can pay the fare myself, if—"

"That will not be necessary," said Sven in his deep voice. "It is kind of you to offer, but we can pay. Will Erik be in trouble when he gets back?"

Sergeant Wright looked at Mrs. Johansson and hid a smile. "Well, now, not so far as I'm concerned. He did a mighty foolish thing, but he didn't hurt anybody. I don't know what the authorities in charge of the orphans will say, but nothing much, I don't imagine. So that leaves it up to you folks, I guess."

Mama's lips tightened. She said nothing. Hilda drew breath, but Sven laid his hand on her shoulder, heavily, and she desisted.

"Ma'am, if you'll allow me to have a word, I wouldn't be too hard on him," said the sergeant. "He's never been in trouble before, has he?"

"Only the things every boy does," Hilda said before Mama could open her mouth. "He has been discharged from many jobs, but he is young and he is not used to American ways. I think maybe he ran away to be on a farm, like in Sweden. He is good with animals. I—had thought he might get a job here in the city as a stable boy. He would like that, and he can work very hard when it is with horses."

Sergeant Wright nodded thoughtfully. "That sounds like a good idea, Miss Johansson, and if I might suggest—the police department is always needing stable boys for our horses. 'Course the stables are a few doors away from the station, now we've moved to City Hall, but I could ask if we need anybody just now. The boy does speak English?"

"He speaks very good English," said Hilda quickly, "better than me, more like a real American."

"Well, then, I'll see what I can do. That's if you approve, ma'am?"

Mama looked dubious. Her boy working for the police? It was a new idea, and not entirely a welcome one. He might behave, with the police there to keep an eye on him. On the other hand, if he did *not* behave, the consequences could be swift and terrible. These American police were said to be different from the ones back in Sweden, not so severe sometimes. And this sergeant seemed nice enough, but she had heard other things about the South Bend police, that they were corrupt, perhaps . . .

Sergeant Wright took a healthy swig of his coffee and gave an admiring shake of his head. "This coffee's better than what my mother makes, ma'am, and I never tasted such cookies. I reckon you're a fine woman and a fine mother, and whatever you decide to do about your son will be right and proper, ma'am."

"You may ask about the yob," said Mama, still stiffly, but less stiffly than before. "It may be dat what Hilda says is right, and Erik needs a yob more like what he knows."

"Good!" said the sergeant heartily. "And you won't punish him too much? I know he's worried the daylights out of you, but likely he didn't mean to."

"I will t'ink on it," said Mama.

"Well, I'll be on my way, then. The next train's due in at seven-thirteen. I reckon one of you'll want to meet the young rascal when he comes home."

"I will meet him," said Sven grimly.

"And give him a smack or two where it'll do the most good, I guess? Well, that'll do him no harm. Good day, ma'am, sir. Good day, Miss Johansson. I hope to see you again at a happier time."

He bowed his way out the door.

10

*Difference of religion breeds more quarrels than
difference of politics.*

—WENDELL PHILLIPS, IN A SPEECH,
NOVEMBER 7, 1860

THEY all sat in the exhausted silence of relief when he had
gone. Elsa had stopped sniffling and was reaching for a
third or fourth cookie when Mama spoke in Swedish.
"Hilda, how do you know this man?"

"I told you, he found Fritz Schlager."

"And you, what have you to do with Fritz Schlager?"

Hilda had been very careful to tell her mother nothing of
her involvement with the disappearance and rediscovery of
the boy. Slight as it was, it was sure to incur parental wrath.
Now it seemed she had no choice but to tell.

"I gave the sergeant an idea of where he might be, that
is all."

Mama said nothing. Hilda waited.

"He likes you," said Mama finally.

Hilda, prepared to defend herself against charges of med-
dling and putting herself in danger, was taken aback. To her fury,
she blushed. "He is a pleasant man, that is all. He is polite."

Mama snorted. "If you cannot tell the difference between

courtesy and attraction, you are more of a child than I imagined. He likes you, and you know it perfectly well."

Hilda could, in what she considered a good cause, lie fluently to almost anybody—except Mama. "He—I—" she stammered.

"And he is not Irish," Mama pursued.

That was undeniable.

"He is a good admirer for you to have," Mama pronounced. "I do not care for the police, but he is not like some. Ask him to Sunday dinner one day."

"Mama, I do not know him well enough for that! We have met only because of police business."

"But he would like to know you better, and he wants to see you again. He said so. And we owe him our gratitude for finding Erik so soon, and maybe finding him a job. Invite him to dinner, Hilda."

Hilda looked at Sven, who shrugged.

"We are too many here for dinner already," said Hilda doggedly. "How can we fit in one more?" It was a last-ditch effort, and she knew it.

Mama stood. "I will borrow a chair. There will be room at the table. This Sunday, Hilda."

Hilda did not stay to welcome Erik home, if welcome was the word. She had to be back at Tippecanoe Place by sundown on her days out; that was shortly after eight, this time of the year. She was sorry she couldn't be there to soften Mama's wrath, but perhaps it was just as well. She was tired, footsore, and annoyed, and she might have lost her temper with an impenitent Erik. Which, knowing Erik, was likely to be his attitude.

Erik wasn't her only problem, either. As she limped home—really, she had to do something about these boots— she fretted over Sergeant Wright.

He *did* have nice manners. Hilda admitted that. And he

had done the Johansson family a good turn. Runaways were often treated severely by the police—if they were found. Hilda's worst nightmare, that Erik wouldn't be found, had been forestalled. The sergeant had really been a big help.

If only he weren't so—so—

Hilda couldn't think of the word, even in Swedish. He had done nothing incorrect, made no improper advances. He had a right to call on her, to ask her on an outing. But—

But there was Patrick. She had told Patrick the sergeant meant nothing to her, or she had asked Norah to tell him, which came to the same thing. Now Mama was insisting she invite the sergeant to a family dinner, and what would Patrick think about that?

Never had Patrick been invited to cross the Johansson threshold. He had met her siblings only two or three times, and not under the most friendly of circumstances. Sven and Gudrun, especially, had accepted him only grudgingly. Mama had never met him and never intended to. She had said so, in so many words. Of her whole family, only Erik treated Patrick like a person, like a friend, and that was probably because Erik, like Hilda, was a rebel.

"He is not Irish," Mama had said of Sergeant Wright. "He is not Catholic," was what she had meant.

Hilda brightened at the thought. Maybe the sergeant *was* Catholic. Lots of people were who weren't Irish, or Polish, or Hungarian. Sergeant Wright might even *be* Polish or Hungarian. The name sounded English, true, and he spoke with an American accent, but his father might have had his name changed at Ellis Island. It certainly happened often enough, usually when the officials couldn't pronounce foreign names. And if the sergeant had been born in this country, he would probably speak like other native-born citizens.

Well, maybe not if he was Polish or Hungarian. Even Hilda's determined effort at optimism couldn't quite make her believe that. Polish and Hungarian families tended to resist being Americanized. They spoke their native language in the home, sent their children to parochial schools where they could, most of the time, use that same language, and organized their social life around their churches and the numerous Polish or Hungarian clubs. Hilda knew some third-generation Polish-Americans who still spoke English with a pronounced accent.

He could still be Catholic, thought Hilda stubbornly. She would figure out a way to ask him. If he was, Mama would never again bring up the invitation to Sunday dinner!

That wouldn't solve the Patrick problem, though. Even when Patrick came to his senses and stopped acting like a jealous infant, he would still be Irish and Catholic, and their marriage would still be out of the question.

Hilda received a note the next morning. It was delivered by a small boy and handed in at the back door to Anton, the footman. He brought it upstairs to Hilda, who was dusting the library.

"I didn't let Mr. Williams see," he whispered with a conspiratorial grin.

"Thank you, Anton." Hilda grinned back. She wondered fleetingly, as she opened the envelope, if the butler had any idea of the extent to which the staff was allied against him.

The note read:

Dear Miss Johansson,

I thought you might like to know that Erik is home, safe and sound and none the worse for his experience, though he may have trouble sitting down for a day or two. I have looked into the matter of a job for him and found that our downtown stables do need another boy. Your mother has given me permission to try him for a week to see if he will settle into the position.

May I call on you on Sunday afternoon? I thought you
might like to see where Erik is working.

Yours respectfully,
Sgt. Richard Wright

"The boy is waiting for an answer," said Anton.

Hilda thought for a moment, then picked up a pencil from
the desk and wrote on the back of the note:

Dear Sgt. Wright,

I must go to church on Sunday, and then to dinner with my
family. I do not know when you are free after Mass. Perhaps there will not be enough time to go to the stables.

H.J.

She wasn't entirely pleased with her wording. It was foolish to suggest that even the latest Mass might occupy his
whole afternoon, but it ought to tell her what she needed to
know. She sent it off with Anton feeling mildly satisfied with
herself.

She felt less satisfied half an hour later when Anton
trudged upstairs once more with the reply:

Dear Miss Johansson,

I am a Methodist. In fact, I attend the new St. Paul's
Church with your employers. I will be free shortly after
noon on Sunday.

I could call for you at your brother's house at about
three, if that is convenient?

R. W.

She sighed. There was no help for it, after all. Well, she
might as well get it over with. Perhaps sooner was better than
later, anyway. Dinner with her family now would seem more

like gratitude and less like—something else. Her reply was brief and to the point:

> Perhaps you would like to come and have Sunday dinner with us after church, if you have no other plans. We eat at about twelve-thirty.
>
> H.J.

The rest of the week seemed very long, with no word from Patrick. Hilda spent most of her working hours and nearly all the time when she should have been at rest debating with herself about what to do. Should she send Patrick a note? But where would she send it? His mother would be extremely annoyed if she sent it to his home. Mrs. Cavanaugh no longer disliked Hilda quite so much as she had. Hilda had, after all, defused a family situation that could have been scandalous, at best, and fatal at worst. So Hilda as a person was deemed to be acceptable. Hilda as a possible daughter-in-law, however, was an entirely different kettle of fish, and Mrs. Cavanaugh made no bones about her strong disapproval.

A note sent to the firehouse would be almost as bad as a visit there, which Patrick had specifically discouraged.

And what would she say? No apology was called for, Hilda thought fiercely. She had done nothing wrong. To deny that there was any relationship between herself and Sergeant Wright would be to suggest the opposite. Anyway, it wasn't quite true. Hilda was being forced into at least a friendship with the policeman, if nothing more than that.

What she wanted to say was that she missed Patrick and wanted to see him and wanted this silly quarrel to end. But a self-respecting woman couldn't allow her pride to be defeated in that way. If Patrick wanted to see her, he knew where she was. If he did not—Hilda swallowed hard and raised her chin a notch—if he did not, then that was that. It was not a woman's place to seek a man's affection.

Only, she was so lonely.

She longed also to see her family, talk to Erik, find out what was happening. Was Erik now working in his new job? How was Mama treating him? Was Mama still upset about Erik running away? She would, in times past, have had no qualms about taking her rest time to sneak away and talk to Freya. Though the butler at the house where Freya worked didn't like Hilda, the sisters could usually find a way to exchange a few words when a crisis was afoot. These days, however, Hilda was watched too closely. She dared not slip out of the house except on a legitimate errand. Indeed, when she felt a headache threaten on Friday afternoon, and asked Mr. Williams's permission to go to Cimmerman's for some of the wonderful headache powders, he sent Anton instead. She fumed, but she was helpless.

The note she had received from Sergeant Wright, accepting her invitation to Sunday dinner, didn't brighten her mood. His presence would mean that, except for the few minutes' walk from church to Sven's house, she would have no chance at all for family talk. Unless, she thought with a brief lift of her heart, unless she talked to one of them in Swedish. But no, neither Sven nor Gudrun would permit that. Speaking Swedish in front of someone who didn't understand it was rude, and rudeness was not tolerated in the Johansson household. Especially not on Sunday.

She couldn't even talk to Norah about her troubles. Norah, these days, walked a few inches above the floor, enveloped in a pink cloud. Any conversation that didn't involve Sean and their plans simply didn't penetrate the cloud.

In one way and another, the male sex was giving Hilda a good deal of grief.

11

Shameful Abuse of Infant Boy Is Charged
Nineteen-Months-Old Child Said to Have Been
Cruelly Treated by Aunt
      —SOUTH BEND *TRIBUNE,* MAY 27, 1903

SUNDAY morning dawned so bright and glorious that
Hilda couldn't stay gloomy, even with Sergeant Wright
in prospect. He was a nice enough man, after all, she
thought charitably as she tasted her coffee, which was no better than usual. Mrs. Sullivan could cook almost everything
exquisitely, but none of the Irish knew how to make good coffee. Except Patrick, of course. Hilda had taught Patrick to
make proper Swedish-style coffee.

Patrick. She sighed. She had still heard nothing from him.
The trouble, of course, was that Patrick could be almost as
stubborn as Hilda. When she could talk to him, she could always talk him around, eventually. Well, after today she could
wash her hands of Sergeant Wright and could work out a way
to make Patrick see reason.

She hurried through her few morning duties so as to arrive
early at church. She was rewarded by the sight of her family
coming up the street, all seven of them. It didn't take Mama's
cheerful wave for Hilda to know that all was well. Erik's walk

was a positive bounce; he would certainly have broken into a
run if it hadn't been Sunday. The others, from Sven right down
to Birgit, looked as though a heavy burden had been lifted
from their shoulders.

As perhaps it had. Erik had been a great worry to everyone.
If he was happily situated now, life in the Johansson home
would be much easier, and maybe she could stop worrying so
much about the terrible fate that seemed to lie in wait for some
South Bend boys. Maybe it had all just been a coincidence, after all. Probably that other boy was in a good home somewhere,
and Fritz—well, Fritz was maybe making up stories. She
shoved all mental objections to the back of her mind, walked
inside the church, and said heartfelt prayers of thanksgiving.

She was eager to hear all about Erik and his job, but there
were friends to greet after church—good friends and not so
good. Stupid Olaf Lindahl had given up his courting of Hilda,
to her infinite relief, but his almost equally stupid sisters
crowded around Hilda, full of news.

"Olaf is to be married in the fall," said Ingrid Lindahl with
a broad smile. "He is engaged to Hannah Svenson."

Hilda glanced in Hannah's direction. A tall, thin girl, she
was dressed in the height of fashion in pale green silk, with
tucks, flounces, and lace wherever they could fit in. No color
could possibly have been more unbecoming to her. Her hat, a
similarly elaborate affair, was worn at the currently proper angle, well forward, which had the unfortunate effect of em-
phasizing Hannah's long nose and receding chin.

"What a beautiful—dress," said Hilda, hesitating just
long enough for emphasis. "Lace is so useful for enhancing
the figure."

"Her father is with the Merchants National Bank, you
know," went on Ingrid, bridling at the implied insult. "The
Svensons are *most* pleased that Hannah is marrying such a
fine, upstanding man as our Olaf."

"And I am sure Olaf is to be congratulated on a bride-to-
be with such a wealthy—such an *illustrious* family." Hilda

smiled sweetly and moved away. She had suffered much over the years at the hands of Olaf and his family.

She cut Freya out from a herd of young women and pulled her into a quiet corner of the lawn. "Quick! Tell me about Erik! Why did he run away with the orphans?"

"Trouble at work, as usual. Something about some type being spilled, or disarranged, or something—I did not understand it all, but they blamed Erik, and when he came home Mama scolded him, too, and he decided nobody appreciated him and he'd run away."

"And now?"

"Happy as a cat with cream," Freya said with a grin. "I do not know where you found that policeman, but Mama thinks the sun rises and sets on him now. He got Erik that job with no fuss at all, and that boy has changed so much you would hardly know him. Goes to work early, comes home late, and cannot wait to go back the next day. They paid him a little yesterday, even though he had not worked the full week, and he turned all the money over to Mama without a word of complaint."

"All? But that is not fair, he should—"

"She gave most of it back. She said when he got his regular wages she would take half, for food and clothes, and he would save half of what was left, but the rest was his to do with as he liked. What do you think of that?"

"I think it is a miracle," said Hilda devoutly.

Maybe Mama heard that remark as she came up behind them, or maybe she didn't. She smiled somewhat austerely. "Come, girls, we must hurry home. We do not want to keep Sergeant Wright waiting."

Freya grinned at Hilda, Hilda raised her eyes to heaven, and they fell into line behind Mama and the rest of the family.

It was as well that they had hurried. Mama and Gudrun had just gotten their hats off and their aprons on when the knock came at the front door. "Go, Hilda," urged Mama. "We have everything done, almost. You go and entertain your guest."

"Mama, he is your guest, not mine!" But she went, not too

unwillingly. She could, after all, question the sergeant about Erik.

Sergeant Wright, once he had been introduced to the entire family, was only too happy to talk about Erik. "Getting along fine, so far," was his verdict. "Nice kid."

Erik muttered something and left the room, but Hilda thought he was pleased. "He does not like to hear people talk about him," she explained. "He is not rude."

"No, no, nice kid," the sergeant repeated. "Good with horses, too. He'll do all right if he keeps it up."

"We are very grateful to you for finding him the job," said Hilda formally.

"Happy to do it, only too happy," he said. His smile was for the whole family, but it lingered longest in Hilda's direction.

"Good," she said brightly. "Please sit down at the table, just there, and I will help bring in the dinner."

She seated him in a chair next to Sven, far removed from her usual place, but when she returned from the kitchen with a platter of succulent roast pork, she found that Sven had moved. "So that you can talk to your friend," he said with a smile. "Sit down, Hilda. Gudrun has plenty of help with the food."

Hilda frowned at Sven, but sat.

"So, Miss Johansson, you're pleased with Erik?"

"I hope that he will stay longer at this job than the others," she said tartly. "Erik can find many ways to get into trouble."

The sergeant sighed. "He's not the only one. That Chapin Street gang—"

"Andy is a nice boy! He helped me find Erik."

"A lot of them are nice kids, or could be, but they don't all come from a very good background."

Hilda frowned. "They are from immigrant backgrounds, you mean?" There was a dangerous edge to her voice.

"No. That is, yes, they're immigrants—Poles and Hungarians, mostly—but that wasn't what I meant."

"Many people think that immigrants are stupid, or lazy, or that they drink too much," Hilda pursued relentlessly.

"I know better than that, Miss Johansson! Immigrants are like everyone else. Some are fine, upstanding people and a credit to the community. Some are not."

Gudrun brought in the final touches just then and sat down, Erik trailing behind her. Sven said a long and solemn grace, they settled down to eat, and Hilda was able to escape conversation with Sergeant Wright.

Not that general conversation around the table was much better. The family were accustomed to speaking Swedish with each other, and Mama was not yet very comfortable in English. Erik and Birgit, the two youngest, were most at home in the language, but children were not to speak at the dinner table unless spoken to, so they were content to feast quietly on the good things they had been too poor to afford in Sweden. After general agreement that the weather was fine, yes, a beautiful day, spring was here at last, and a few more variations on the same theme, a silence fell.

Sergeant Wright cleared his throat. "Well, Erik, how do you like your new job?"

"Mighty fine, sir," said Erik, beaming. "The horses are good and healthy, and Patrolman Parker said he'd let me start exercising them next week. He found out I know all about horses, y'see, after I told him about the farm in Sweden. I reckon he thinks he's lucky to have someone working there who knows so much."

Hilda grinned. "We had one horse in Sweden, and an old nag at that. How is it you know 'all about horses,' eh, little one?"

"I rode the Lindborgs' horses, too," retorted Erik, stung, "and helped take care of them! That was after you went to America. You don't know how good I am. I can ride bareback or with a saddle, and I can drive a wagon, and I know all about the harness, and—"

"That is enough, Erik. Be quiet," said Mama. "You are de lucky one, I t'ink, to get such a good yob."

"That's right, ma'am, he is," said the sergeant. "Not to puff myself up, but I'm right pleased to see him settled, and I kind of hope he can go on working some, even after he starts back to school. There's a lot can happen to a boy in this town."

Hilda frowned. "What do you mean? Erik is a good boy."

"I'm not saying he isn't. But read the newspaper. Something is forever happening to children in these parts. If they don't run away, they get abandoned, or beaten and starved. Look at that case just a few days ago, that aunt who left her baby nephew alone in the house with no heat, and beat him, and all—and him only nineteen months old!"

Mama made a shocked sound, and Hilda, strongly disapproving, said, "Yes, but none of those things could happen to Erik. We love him and would never mistreat him or abandon him. Do not be foolish, Sergeant Wright."

"I'm sorry, Miss Johansson. I didn't mean to say you would. Erik has a good home. But there's other things. He could get into bad company, like the kids I was talking about earlier."

This time it was Erik who frowned.

Sergeant Wright persisted, doggedly. "Erik, I know you like those boys, but some of them steal, you know. I've caught them at it myself. You remember last January, when they attacked a newsboy and robbed him? And they insult the women who work at Wilson's."

"That's so," said Elsa. "They have called out rude things to me when I pass by. You know they have, Mama."

"Yes," said Mama grimly. "Dat is reason why I tell Erik he not talk to dem!" She broke off and addressed agitated Swedish to Hilda, who translated for the sergeant.

"Mama says she is sorry, but she does not know how to say in English that she has forbidden Erik to have anything to do with the boys on Chapin Street. She is afraid he might get into trouble with them. She says, too, that she wishes the police would do something about that gang. They are a menace to the whole neighborhood."

"They are not!" Erik burst out, unbidden. "Some of them are pretty rough, but most of them are nice. Nice to me, anyway. And I told 'em I'd lick 'em good if they said anything else to my sister and my mother, and they haven't, not lately. Have they, Mama?"

"Be silent, Erik!" said Mama, at the same time that Sven admonished, "Silence is golden, remember." Shyly, Elsa dared say, "It is true, Mama. It is a little time since they said anything."

"I think we will have no more talk of this," said Sven. "Erik will have no time now to run with these boys." Erik looked rebellious, and Sven continued, "If there are some of them, Erik, who are well-behaved, you may play with them, but Mama or I must meet them first, and we would like to know who their parents are."

"That's a good idea," said the sergeant heartily. "I'm sure they're not all bad, but it's just as well to know the families. Make sure there's no smallpox there, for one thing, or typhoid." He pushed back his plate. "That was a mighty fine dinner, ma'am, and I'm much obliged. Now, Erik, would you like to show Hilda where you work?"

Hilda went off with the two of them feeling sure that Sergeant Wright, despite his protestations, had an aversion to certain kinds of immigrants.

12

Stubbornness is as iniquity. . . .

I SAMUEL, 15:23

ERIK, you may run, if you like. We will follow." Hilda gave her brother a pat on his rump, and he very willingly ran on ahead.

Sergeant Wright smiled at Hilda. "So now we can talk, eh, Miss Johansson?"

"Yes," said Hilda briskly. "We can talk about Fritz Schlager. What has happened? Have the police found Mr. Shaw? I have not been able to read the newspapers for several days."

The sergeant's smile faded. He sighed, almost inaudibly. "Not a trace of him. We've caught up with a couple of members of the troupe, the ones who aren't part of the family. Man and wife, tightrope walkers. Found them in Fort Wayne, looking for work. They said they traveled with the circus on the train, not with the Shaw family in the wagon. They waited in Fort Wayne at the fairgrounds for the wagon to roll up, but it never did. There they were, left high and dry, without their equipment even."

"What equipment does a tightrope walker need, besides a rope?" Hilda asked, momentarily diverted.

"Dunno, but that's what they said. Those long poles they use to balance themselves, maybe? Anyway, seems everything for the act traveled in the wagon. Must have been pretty crowded, with four people, but that's the way the Shaws wanted it."

"I do not understand about the train. I thought the circus traveled always in their wagons."

"Just the parts that can't go by train, from what they tell me. The animals travel in wagons, of course, and the acts that need a lot of gear. The band, say. There's one big wagon that carries all the instruments, music, uniforms—all that. But the musicians go by train, see. Same with the clowns. Those big hoops they jump through, and all that, that goes by wagon. But the people take the train."

"I see. And the tightrope walkers, they did not know where the Shaws went?"

"Never had any idea they were going anyplace. I guess they were pretty disgusted when they figured it out."

Hilda frowned. "Me, if I were looking for them, I would look where there are other circuses, small ones. These people must somehow earn money, and if circus work is all they can do, they must find a circus."

"We're doing our best, Miss Johansson. It isn't easy."

Hilda looked affronted and the sergeant hastened to make amends. "Not that your idea isn't a good one. We're trying to follow up on that sort of thing, but we don't have enough men to send someone out scouring the countryside. We've sent wires to towns where we know circuses are coming, but there are a lot of these little outfits, you know."

"I know, but—" Hilda stopped and shut her mouth. Erik was waiting for them on the corner.

"Come *on*, Hilda, hurry up!" Erik grabbed Hilda's hand to urge her on, just as he used to as a baby. Hilda smiled at him.

"Yes, little one. We will hurry." Trying to ignore the pain in her feet, she stepped up the pace, and Sergeant Wright followed with another sigh.

The police stables were new and very nice. Erik pointed out the salient features with pride. "There's electric lighting, see? It's safer than gas or lanterns, with all the straw around. And it means that even if the patrolmen have to go out at night, they can see to harness up the horses. Pretty fancy, huh?"

Hilda agreed that it was pretty fancy.

"And look at the paddy wagons! Three of them, all Studebakers. I guess you're pretty proud of that!"

Hilda expressed her pride in Studebaker paddy wagons.

All the horses had to be introduced and admired. "They are fine animals, Erik. You look after them well."

"And they all know me, even after just three days. Don't you, Admiral?" He patted the nose of a handsome bay. The horse snorted gently and nuzzled Erik's shoulder. Delighted, Erik took a lump of sugar (filched from the family dining table) from his pocket and held it out on his flat hand for Admiral.

Sergeant Wright chuckled. "He has a way with horses, young Erik does. Admiral, now, he's a stubborn one. Likes to make up his own mind. If it isn't his idea, he won't even take treats, usually. But Erik won him over right away. Don't you spoil them, now," the sergeant cautioned Erik. "They're working animals, not pets. Don't forget that."

"Oh, no, sir, but you can't spoil a horse with love. That's what Mr. Lindborg always said, and I reckon he's right."

"I reckon he is," said Hilda thoughtfully, giving Erik a hug. "Sergeant Wright, thank you for showing me the stables, but Erik and I must go now."

"Oh, but I had thought—maybe some ice cream at the Philadelphia—"

Erik looked pleadingly at Hilda, but she shook her head. "No, thank you. Come, Erik." With her arm still around his shoulders, she urged Erik to the door.

"Maybe another time?" said Sergeant Wright, but Hilda, already outside, pretended not to hear.

"No ice cream?" said Erik as Hilda hurried him down the street. "Why not?"

"Erik, I will buy you ice cream another day. Not today."

"Why not?" he repeated.

"Because my feet hurt and I want to go home and take my boots off." It wasn't the main reason, but it was true enough, and would do for an excuse.

"But my feet don't hurt. You could have let him take me."

"Erik, do not tease. And walk slower, please. It is hot today, and anyway, it is Sunday. You should behave yourself."

"You let me run before," said Erik, but he said it very quietly. Hilda could be pushed only so far.

"That was because I wanted to talk to Sergeant Wright."

"Is he your new beau, Hilda?"

"No!" She said it with such vigor that Erik chuckled.

"Reckon he is, though, coming to Sunday dinner and all. Reckon he thinks so, anyway."

"If he thinks so, he will not think so for long."

"Why not? He's a nice man, and he likes you."

"He is all right, but he is not . . ." Hilda didn't finish, and Erik, after one sharp look at her, had the sense to keep quiet.

Hilda, too, was quiet. She was thinking hard.

Nearing Tippecanoe Place, they turned up Taylor Street, toward the back drive. Erik started to walk on home, but Hilda took his hand. "No, come in with me."

Erik's eyes widened. "You never let me come inside before. Will you get in trouble?"

"Not if you are quiet and good. Most of the servants will be out, and if Mr. Williams is in, he will be taking his nap. You must not wake him!"

Erik shook his head solemnly. He knew all about the tyrannical Mr. Williams.

The two of them went down the outside stairs quietly and stole in the back door. Hilda put her finger to her lips as Erik followed her to the servants' room.

It was empty. She relaxed and allowed Erik to enter.

"Sa-ay! This is *some* place, all right! A fireplace, even! And look at all the fancy stuff!" He turned around slowly, taking in

tables, oil lamps, the gas chandelier, vases filled with late daffodils and tulips.

"And all that 'fancy stuff' has to be dusted, little one."

"Do you have to clean it all?"

"No, the underhousemaids do this room. It does not matter so much if it is not done perfectly, because only the servants ever see it. This is where we eat and where we sit when
there is time to sit."

"Can I see the rest of the house?"

Hilda considered. "Not all of it, not today. You may look at
the breakfast room and the dining room. No one will be in
there now. Go that way, through the butler's pantry, and be sure
that you touch nothing."

Hilda hoped he would obey. She didn't even want to think
about the consequences if anything were broken or damaged.
She really ought to have gone with him, but she had something else to do. She sat down at a small writing table, found a
pencil, and pulled out the pad Mrs. Sullivan used for her gro-
cery lists.

When Erik returned a few minutes later, he was full of
questions. What was that stuff on the dining room walls and
ceiling? (Leather.) How many people could eat dinner at the
same time? (At least one hundred, if the breakfast room and
the reception room were also used. Fifty or thereabouts in the
dining room alone.) Sa-ay, how much would it cost to feed
that many people?

"I do not know. It is not polite to ask that kind of question."

"Why not?"

Hilda laughed. "I do not know, really, but in this house we
do not talk about money. Maybe it is because there is always
enough, and more than enough, and the family does not need
to talk about it."

"I'd talk about it, if I had that much!"

"You are not likely to. Now, Erik, I want you to do something for me."

He became instantly wary. "What? Why?"

"I want you to take a note to Patrick for me, because I cannot go to his house."

"Why not?"

"Oh, Erik, you ask too many questions. You know why not. Mrs. Cavanaugh does not like me. She would be angry if I went to the house. But you, she does not know you. She will answer the door to you."

Erik looked skeptical. "What if she won't let me give him the note? If she doesn't like you, she might not."

"You will not say the note is from me. You will go to his house. It is just up Taylor Street, past St. Patrick's Church." She gave him the street number. "You will ask if Patrick—but say 'Mr. Patrick'—you will ask if he is at home, that you have a message for him. Do not say that it is a note, just a message. And if he is there, give him the note. If he is at the firehouse, take it to him there."

"Say, Hilda, how come Patrick isn't here? How come you didn't spend Sunday with him, like you always do?"

Hilda hesitated, and then decided to trust Erik. "We have quarreled. It was not all my fault, but partly, it was. It was silly, and I have been too stubborn to say I was sorry."

"Oh. Like Admiral."

"Exactly like Admiral, little one. Now go. I will wait for you on the bench by the back drive."

"If Patrick comes back with me, can we have some ice cream?"

"*Go!*" She gave him a little push, but she was smiling as she moved toward the back stairs. Erik was a good boy, and he was safe, and she was about to make up with Patrick, and she was about to get out of her pinching boots.

Clad in slippers she had knitted herself, with soles salvaged from some moccasins Mrs. Clem had decided she didn't like, Hilda walked back down the stairs and out the back door. She didn't like going outside in slippers, but her blisters were painful enough that appearance was a secondary consideration. Walking on the soft, thick grass in soft slippers was bliss.

Sitting on the bench, waiting, she had time to worry about her note. Had she said too much? Not enough? Had—oh, horror! Had Mrs. Cavanaugh taken the note from Erik and read it?

It was a very simple note, saying only that Hilda hoped Patrick was not angry with her, that she was sorry she had upset him, and that she hoped they could meet this afternoon. Only that, but if Mrs. Cavanaugh saw it—

Erik returned soon, and alone. He was out of breath, and Hilda had to wait anxiously till he could speak.

"He's at home," Erik managed at last. "He said—to tell you—that he can't come today—but he'll be here Wednesday—and he's sorry he lost his temper." Having gasped that out, Erik took a deep breath and asked hopefully, "Can I have some ice cream anyway? I ran all the way, both ways."

Hilda laughed. "And I am to reward you for running? On a Sunday, too! *And* in your best shoes, which I hope you have not scuffed."

Erik was not at all put out. Hilda's words might scold, but her tone was indulgent. "So can I?"

She reached in her pocket and fished out a nickel. "You go by yourself. I cannot walk to the Philadelphia in carpet slippers, and I have no wish to put my boots back on." She stood and smiled at Erik, ruffling his hair. "It is well, little one. Enjoy your ice cream, but do not talk to strangers. And do not be too late going home. Mama will worry."

Erik started to run down the drive, then turned around, grinned at Hilda, and walked off sedately. She laughed again and went into the house for a nap.

13

Fire is the best of servants, but what a master!
—THOMAS CARLYLE, *PAST AND PRESENT*, 1843

HILDA did a great deal of thinking between Sunday and Wednesday. A maid's work is hard, it is constant, it is tedious, but it requires only a fraction of one's mind. While the hands dust and polish and scrub, the brain is free to deal with other things. So while she was on hands and knees scrubbing the tiles on the bathroom floors, while she was on ladders polishing the elaborate chandeliers, while she dusted Colonel George's office, careful not to disarrange his papers, she thought about Patrick. She thought about Erik. She thought about Fritz Schlager.

When Patrick arrived after lunch on Wednesday, she was ready for him.

Patrick greeted her with an odd diffidence. The truth was that he was more than a little nervous. He was aware that the coolness between them had been mostly his doing, and he hated feeling guilty. Then, too, Hilda had sent him a conciliatory note, which was most unlike her. Their past quarrels had always ended with him being the one to give in. Would she have regretted that note by now? Would her famous temper be roused? Should he bluster and bully, or try to placate?

Hilda gave him no chance to try either approach. She was waiting for him, sitting on the bench because her feet hurt, but she sprang to her feet when he came up the drive.

"There you are! Good, first we go to White's, for I must buy a new pair of boots. These I can wear no longer! Then we go maybe to the park?"

"It looks like rain," said Patrick dubiously. The afternoon was warm—all of May had been unusually warm, after the terribly cold April—but there was a thundery feel in the air, which was thick and hard to breathe.

"If it rains we go somewhere else, somewhere we can talk. There is much I want to talk to you about, Patrick!"

He gave her a sidelong look, but there was no menace in her tone, only her usual confident enthusiasm. He shrugged. "The park if it doesn't rain, then. Here, you'll step right out of those boots. They're unbuttoned at the top." He almost blushed; only a mighty effort kept him from it. One did not lightly mention to a lady that her apparel was not properly fastened.

"I know. I cannot button them up anymore. They will not fall off; they are too tight. And my skirt covers them, mostly. But I am glad White's is not far away."

There were a number of shoe stores in the one-hundred block of West Washington; White's was the closest and the cheapest. "No shoe over $3.00" was their motto, and Hilda hoped to pay a good deal less than that. There were ladies' boots in the Sears, Roebuck catalog for $1.98 that looked perfectly all right, and Hilda would have bought them if she had been prepared to wait for delivery. She had decided her feet hurt too much for her usual strict economy.

Once in the store, Hilda had to try on half the stock, walk around in several pairs, and firmly rebuff the clerk's attempts to sell her extra laces, boot polish, and a shoe horn. Patrick would have been extremely bored had he not been beguiled by the sight of Hilda's pretty feet and neat ankles. He began to feel that the life of a shoe clerk had a few things to recommend it.

When they finally left the store, the clouds were thicker and darker than before, and a distant rumble of thunder could be heard, no more than a shudder, but ominous, all the same.

"Not the park," Hilda said in answer to Patrick's lifted eyebrow. "But I do not want to go back home. There is no privacy there. Mr. Williams might listen."

Patrick guffawed at that idea. "No need to worry about that. He'll be having his nap. But why don't we go get some ice cream somewhere?"

"Not ice cream," said Hilda, "not for me. I am not hungry. But something to drink, something fizzy, yes. We must hurry, though. It is going to rain very soon."

They didn't make it as far as the Philadelphia. Nobile's, smaller but nearer, was their refuge just as the storm began.

The place was crowded. Many shoppers had sought shelter from the storm, and in the hot, close atmosphere the soda fountain was doing a roaring trade. The front door stood open, and from time to time a gust of cooler air would blow in a slash of rain. Thunder cracked, lightning flashed. In one corner of the shop a brand-new electric fan (of which Mr. Nobile was very proud) did its rattly best to cool the air.

With all the noise going on, it was a perfect place to talk privately. Hilda wriggled onto a stool at the far end of the counter and asked for a strawberry phosphate. Patrick, wedged beside her, ordered a Coca-Cola.

"Now," said Hilda quietly, but in a businesslike tone. "It is about Fritz Schlager. Patrick, I do not think the police are doing very much to find the man who mistreated him."

"Well, you'd know, wouldn't you? Goin' around with that Wright all the time." Patrick had come out determined to avoid a quarrel if he could, but at the thought of the other man, his jealousy rose to swamp his common sense.

Hilda, however, was in command of herself. "Patrick. I do not go with him all the time, only when I cannot help myself. I will tell you, since you will find out anyway, that he had dinner at our house on Sunday. Mama made me ask him. He wanted me to have ice cream with him, but I said no. I think he will try to see me again, but I will keep on saying no."

"Is he botherin' you, then? I'll settle him if he is!" Patrick's eyes gleamed with the light of a thousand battling ancestors.

Outside the storm increased in intensity. Hilda no longer had to keep her voice low. Indeed, she could not, not if she wanted Patrick to hear. "I do not want you to fight with him, Patrick," she said firmly. "For I must maybe ask him some more questions, and I want him to answer them."

"Questions about what?" Patrick's brows came together in a scowl, despite his best intentions. His voice, also raised to compete with the storm, sounded both surly and suspicious.

"About Fritz Schlager," said Hilda with a sigh. "Pay attention, Patrick." She sipped at her strawberry phosphate.

A flash of lightning was followed instantly by a crack of thunder, so loud and menacing that several ladies screamed. The electroliers over the counter flickered once, twice, then stayed on.

"That was close," said Patrick. He tried, over the tumult within and without, to hear the bells and whistles of a fire wagon. "I'll need to go, Hilda, if a building was struck."

"Yes." Hilda shivered and pushed her drink away. The wind coming in the open door was cold, now, and strong, shrieking like a thing in torment. Mr. Nobile moved hurriedly to close the door; the candy in the front window was getting wet. He had to have help to force the door shut.

"But listen, Patrick. I want this man Shaw to be caught and punished. It is not safe for men like him to be free. Other children, even Erik, maybe . . ." She shivered again, not this time from cold.

Patrick nodded soberly. "It's bad, all right. He's a menace. But how're you thinkin' you can help? He's likely miles from here, now."

Quickly she reiterated her ideas about small circuses.

Patrick shrugged. "Makes sense. But the police've surely thought of it, and they can do that kind of thing much better than the likes of us."

"But they have not found him, Patrick! I think they do not try hard, because the Schlagers are immigrants. Think, Patrick! If it were a little Studebaker boy who had been hurt, or an Oliver, or Mayor Fogarty's son, they would send out every man, the army maybe, even, and not rest until Mr. Shaw was found. But Fritz is only the son of a German laborer. So we must help find the man, Patrick, you and I and other immigrants who care. We must—"

Patrick held up his hand. Now, rising above the clamor of wind and thunder, he could hear the wild clanging of the bells. Loud, insistent, they approached nearer and nearer. "I've got to go, Hilda. That's more than one wagon. It could be bad. I'll come to the house later, if I can. And I'll try to help you, if I can figger out how!" He forced his way through the patrons, who were crowding around the door to try to see the fire. Hilda lost sight of him.

She let out a long breath. She had not dared admit to herself how afraid she had been. Afraid that Patrick would refuse a reconciliation, would refuse to have anything to do with investigating the crime. Now things were back to normal, or as normal as they could be with a dreadful criminal at large. Together she and Patrick would work for justice, as best they could.

There were more bells. The storm had abated now, the rain a mere drizzle, the thunder grumbling itself away. Hilda could hear the clanking of horseshoes on the brick pavement, the singing of steel tires as they sped toward the fire.

She could smell the smoke.

Fear gripped her, so suddenly she thought she might

swoon. Somewhere out there, somewhere very close, a big fire raged, and Patrick was in the thick of it!

The other customers were afraid, too, afraid for themselves if the ice-cream parlor caught. Or perhaps they were merely curious. Now that the rain was nearly over, they poured out of the shop to see what was happening. Hilda tried to battle the tide, get to the front, find Patrick, but she was caught up with the rest, jammed into the middle, and it was several minutes before she could fight her way clear, climb on a bench, and see for herself.

It was the building across the street, a small two-story brick building housing a drugstore and a haberdashery on the ground floor, with offices and a rooming house above. Hilda could see little through the thick clouds of smoke that surrounded the building and now and then billowed toward her, stinging her eyes and filling her throat. Fire wagons filled the street, the firemen busy spraying streams of water on the burning building and adjacent buildings. Firemen out of uniform, or perhaps just helpful citizens, were trying to quiet the horses, unharness them, and lead them to safer environs. Policemen were attempting, with little success, to keep the crowd out of the way of the firemen. It looked to Hilda like complete chaos.

Nowhere could she see Patrick.

It seemed she had stood there, terrified, for hours when strong arms closed around her waist and lifted her down from the bench. She whirled around to scream.

"The roof's going," said Patrick in a matter-of-fact tone. "You'd best get away. There'll be sparks—why, what's the matter, girl?"

Tears streamed unchecked down Hilda's cheeks. "I thought you were—" She couldn't finish.

"Well, I'm not, am I? Nor anybody else, neither. We got everybody out safe and sound. The building's a goner, but we've saved the rest of the block. So come *away*, darlin', before she caves in on us."

Wet and sooty though Patrick was, Hilda clung to him as he drew her away from the danger.

With the collapse of the roof, the firemen's work was nearly at an end. They would continue to wet down the ruins of the building, lest a spark reignite the blaze, but the rain had picked up again, and was doing much of their work for them. Patrick sent Hilda home, saying he'd be there soon. Hilda plodded down Washington Street through the rain, her new boots becoming more sodden with each step.

When she left the business district behind, she realized just how bad the storm had been. Leaves and twigs were everywhere, as well as a few large limbs, wrenched from the trees by the fury of the wind. One young maple tree, heavy with new foliage, had been torn up by the roots and lay blocking the street. Here and there slates had been torn from roofs. One front window was smashed.

Even Tippecanoe Place had not been spared. Tree limbs littered the lawns, and the lilacs looked as though they had been trampled by a herd of buffalo.

Norah, accompanied by Sean, greeted her when she came in the back door. "So there you are, and us worried sick about you! And by the blessed saints, girl, you look like you've been huggin' the coal bucket!"

"Near enough," said Hilda. She could almost smile about it now. "There was a bad fire, downtown, and soot everywhere. That is how I got so dirty."

"*And* wet through," observed Norah. "Me and Sean was at me mother's when the storm hit, so we're almost dry. We came here as soon as it was safe, to see what the damage was."

"And your mother's house? Is it all right?"

"Not touched at all, at all. Yours?"

"I do not know. I must change my clothes, and then I must go and see."

"I heard that part of town wasn't bad hit," Sean contributed. "But I've never seen such a storm as we had here! A cyclone, some say. Don't know how a fire could last against that rain."

"It was caused by lightning. It struck just across the street from Nobile's. Patrick and I were having sodas there."

Sean saw nothing unusual in the remark, but Hilda was gratified by the look of delighted surprise that flitted across Norah's face.

"And I bought my new boots, and now they are wet and dirty and I do not know if I can save them!" Hilda, having dealt with several big problems, was beginning to fret about the small ones.

"Hand 'em over, then, and I'll see what I can do. They look like good leather. I expect they'll clean up all right."

Hilda pulled off the boots with exclamations of dismay and squished up the back stairs in her stockings to change her clothes. She had, of course, worn her good summer dress to go out with Patrick. This was only the second year for it, and it was still in beautiful condition, or it had been. Now she wondered if the stains would ever come out.

She descended again, in her uniform and carpet slippers, just as Patrick knocked on the back door. She stepped outside. He was a sight to behold, even wetter and grimier than when she had last seen him.

"Don't get close to me, darlin'," he said with a tired grin. "I'm not fit to be in a lady's company, and what me mother'll say when she sees me good suit I'm sure I don't know."

"Tell her you saved the lives of the people in that building," said Hilda shrewdly. "She will be so proud of you she won't say anything. But I can brush you down and make you look a little better before you go home."

"No, I'll not come in. I stopped to say I'll try—" He lowered his voice and peered in the screen door. "Where's your boss, then?"

"I do not know. I have not seen him since I came back."

"Better safe than sorry." Patrick's voice lowered still more, to little above a whisper. "I'll try to come by tomorrow, about five, as usual. All right?"

"Yes." It was all she said, but her smile nearly flattened Patrick.

"And I wanted to let you know—mind, it might not mean much—but you'd want to know—"

"What? Tell me!"

"Well, that other boy, the one who went missin' last year?"

"Yes. Tom Brady. What do you know of him?"

"Nothin' about him, but his mother—well, she was livin' in the buildin' that burned. And, Hilda, as things was just startin' to settle down, I thought I heard someone talkin' about Shaw."

14

Tyranny is a habit . . . and at last becomes a disease. . . .

—FYODOR DOSTOYEVSKY,
THE HOUSE OF THE DEAD, 1861

WHAT? What did they say?"

"Don't know. We was busy, still, and there was still a lot of noise and confusion. All I heard was the name. Don't even know who was talkin'. I turned around, but there was people everywhere and smoke, still, and—well, I didn't have time to go askin' about it."

"No." Hilda thought for a moment, then opened the door and touched Patrick's hand. "Thank you. I must go. We will talk tomorrow."

Mr. Williams, apparently just wakened from his nap, was coming out of the kitchen as Hilda reached the stairs to her room.

"Ah, there you are. Back in good time, I see, and just as well. There is a great deal of cleaning up to do. The rain came in several windows before we could get them shut. Really, it's most inconvenient to have the entire staff out at the same time. But since you're here, and ready for work, I want you—"

"I am not ready for work," said Hilda calmly, interrupting.

"It is a long time before I must go to work. I changed into my uniform because my dress was wet and dirty and my boots needed cleaning. I must go now and see to my dress."

Turning her back, she started up the stairs, leaving Mr. Williams openmouthed.

She had no intention of going to her room just yet. Her dress needed attention, yes, but she had a far more important errand.

Colonel George's office was very near the back stairs. She climbed the few broad steps and tapped on the open door. "Sir? May I speak to you, please?"

Colonel George turned quickly from his desk. He was studying an important business document, but few things could be allowed to come before a servant's ominous request to "speak to" the master of the house. Something unpleasant was nearly certain to follow, and Hilda was a good maid. Mrs. George would have several things to say to her husband if Hilda was allowed to slip away from the household. "Yes, of course," he said, therefore. "Come in. Sit down."

"Thank you, sir." She sat as bidden, something she almost never did in the presence of any of her employers.

"I hope there's nothing—that is, you're not unhappy here, are you, Hilda?"

"I am happy with my job, sir," she said carefully. "I am un-happy only with Mr. Williams."

Oh, dear. This was worse than he had anticipated. If Hilda was a good servant, Williams was priceless. His English manner was perfect, he kept the silver polished and the household running smoothly. If it came to a choice between Williams and Hilda . . .

Hilda knew exactly what was running through Colonel George's mind. She allowed him a moment to consider his predicament, and then went ahead. "It is not a big problem, sir, and I think it can be solved easily."

Colonel George was an important businessman. He didn't allow a sigh of relief to escape, but he couldn't help relaxing a little, and Hilda saw it. "Perhaps if you'd explain," he said, and Hilda was virtually certain she'd won.

"You see, sir, he allows us, the other servants, I mean, very little freedom. His rules are rules meant for children. I think you may not know that we may never have an evening out, that we must be back by sunset even when we have our days off, that we may not leave the house at all when we do not have time off, even if our work is done."

She knew perfectly well that Colonel George didn't know Williams's rules. Employers never did know, nor did they care, so long as the servants performed satisfactorily and gave no trouble. Mrs. George might know a little more, the servants being really her responsibility. That was why Hilda had come to Colonel George.

The master cleared his throat. "Yes, that does seem a trifle—er—peremptory. But wait, didn't I hear something about you going to the circus the other evening?"

"Yes, sir. I got special permission, and had to give up my afternoon out to do it. I have worked here for six years, sir, and that is the first time I have ever been out of the house at night." Well, it was the first *legitimate* time, except once when she had special leave to investigate a disappearance. She didn't think Colonel George knew about the illegitimate nocturnal escapades.

"I see. Well, what is it exactly that you want, Hilda?"

"You know, sir, that I am good at finding things out." And well he should know. The last investigation had been with his permission, almost under his orders, to try to help some friends of his. She had succeeded, too.

He nodded, something that might almost have been a grin playing at the corners of his mouth.

"There is something now that needs to be found out, something important. It is to do with the little boy, Fritz Schlager."

Colonel George looked a little shocked. The details of Fritz's ordeal were not such that a young unmarried woman should be privy to them.

"My family knows his family, sir. The police have not yet found the man who beat Fritz." She had seen the shocked look and decided an expurgated version was in order. "I wish to help, but I cannot when Mr. Williams is—is blowing on my back—that is not right, is it?"

"'Breathing down your neck,' do you mean?"

"Yes! That is it! When he is breathing down my neck all the time. Always he watches me. Always he thinks I do something wrong. I was not allowed even to go myself to the drugstore for headache powders." She saw that she was taking too much time. Colonel George was getting bored. "What I want, sir, is to be allowed to leave sometimes when I must, so long as I do all my work and do nothing improper. I would not wish ever to be away for very long. I do not mean to act as if every day is my day out. I would not wish to be out late at night, or to go to anyplace where a young woman should not go, but I wish to be treated as a grown, respectable woman, not a silly child. That is all, sir."

Colonel George frowned. "You can't expect just to leave anytime you feel like it, you know. What if I want you, or one of your mistresses does?"

"But you never do, sir. If you need something, you ring for Mr. Williams or your valet. If the ladies need something, they have their maid, Michelle. Never am I needed except to do my job, and I always do my job, sir."

The colonel found another objection. "What would the other servants say? I can't give you special privileges."

That was the stickiest point. Hilda took a deep breath. "We are all allowed to rest after luncheon, unless there is a special dinner party or something else to prepare. If I, or any other servant, would wish to go out at that time instead of resting, I do not see that it is a thing that should be forbidden."

He wished she had gone to his wife instead. Ada might see some pitfall here that he did not. But Hilda had not gone to Ada, she had come to him, and his right to authority must not be open to question.

"It sounds reasonable enough to me, Hilda. I'll speak to Williams about it. I can trust you, and the others, not to abuse the privilege?"

"Yes, sir. And, sir, when you speak to Mr. Williams, perhaps you would not mention our talk?"

Colonel George had never had any intention of telling the butler that the maid had talked him into interfering. He cleared his throat again. "No, I don't think that will be necessary. Now, was there anything else?"

"No, sir. Thank you, sir. I must go now and mop up the rainwater under the windows." She curtsied politely and waited until she was down the steps and out of sight before she danced an awkward little jig in her carpet slippers.

She had taken a great risk, and she had won. To tender a request directly to the master of the house, without submitting it through the butler, was strictly forbidden. The butler was as absolute a monarch over his little kingdom as ever held sway over a great one. She had gone beyond the monarch to the emperor, and she had prevailed.

Mr. Williams wouldn't like his new orders, and he would strongly suspect who was responsible for them, but he dared not disobey.

With one bold stroke, Hilda had opened the prison doors!

The only thing she regretted was that she could tell no one. The other servants would wonder at their new freedom, and Hilda could not take the credit. She could not, she decided with great reluctance, even tell Patrick. Patrick and Norah were cousins in some degree or other. If Patrick knew, even if he were sworn to secrecy, Norah would eventually know. Hilda knew enough of the dynamics of a large Irish family to be sure of that. So she had to hug her victory to herself.

Wiping the delighted smile off her face, she went down to the servants' room to see if her boots were decent enough to resume.

They were clean, but not yet dry. Norah had stuffed them with old newspapers to keep their shape, and had put them in a corner of the room. "You want to get them really dry before you wear them again. Then they'll want to be polished with a good dressing. Anton can do it tomorrow," said Norah. "They'll be good as new, but they've got to dry natural. Put them in front of a fire, or even the stove, and they'll be hard as wood."

"Tomorrow! But I must go to see my family, make sure their house is not damaged, and I cannot walk there in carpet slippers."

"Would you like me to go and see, Miss Hilda?" asked Sean. "It's nearly time I got back to me own family, anyway."

"I do not live nearby," said Hilda, hesitating. "It will be a long walk for you, there and back."

"Pooh," said Norah. "It's not all that long. I'd go with you, Sean, but there's work to be done here, and it's wet out there. My boots aren't new, like some people's, but I want to keep them dry if I can."

"I'll be off, then, and back to report in no time at all, at all. If you'll tell me just where you live, Miss Hilda?"

Hilda told him, thinking as she did so about Mama's probable reaction to an Irishman on the doorstep. Oh, well, she might as well get used to it. The world was changing. She, Hilda, had helped make a little change today.

Restraining a deplorable tendency to whistle, she collected rags and buckets and went with Norah to mop up rainwater and assess the damage to floors, rugs, and curtains.

15

Those who expect to reap the blessings of freedom must . . . undergo the fatigue of supporting it.
—THOMAS PAINE, *THE AMERICAN CRISIS,* 1776

ONLY a firm resolve kept Hilda from telling anyone what she had done—a firm resolve and the knowledge that important matters were at stake. The rest of that day, throughout the storm cleanup, the good news from Sean that the Johansson family home had sustained no damage, the evening of washing her dress and other odd jobs, she maintained a closemouthed cheerfulness.

Norah looked at her oddly more than once, and when they at last went up to bed, she plumped herself down on Hilda's bed and demanded an explanation.

"You've been lookin' mighty pleased with yourself ever since you got home. Has Patrick got over his snit, then?"

Hilda was grateful that she could tell the truth about that. "He has. I began it."

"You don't mean to tell me you gave in first!"

"I did. You are surprised. I surprised myself. But it was this way."

She told Norah the story of Admiral, the horse so stubborn he would even refuse a treat, and her sudden suspicion that she was behaving just like Admiral. "So I sent Patrick a note, and today he met me. We went to buy my new boots and then sheltered from the storm at Nobile's. We had a good talk, but then the storm became worse and the building across the street was struck and Patrick had to help fight the fire. Norah, the smoke was so thick I could not see Patrick, and for a little time I thought—"

Her chin wobbled a little at the dreadful memory. "But he was not even hurt," she went on hastily, "and he will come to talk to me tomorrow."

"Huh! Hope you don't get caught. You know what His Nibs is like these days."

Hilda had to look down, then, afraid, even in the dim light of the gas fixture, that she would be caught smiling. "Is that a hole in my stocking?"

"Where? It's too dark in here to tell."

Hilda rolled off the perfectly intact stocking and pretended to examine it. "No. It must have been my eyes playing tricks. Do you think it is true that Colonel George will put in electricity?"

"I surely hope so. I wouldn't mind bein' able to see my hand in front of my face at night. And we could maybe have an electric fan up here, for when it gets so hot we near broil alive."

"That would be good," said Hilda, "but they are very expensive, electric fans. Mr. Nobile has one, did you know? He had it on before the storm came."

"And did you ever see such a storm in all your life?" said Norah. "Sean and me thought it was the Judgment Day for sure, it got that dark!"

By the time the two had exhausted the topic of the storm, Norah had forgotten about Hilda's unusual cheerfulness, or had put it down to the reconciliation with Patrick.

Next morning, Hilda thought she had better be very careful indeed. She was supposed to know nothing about any change in the rules until Mr. Williams announced it to the staff. He might do this at breakfast or at one of the other meals, depending upon when Colonel George remembered to talk to the butler and when Mr. Williams decided to pass along the news. Hilda hadn't dared to suggest to the colonel that she was in a hurry, so he might wait quite a time.

Hilda sighed rebelliously. She wasn't sure of her acting ability. It would be better if she were not present when the announcement was made. She could absent herself from breakfast on the excuse of heavy work. That was not unusual, and breakfast was an informal meal with no fixed hour. She couldn't skip lunch, though. She worked too hard to miss more than one meal, and besides, everyone was expected to be there for luncheon and dinner. She hoped Mr. Williams would get on with it.

She need not have worried. She was scrubbing the floor of the back porch and trying to decide what was to be done about sodden chair cushions when Norah found her.

"You'll never guess what!"

"Norah, do you think these will ever get clean? The storm, it drove leaves and rain and dust onto the porch, and the chairs—"

"Stop fussing with those silly cushions and listen! You'll never guess what Himself said to us at breakfast."

"No, I will not guess," said Hilda, still studying the spots on the cushion, "so it would be better for you to tell me."

"We're all to get extra time off! Every day!"

Hilda tried to look suitably astonished. "I do not understand. We cannot have every day off. Who would do the work?"

Norah sighed. "It isn't that way. Listen, will you? He said Mrs. George said it wasn't right we had so little time to ourselves, and she decided we could go out during our rest time if we wanted to. Oh, old Williams tacked on a lot of stuff about using the time for necessary errands and making sure our work got done proper and all that, but that's what it amounted to. Aren't you glad?"

Hilda pretended to consider. "I am not sure. Yes, I suppose, but many days I need my rest. I work hard."

Norah rolled her eyes. "You great gomerel, you don't *have* to go out. You can if you want to. I thought you'd be excited. It'll give you time to go poking around in those crimes of yours without having to sneak out, don't you see?"

Hilda decided an attack was a good idea at this point. "What do you mean, crimes of mine? I do not commit crimes, Norah! It is not my fault that sometimes things happen, and sometimes I want to find out about them."

Norah frowned. "Sometimes, my foot. You always want to find out. Why're you actin' so funny about this? You've got some scheme in your head, don't you? Or else—"

"Hilda! Why are you standing about when there is so much to be done?"

Every now and then a tyrant can come in handy. Hilda nodded submissively and began to discuss the state of the cushions with Mr. Williams.

Norah left to do her own work, but with a speculative gleam in her eye.

Hilda avoided Norah for the rest of the morning, an easy thing to do since the storm had created so much extra work. In mid-morning she was ordered to help Mrs. Czeszewski, the laundress, with the window curtains. The heavy velvet draperies had already been taken down by the underhouse-maids and sent out for cleaning, but the lace curtains were Mrs. Czeszewski's responsibility, and the bedroom ones, at least, had to be done today. No decent person could prepare for bed in an uncurtained room.

Hilda thanked all the gods, the old Norse ones included, that the storm had come from the southwest and many of the bedrooms were on the north and east sides of the house. Still, there were what seemed like hundreds of panels to take down, wash, starch, hang out to dry, iron, and rehang, and all the work had to be done with the utmost care. The curtains for the family bedrooms were of priceless Brussels lace; no curtain stretchers were allowed near them.

By lunchtime Hilda, Mrs. Czeszewski, and all the underhousemaids were exhausted and bad-tempered, but all the curtains were clean and drying nicely in a brisk breeze. The storm had brought a welcome change in the weather. Hilda thought, as she sat down to her meal, that she would have had a headache after all that work if the heavy heat had continued. As it was, she was tired, but exhilarated. Fresh, cool air always acted on her northern blood like a tonic, and today she also had a major victory over tyranny to celebrate. Not only that, she had Patrick's tantalizing bit of news to think about, and Patrick was coming to see her later.

She ate her lunch slowly, hoping to avoid further private conversation with Norah, who, Hilda was sure, intended to take full advantage of the relaxation in the rules. If Hilda dawdled, surely Norah would be out of the house before Hilda went upstairs.

But Norah was not to be thwarted. She did go upstairs before Hilda, but waited for her.

"I've figgered it out," Norah said in a whisper as soon as Hilda appeared at the head of the stairs. "You did it, somehow, didn't you?"

Hilda was suddenly tired of secrets, of devious stratagems and machinations. "Yes," she said wearily. "And if Mr. Williams finds out, I will lose my job."

"Well, you didn't think I'd tell, did you? I just wanted to know, that's all. How'd you get 'round Mrs. George?"

"I did not. I went to Colonel George."

Norah held her hands to her face to stifle a delighted giggle. "Poor man! I'll bet he was scared stiff, havin' to deal with a servant problem!"

"We-ell." Hilda allowed a smile to crack. "He was worried enough to say he would do what I asked." At Norah's further giggle, though, Hilda's smile faded. "It is a good story, *ja*. I also wish I could tell it. But, Norah, Mr. Williams must never, never know!"

"I know." Norah sobered and drew her hand across her breast. "Cross me heart, I'll not tell a livin' soul."

"Not even Sean," Hilda warned.

"Not even Sean. You goin' to tell Patrick?"

"Yes," said Hilda tartly, "and print it in the South Bend *Tribune*, also. Of course I will not tell him! Are you going out, then?"

"Just to prove I can. Let's go someplace together."

"Me, I stay in today. Because," she went on in reply to Norah's astonished look, "I am really tired, and I have important things to think about, and also because Mr. Williams will be less suspicious of me if I do not go right away."

"That would *make* me suspicious."

"Yes, but you know me better than he does. Also you are smarter."

Norah, on a renewed tide of giggles, retired to her room to take off her cap and apron, and Hilda closed her door, carefully removed her new boots, and lay down on her bed.

Her body was glad of a respite, but her mind had no desire for anything as insensate as sleep. She had a problem to solve.

Who had spoken of Shaw, and to whom? Did the conversation refer to the trapeze artist, or to someone else altogether? Shaw was a common name. Hilda's fingers drummed irritably on the white cotton bedspread. It was a pity the circus family didn't have a strange name, something Polish and difficult, perhaps. Though, now that she came to think about it, there was no shortage of difficult Polish names in South Bend, nor of people bearing those names.

Forget about the name, for now, anyway. Someone in that burning building had spoken of Shaw, to someone. Mrs. Brady, perhaps? All the people in the building had escaped, thanks to Patrick. And his fellow firemen, her mind added in fairness. Patrick would know where those people were.

That was the first thing, then, find Mrs. Brady. Find out if she had talked to someone about Shaw. Hilda could do that herself, once she knew where Mrs. Brady was. There was, she realized, a good deal Mrs. Brady might be able to tell her.

Then there was the other thing: try to find Mr. Shaw. The

police, if they had been doing their job, could do that much more easily than Hilda, but apparently they were not doing their job. It was going to be very hard for her, limited in her freedom as she still was, but she would find a way.

She snapped her fingers. Norah's cousin, the one who worked for the Lake Shore and Michigan Southern railroad! He traveled all over the place, and he knew other men on other railroads. He could keep an eye out for small circuses, and could ask others to do the same. And when they found one with a new troupe of trapeze artists—

Yes, what then?

Hilda, deciding to face that step when it arose, turned over and closed her eyes. Might as well nap when she could. She was going to be busy for the next few days.

16

*You shall seek all day ere you find them, and when
you have them, they are not worth the search.*
—WILLIAM SHAKESPEARE,
THE MERCHANT OF VENICE, 1597

AT five o'clock precisely, Hilda walked out the back door,
stooping to no subterfuge, not even checking to see
where Mr. Williams was. This was not the time of day
that the servants had been given leave, but it was a slack time,
and Hilda's work was well up to schedule. She felt a principle
had been established that work properly completed freed one
of overly rigorous supervision. She intended to test that principle to its limits.

Patrick was waiting for her in the usual spot, a secluded
corner by the porte cochere where they could not easily be
seen by anyone either inside or outside the great house. Hilda
greeted him cheerfully.

"Patrick, let us go and sit down. I am tired and so are my
feet. These boots, they are much better than the old ones, but
they are new and still stiff."

"But won't the old ogre see us?"

"It does not matter," she said calmly, leading the way to
the bench by the drive.

"Hilda! You haven't gone and got yourself sacked, have you?"

"No. Something good has happened. Mrs. George has made Mr. Williams change the rules. We may go out now in our rest times, if we wish. And I think at other times, too, if we do not stay long. So now tell me slowly all you can remember about those people talking about Shaw."

"I've thought and thought, Hilda, me love, and not come up with anything much. It was a man talkin', I think, and I might've heard a woman answer. That's all I know. I'm sorry."

"It does not matter. You were working hard, Patrick. And you saved those people's lives, and I am very, very proud of you!"

Patrick's chest expanded. He beamed.

Hilda went on to business. "Now. I want to talk to Mrs. Brady. Do you know where they went, the people who lived in that building?"

"Hotels, likely, or to stay with family."

"Can you find out for certain?"

"I'll do what I can, but I'm on me way to work, and I'm on duty till mornin'."

"Then you could talk to the other firemen, and tell me what you have learned on your way home tomorrow? I will come outside if I can."

"I thought you were goin' to do as you pleased, and blast old Interference."

"You should not be rude, Patrick. And I am not so silly as that. I will be so obedient you would not know it was me. It is better that way. And I will see you tomorrow?"

He accepted his dismissal and rose. "You will. What're you plannin' for Sunday?" he added casually.

"It will depend on the weather. If it is a nice day, I thought maybe the river?"

"Suits me." Patrick's smile said it more than suited him.

"Maybe with Erik?"

"Oh. Well, sure, if he wants to come."

"Patrick, we need to talk to him, you and I. It may be that he has talked to Fritz, and knows something. We can send him home later." She smiled beguilingly and Patrick had to swallow hard.

"Okay with me. See you tomorrow, then." He squeezed her hand, debated for a moment about kissing her on the cheek and decided he'd better not, and whistled his way down the back drive.

"And where have you been, miss?" demanded Mr. Williams when she went back inside. He looked as though he'd been lurking just by the door.

"Talking to Patrick." Her head was held high. "For five minutes, maybe less. My work is done, Mr. Williams. I have time even to go and help Norah. Excuse me."

Much of a tyrant's power is destroyed when his victims no longer fear him. Highly irritated, but impotent, Mr. Williams watched Hilda sail in the direction of the dining room.

She was up the next morning before the alarm rang at five, and was outside waiting for Patrick when he walked wearily up the drive at a few minutes after six.

"I made a list." He handed her a folded piece of paper. "Just some of the places the men knew of where folks had gone. It's not every place, but it's the best I can do." He yawned widely. "Sorry."

"You look very tired. Was there a fire last night?"

"Only a little one, but it was down next door to the library, so we had to stay most of the night to be sure it didn't flare up again."

Hilda shivered. "Ooh, yes, it would be terrible if the books were to burn. Patrick, I thank you for the list."

"Glad to do it." He yawned again, almost cracking his jaw.

"Go and rest," said Hilda. "I will see you at five o'clock." She gave him a peck on the cheek and ran into the house.

Patrick suddenly felt a good deal better.

Hilda, however, was greatly annoyed. Not with Patrick, of course. He had done exactly what she had asked, and a little more. It had, however, not occurred to her just how hard it was going to be to find Mrs. Brady. If she wasn't in one of the places listed, the search could be long.

There were many hotels in South Bend. The Oliver was a showplace renowned throughout the Midwest, and there were several others, not as new or as splendid, but large and comfortable and highly respectable.

Then there were the others. If Hilda were to visit one of those, even with an escort, her reputation might not be the only thing destroyed.

If it were easy, she told herself firmly, anyone could do it. Me, I work harder than most people. Also I am more stubborn. I will not give up.

Buoyed by her excellent opinion of herself, she went about her morning's tasks with vigor and precision. While cleaning the library she stole a few moments to copy from the city directory the list of hotels.

She rushed through her lunch, ran upstairs only to remove her cap and apron, and sallied forth, Patrick's list and her own in hand.

Mrs. Brady was not staying at the Hotel Royal on Washington, according to the clerk at the front desk. Nor was she at the Sheridan House, the Bonaker House, or the Columbia Hotel, all on Michigan Street.

By the time Hilda had asked at all of these, it was time for her to return to work, warm, tired, and in no sweet temper.

She met Patrick as scheduled at five and poured out her woes. "Four hotels in an hour, Patrick! It could take days to find her. There are twenty-two hotels in town. I made a list. And there are even more in River Park and Mishawaka, and she might have gone there. And some of them, Patrick—there are some I cannot go to."

"I should say not! Have you got your list with you?"

Hilda fished it out of her pocket.

"Right you are. I'll take this one myself, and these two." He pointed to some of the more dubious addresses on the list.

"And these—I don't think we even need to bother with these. A decent woman wouldn't go to places like these."

Hilda was somewhat cheered. "And The Oliver is too expensive, yes?"

"For the likes of her, it is. But, Hilda, she's most likely staying with family or friends. That's what you or I would do, and she's probably like us."

"But then—oh, you are right, Patrick." She sighed. "I am tired now, and the time and work make it all seem too hard, but I will not give up. Tomorrow I will look in the city directory for Bradys and try to talk to some of them. The trouble is that they are probably working people, and they will not be at home when I can call on them."

"But some of 'em'll have Saturday afternoons off, maybe. You might have some luck. I'm off duty all weekend, so I can do some lookin' meself. I'll ask around at the firehouse tonight, too. Some of the men might know somethin'. But you do understand, that bit I overheard might not have anything to do with anything?"

"I know. I am not stupid, Patrick!"

Patrick grinned. "Never said you were, darlin'. Smartest girl in town, I say."

Hilda ignored the blandishments. "And very, very tired. I need my rest time, Patrick. I do not know if I will be able to go out every day."

"We'll manage somehow, together. I've got to get meself to work now."

Weary and discouraged though she was, Hilda liked the sound of that word "together."

On Saturday, unfortunately, she was able to accomplish nothing. She had completely forgotten that Mrs. Clem was giving a small dinner party for a few of her closest friends and members of her Mishawaka family. A dinner party always meant extra work for everybody. Hilda was able to rest briefly in the afternoon, but there was no chance for anyone to leave the house even for a few minutes. She fumed all day. Saturday, when she might find people at home, and she couldn't get out! Well, she was just going to pursue her inquiries on Sunday, no matter what Mama or anyone else thought.

Sunday was another perfect day. It was, Hilda thought as she dressed for church, going to be very warm later on. She thought with longing about the cool, shady river. A walk from house to house, even with Patrick, wasn't nearly so attractive a proposition.

Sunday dinner was mostly cold on a day like today: pickled herring, the beets Erik hated so, cold boiled potatoes, smoky ham, a rice pudding for dessert. Hilda ate with a good appetite, but finished as quickly as she could.

"Now, little one," she said to Erik, "I have a treat for Admiral. Do you think he would take it from me if we went to see him?"

Erik jumped up eagerly, but so did Birgit. The youngest girl at thirteen, she was one of the docile Johanssons, taking more after her placid father than her volatile mother, but today she chose to be difficult.

"I want to go, too," she said firmly.

"You can go anytime," said Erik. "You work downtown, next door to the stables, almost. You've never wanted to see them before."

"I want to see them now. I want to go out with you and Hilda. You're always going places with her. I want to go."

This didn't suit Hilda's plans at all. She had intended to have Patrick take her and Erik for ice cream, question Patrick about small circuses, and then send Erik off, leaving her and Patrick to hunt an elusive woman.

She couldn't come up with an excuse quickly enough. Mama nodded approvingly. "Yes, Hilda, take Birgit with you. She works hard all week. She deserves a treat. Perhaps you will see that nice policeman again."

Birgit darted off to get her Sunday hat, an elaborate creation she had made herself out of scrap materials at the millinery shop where she was employed, and Hilda was left to make the best of matters. Maybe she could distract Birgit somehow. Maybe she could contrive to spill some ice cream on Birgit's dress. Birgit was fussy about her clothes and would immediately go home.

Then Hilda was ashamed of herself. Birgit loved her new Sunday dress, made with a sailor collar and decorated with braid Mama had brought from Sweden. Mama had finished it only a month before, and it was probably the last short summer dress Birgit would ever wear; she was growing up. Hilda couldn't spoil the dress.

With a martyrly sigh, she donned her own hat and set out, Birgit walking sedately beside her and Erik grumbling his way ahead.

17

Truth is on the march and nothing can stop it.
          —ÉMILE ZOLA, J'ACCUSE, 1898

ILDA thought furiously as they walked. Could she simply go to the stables, without Patrick, and then send Birgit home?

Not if Birgit wouldn't go. Birgit might be quiet, she might be placid, but she had inherited the Johansson stubbornness in full measure. Besides, to be fair, Birgit *did* deserve a treat and Hilda *had* treated her rather shabbily ever since the family had been reunited.

Could she, then, get Patrick to take both her siblings for ice cream after seeing the horses, and then send them both home? That would give Birgit her treat and probably satisfy her.

But then Hilda would have no chance to talk to Erik.

She considered confiding in Birgit and abandoned the idea at once. Birgit wasn't a tattletale, not exactly, but she was almost annoyingly obedient. She wouldn't go out of her way to tell Mama that Patrick and Hilda were involved, with Erik, in some interesting investigations, but neither would she withhold the information if someone (like Mama) were to ask.

Hilda sighed, at the same moment that Erik found an old, battered tin water dipper by the side of the road and gave it a vicious kick. Hilda had to grin at that. Two minds with but a single thought!

As they drew near Tippecanoe Place, Hilda had a moment's impulse to walk on past. Patrick would understand when she explained later.

But he might not understand, and there had been too much misunderstanding between them. And there had been too much stealth, too many subterfuges in Hilda's life of late. Let Birgit think what she would, report to Mama what she wanted. Hilda intended to spend her afternoon with Patrick, even if they couldn't spend it as she had planned.

If Patrick was surprised, and not a little displeased, to see Birgit, he did his best not to show it.

"Patrick, this is my sister Birgit. Birgit, you have heard me speak of my friend Mr. Cavanaugh."

Birgit curtsied politely. "I am pleased to make your acquaintance, Mr. Cavanaugh."

Erik snorted. Hilda frowned at him.

"Patrick, Birgit asked if she might come with us today. She wants to see the horses Erik looks after."

To Hilda's amazement, Patrick smiled and nodded. "That sounds like a good plan to me. And afterward, Miss Birgit, I'd be pleased if you'd all come boating with me. Me aunt Molly packed a bit of a picnic, some lemonade and cookies, and it'll be pleasant on the river." He gestured toward a small basket tucked under a shrub to keep cool.

Erik gave a squeal of delight. Birgit responded demurely, "Thank you, Mr. Cavanaugh. I would like that."

"But, *Patrick*," Hilda whispered urgently.

"Not now," he mouthed. "Later, when the kids can't hear."

So Hilda fumed inwardly while they visited the horses, all of whom had to be introduced to Birgit and Patrick and given their treats. She fretted on the way to Leeper Park, where Patrick rented a boat.

"Now, you'll understand you've got to sit still. No capering about, Erik, or you'll have us over, and the river's dangerous. Got that?"

"Yes, sir," said Birgit, looking a little scared.

"Yes, sir," Erik mimicked, looking cocky.

Patrick laid a hand on his shoulder. "Erik, me lad, I'll leave you behind unless you promise, on your honor, to do exactly what I say. And I'll flay you alive if you break your promise."

"And I," said Hilda more practically, "will throw the picnic basket overboard if there is any trouble."

Erik grinned at that. "I promise I won't upset the boat."

"And you'll do what I say, when I say."

"Yessir, Mr. Patrick."

"Right, then. You first, Hilda, to keep the boat steady."

He situated them, Hilda on the seat facing him in the stern, then Birgit in the middle and Erik in the bow, facing each other.

"Now, you two," said Patrick when he had seated himself at the stern. "Ever been in a rowboat before?"

"No," said Erik cheekily, "just a big boat coming to America."

"Well, you'll find a small one very different. But there were rules on the big one about what you could do and what you couldn't, and there are rules on this one. Never stand up. In fact, plant yourself on the middle of that seat and stay there. Don't shift about. And keep your two hands on the gunwales—that's the sides of the boat—all the time. No trailing them in the water, no leaning over. Sit. Look. Make all the noise you want, but sit still."

"How can I eat cookies and drink lemonade with my hands on the side of the boat?"

That, of course, was Erik. Hilda giggled in spite of herself.

"When we get hungry, I'll pull the boat to the side of the river where there's very little current. *Then* you can take your hands off the gunwales. And if I hear another peep out of you, me boy, you'll find yourself ashore. Hilda, doesn't your mother teach these young ones that children should be seen and not heard?"

"She tries," Hilda replied. Erik grinned broadly, opened his mouth, and then shut it again hastily. The grin remained, however.

The river was pleasant in this stretch, though somewhat crowded with boats on a hot, pleasant Sunday afternoon. Hilda would have enjoyed herself very much if she hadn't been impatient to get on with her investigation. The search for Fritz's captor was very important to her, and she wished Patrick would hurry up and get this over with so they could send the children home and get about their business.

Patrick saw her impatience and smiled. "Wait a bit," he said softly.

She frowned in puzzlement, but in only a few minutes she understood. Patrick was steering their boat toward an area of the river she didn't know well, and when they rounded a bend she saw why.

There was a small park on the flat west bank of the river, with a bandstand, and within the ornate white structure Elbel's band was performing with vigor.

"Ooh!" shouted Erik with a wriggle.

Patrick instantly fixed him with a glare that might have singed the hair on his head. "And didn't I tell you not to move?"

"Yes, and I'm sorry, but can I get out and go listen to the band?" Erik loved bands almost as much as he loved horses.

"You can hear it perfectly well from here."

"Yes, but I can't *see* it! I like to see the men with the big horns, the—" He mimed a huge bell and the puffed cheeks of someone playing it.

"The tubas, yes, and I suppose the trombones, too?" Patrick moved an imaginary trombone slide out and back in.

"Yes!" Erik bounced again in his seat. The boat rocked.

"Oh, for the love of Mike, if I don't let you get out, I suppose you'll have us all in the river. All right, but you'll have to jump for it. I'll get in as close as I can, but there's no dock." He half-rowed, half-poled the boat to the sandy bank while Erik rid himself of shoes and stockings and joyously jumped into the inch or so of water. As he ran up to the bandstand, Patrick turned to Birgit.

"Miss Birgit, if you'd like to go ashore, I'll be happy to lift you out."

"No, thank you," came the prim reply. "I wouldn't like to get wet."

"Good, we'll all wait here for your brother, then."

The noise of the music, a Sousa march, rose above them. Patrick turned to Hilda. "So you see," he said in a voice pitched only for her, "we have all the privacy we want."

"Yes, but we cannot do anything! I wanted to try to find Mrs. Brady, and here we sit in a boat. It is very pleasant, Patrick, I do not want you to think that I am not grateful for your trouble, but—"

"But you're pinin' for information."

"Yes."

"And I have some."

She was instantly alert.

"You'll not like it much, though," Patrick went on, just as the band came to the end of "Hands Across the Sea."

"Why not?" Hilda hissed under cover of the applause.

Patrick jerked a head in Birgit's direction. Hilda rolled her eyes and waited for the next piece to begin.

The band launched into "El Capitan" and Patrick continued. "Yesterday I found somebody who knows Mrs. Brady. And—I'm sorry, Hilda, but—she's lit off for California. The fire was the last straw for her. I guess she has a cousin there or somethin'."

The band went into a quiet passage. Patrick hummed along until the heavy brass took up the refrain and he could continue.

"And before you ask, no, nobody knows her address."

Hilda slumped in her seat while the band went into "The Stars and Stripes Forever." It was her favorite march. She scarcely heard it. When she spoke, it was with a string of vicious-sounding Swedish whose meaning Patrick could only guess. They sat in silence as the music trickled down to a few horns, with the piccolo playing its obbligato. When it wound up again for the big finale, he said, almost in Hilda's ear, "I've got an idea. But let's wait until we take the kids back home."

With the final chorus, the band had apparently reached the end of its program. When the musicians began to pack up their instruments, take off their caps, and run handkerchiefs across their brows, Erik finally gave up hope of more music and came back to the boat. He looked hopefully from Patrick to the picnic basket.

"Yes, o' course. Do you reckon you can get back in the boat without upsetting us all, rapscallion?"

"Reckon I can." He did, too, though it was trickier than it looked. Patrick passed cookies, Hilda poured lemonade, and they looked like any other pleasant family enjoying a Sunday on the river. An observer would, however, have found their thoughts surprising had he been able to read them.

Hilda was wondering about Patrick's idea. Had he worked out a different way to trace Mrs. Brady? Or had he decided she was unimportant and thought up a different plan?

Patrick was thinking carefully about what he was to suggest to Hilda. He had to put it in a way that would keep her from plunging headlong into danger, without appearing to be protecting her, which she despised.

Erik was thinking about his horses. Oh, the police horses, but he already thought of them as his. They were wonderful, and he loved working with them. Sergeant Wright came there a lot to talk to Erik and encourage him. He was all right, Erik thought, but he could understand why Hilda preferred Patrick, who was much more fun.

Only Birgit's face reflected her thoughts. She was concerned solely with keeping crumbs off her new dress.

18

*. . . unmerciful Disaster/Followed fast and
followed faster.*
        —EDGAR ALLAN POE, "THE RAVEN," 1845

THEY walked Birgit all the way home. She could not, of
course, be permitted to walk by herself, and Hilda was
uncertain about Erik's devotion to his sister if a distraction presented itself. Besides, the walk gave her a chance for
a few private words with Erik.

"How is Fritz?" she asked in what she hoped was a casual tone.

"All right, I guess. I don't know. He doesn't come out to
play anymore."

"What do his brothers say?"

Erik shrugged. "Nothin'."

Hilda persisted. "Have you talked to Fritz at all?"

"Not much. I saw him once after he came back, but he
didn't feel good, I guess. He didn't want to play, or talk, or
anything. I guess he was beat up awful bad."

"Did he tell you anything about it?"

"*No*, I said! How come you always want to know everything? Everybody knows what happened, anyway. Fritz got
beat up by that circus man. He won't talk to anybody about it,

his brothers say. He won't talk to me about it, either, and I guess he doesn't want to be my friend anymore and I guess I don't care!"

The last came on one breath, Erik having to get it out in a hurry before tears betrayed him.

Hilda felt a rush of pity that she dared not express. It was hard to lose one's best friend. Maybe, though, Fritz wasn't lost to Erik forever. And meanwhile, if he knew nothing, suspected nothing, he was probably safe.

"It was nice today, the music," she said, changing to a neutral subject. "I was happy you could come."

Erik made no reply.

"And tomorrow, when you go to work, stop at the mansion. I will see if Mrs. Sullivan will give you some carrots for the horses. Maybe you can even persuade Admiral to eat one."

That brought a suggestion of a grin.

After the children were safely deposited at their home, Hilda and Patrick leisurely strolled back to Tippecanoe Place. Hilda was so happy to be back on the old footing with Patrick, so happy that Erik was reasonably content, that she almost forgot about Patrick's idea.

He saw that she had forgotten, and guessed why, and was in such a good mood himself that he nearly decided to abandon the idea. On sober reflection, however, he realized that wasn't a good plan. She might be feeling relaxed just now, but her moods could change in a heartbeat, and when she remembered, and remembered that he had not brought the matter up, there would be consequences.

"Have you fallen asleep, then, darlin', or are you dreamin' on your feet?"

"Dreaming? Asleep? Patrick, do not be silly. I am very awake."

"Then why have you not asked about me great idea?"

"Oh! I forgot, but why did you not tell me?"

"And am I not tellin' you this very minute? You were talkin' a few days ago about circuses, remember? The little ones?"

"Yes. I thought I could ask Norah's cousin, the one who works on the Lake Shore and Michigan Southern. Keith, I think his name is. If he doesn't know of some small circuses near here, he can ask other people. Then—well, then I do not know what. There are many of them, I think."

"Well, for once, I'm one jump ahead of you. Think of that, now! Norah's cousin Keith is me own cousin, too, and I asked him already. He knows of one that's goin' to be in Niles this comin' week. An' I thought maybe I'd take you *and* Erik on Wednesday, and we can ask a few people about new trapeze acts."

Hilda mulled it over. "It will cost much money, Patrick. And Niles—how would we get so far?"

"It's on Keith's line, and he's a conductor. I expect he can manage. Only ten miles or so, after all. And the circus tickets won't cost much, I expect, not for such a small outfit. You see, darlin', it's like this. I reckon if we don't get that brother of yours to a circus soon, he's apt to bust out by himself, and that could be bad. So if we take him, we can kill two birds with one stone. What do you say?"

"But what if there is danger there for Erik?"

"With both of us to look after him? I'll not let anything happen to your little brother."

Hilda stopped, right there on the street, and kissed him on the cheek. "You are a very nice man, Patrick. Maybe I do not always tell you so, because you would get a big head, but it is true. Now, how are we to get permission for Erik to go?"

Patrick cocked his head to one side. "I think you can get that fancy-smellin' policeman friend of yours to let him off work for the afternoon, if you smile at him pretty enough."

"*Patrick,*" Hilda began, before Patrick let his grin begin to show. Then she made a face. "Oh, I do not know why I put up with you." But she let him pull her hand into the crook of his arm.

"And as for your mama, does she have to know?"

"Yes." Hilda nodded sharply. "There has been too much silence and hiding, too much deceit. I will tell her he is going, that is all."

"You'll have a battle on your hands."

"I do not mind that. I will go back now and tell her what you told me, that he is bursting to go, and better with us than to do something foolish by himself. Then if she still will not permit it, we will take him anyway, but I will have done the right thing."

"Seems to me you've let Sunday go to your head," said Patrick. "That's a fine sermon."

Hilda stuck her tongue out at him and turned to retrace her steps yet once more to her brother's house.

It was a fine battle. Patrick had been right about that. Mama didn't want Erik to take time off from his new job that was working out so well. She didn't approve of circuses. She most strongly didn't approve of Patrick. Hilda ignored all her protests and silenced Erik when he would have pleaded passionately. "He goes with us, Mama. I did not want to go without telling you."

It was when Sven fell in on Hilda's side that the tide turned. "Hilda is right, Mama. Erik is willful. He will go one day, allowed to or not. This way is better."

Mama, tight-lipped, said no more. Erik's whole being shone like a lantern, but he had the sense to keep quiet.

"I will come to see you after lunch tomorrow or the next day, little one, to tell you the plans." Hilda tousled Erik's hair. "Try not to get into any trouble between now and Wednesday."

The three-day wait was interminable, but Wednesday came at last, a fine day, warm but not hot. Hilda met Patrick near the police stables.

"So you got him off, did you, you and your blue eyes and your dimples?"

Today Hilda refused to be baited. "I told Sergeant Wright that we hoped to learn something of that Shaw man, and he agreed that Erik might go. The sergeant likes Erik. He says he is doing a fine job and might have more responsibility when he is a little older."

Erik was waiting for them at the stables, quivering with excitement.

"Are you sure you don't want to bring Admiral along?" teased Hilda.

"He'll be all right. Let's go!"

Cousin Keith was waiting for them at the train station with three passes. "I get a few, you know," he replied to Patrick's surprise. "You didn't think I was goin' to sneak you on the train, did you? Up you go, lad." He boosted Erik aboard and assisted Hilda with a courteous hand. "Have a wonderful time, and don't forget the last train back leaves at eight-ten."

"Oh, we will be home before then," said Hilda. "I must be home by sundown." Sundown was coming later and later as the year approached its zenith, but an 8:10 train from Niles was still uncomfortably late.

Patrick was in rare form that day, entertaining Erik on the short ride with stories and jokes, and pretending to find a nickel behind Erik's left ear. "Here, you. Don't you wash your ears? Not the best place to keep money, me boy. Safer in your pocket."

"How did you *do* that?" demanded Erik through giggles.

"How did I do what? Bless me, there's another one!" The right ear yielded a nickel.

"I did not know you could do that, Patrick," murmured Hilda when Erik was distracted by the sight of an automobile close to the train tracks.

"Uncle Dan taught me," said Patrick with a chuckle. "Nobody like a politician for makin' money appear and disappear."

Hilda giggled nearly as hard as Erik had.

They were early for the first show, which began at two-thirty, so they trailed around the sideshows, always keeping Erik firmly by their sides. To Hilda and Patrick, the sideshows at Bigelow's Superior Circus were poor fare compared to the famous freaks and wonders displayed by Ringling Brothers, but Erik was entranced by the two-headed calf and the snake handlers, though to his obvious disgust, Hilda and Patrick wouldn't let him see the tattooed lady.

The tent was half empty when they went in. It was still some time before the show was to begin. "Just take any seats you like, folks. First come, first served."

Erik wanted to sit at ringside, but Hilda preferred to be a little farther away from the sawdust and the massive feet of the elephants, so they climbed the rather rickety bleachers and sat.

"When is something going to happen, Hilda?"

"Soon. The band will parade in first, probably."

"There will be a *band?*"

"I think so."

"Sure and there'll be a band, youngster. Can't have a circus without a band. The acts have to have music, for the beat, you see."

So Erik had to have that explained to him, how the acrobats and trapeze artists relied on the music to keep themselves synchronized.

"And then what happens?"

"Then the horses come in."

"Ooh! How many horses? What do they use them for? What color are they?"

"I do not know, Erik." Hilda's head was beginning to ache slightly. "I have not seen this circus. Wait and see."

"But it's so *long.*" His voice took on a whining note, and Hilda sighed.

"Suppose you tell us about your own horses, me lad," said Patrick. "Admiral and the rest."

"They're all right."

Hilda and Patrick exchanged a glance over Erik's head. Surely he wasn't growing tired of this new job already!

"Somethin' the matter, then? You get blamed for somethin' you didn't do, maybe?"

"No. The horses are fine. I would *never* do anything wrong with them. I love them." He said it fiercely. "It's only—ooh, listen!"

A trumpet sounded a fanfare and the band marched in, rather a small band, but playing with loud enthusiasm. The show was on.

Hilda's attention wandered. The performers were not as competent as in the big circus, the costumes were not as spectacular. When the trapeze artists were announced, they were not "The Stupendous Shaws" but some other name she didn't catch. They were good, she had to admit, nearly as good as the Shaws, though a smaller troupe. As for Erik, he was on the edge of his seat.

The show seemed to Hilda to go on for a long time. She was glad Erik was having a good time, and she was grateful to Patrick for providing it, but so far they had learned nothing useful, and it didn't seem likely that they would. Her head throbbed a little more with each blare of the trumpets, and she couldn't quite remember why coming here had seemed a good idea.

Her relief was great when the parade of all the animals finally wound its way out of the tent and Erik could be persuaded that everything was over.

"That was swell!" he said, glowing with the wonder of it. "Now I know what an elephant is. Aren't they funny? They look as if they're wearing baggy pants. And the monkeys. I *loved* the monkeys. And the horses were the best of all. I bet I could train a horse to do those things. I bet I could ride standing up like that. But I'm thirsty, Hilda. Can I have some soda water?"

"You have the nickels Patrick gave—found behind your ears. Let us see if there is something to drink."

There was no soda water, but there was lemonade, and there was popcorn, and there was ice cream, and there were pretzels. Hilda let Erik spend his money as he liked, and

Patrick contributed a little more. This was Erik's day and he might as well enjoy it thoroughly. If he got sick later, he would at least have had a good time first.

But he was tiring, and so was she, and her headache was getting worse by the minute as the heat and the noise and the smells assaulted her.

"So, youngster, we'd best be headin' for home," said Patrick, eyeing Hilda's face as it grew ever paler. "Your sister's not feelin' so good."

"It is only that it is so hot," said Hilda. "If we could find some shade . . ."

"Here, let's go out the back way. There's trees back where the wagons are. Shade for the horses, I reckon."

Erik perked up at the word "horses," and pulled at Hilda's hand, urging her to hurry.

A fair portion of the crowd had come back here to mingle with the performers, or perhaps they all thought this was a quicker way out than the front gate, which was jammed with people. Hilda tightened her hold on Erik's hand and picked her way through the masses of people, Patrick following close behind. They had nearly reached the back gate when Hilda stopped dead, dropping Erik's hand. Instead she clutched at Patrick. "Patrick! Look!"

She pointed at the last wagon in line, the farthest away from them. It had been newly whitewashed, the gaudy old painting covered up. But no new sign had yet been painted on, and in the slanting light of late afternoon, Hilda could clearly see the outlines of the old sign.

"The Stupendous Shaws" was just decipherable.

Hilda nearly fainted. She stumbled against Patrick, her face white. "Look!" She pointed with a finger that trembled. "It is them after all!" Erik, puzzled, looked from the two of them to the wagon that had attracted his sister's attention.

Suddenly he saw what she had seen, and he screamed. It was a wordless sound of pure rage.

"Erik, *no!*"

Hilda and Patrick both reached out for him, but it was too late. Still screaming something unintelligible, Erik ran straight for the trapeze artists' wagon and disappeared in the crowd.

19

From battle and murder, and from sudden death,
Good Lord, deliver us.
　　　　　—BOOK OF COMMON PRAYER, 1662

ILDA was for a moment unable to move, stricken with
stark terror. Patrick suffered no such disability. "Here,"
he said hastily. "Sit. I'll go." He found a packing box,
dumped Hilda on it unceremoniously, and sprinted off.

Alas, a grown man, even one as fit as a fireman must be,
is no match in a race for a boy, and a boy, furthermore, with
rage in his heart. Erik disappeared in the crowd as quickly
and as thoroughly as though one of the sideshow magicians
had "vanished" him.

It was obvious, however, that he had been making for the
Shaw wagon. Patrick strode grimly in that direction, paying
little heed to the people in his way. He intended to catch up
with Erik and whale the daylights out of him.

The Shaw wagon was quiet when Patrick reached it.
There was no activity of packing up, for the circus had the
evening performance to give before it moved on. Erik was
nowhere to be seen; neither was anyone else.

Patrick climbed the wooden steps at the back of the wagon
and beat thunderously upon the door. There was no response.

After another volley, he tried the door and, finding it unlocked, ducked his head under the low frame and went in.

The wagon was fitted inside much like a gypsy wagon Patrick had seen once back in Ireland. Storage cupboards lined the sides. Patrick assumed that was where the trapeze equipment was stored. In front of the cupboards were wooden benches. A small folding table was set up for a meal. Not a soul was to be seen.

Wherever the performers were, they would be back soon. They wouldn't be pleased to find Patrick there. He turned around to find Hilda trying to climb the steps, much encumbered by her skirts.

"Where is Erik?"

"Not here. I don't know. I'll look."

"I will come with you."

Patrick looked at her doubtfully. "Are you well enough?"

"It does not matter. I must look, Patrick."

Her face was set, whether with pain or determination, Patrick couldn't tell. Both, probably. He would rather have seen her resting somewhere, but he knew no arguments could keep her from the search. He took her hand to help her down the steps, and together they set out to find Erik.

The crowd was thinning, which helped. They could see individuals now, not just a mass of people. At every wagon where there were people, they stopped to ask. "Have you seen a boy, twelve years old, blond, wearing black knickerbockers and a white shirt? With a blue tie and a new blue cap? About so tall?"

No one had seen him except one clown. "Saw a boy like that takin' off like Old Nick was chasin' him, headed that way." He pointed in the direction of the Shaw wagon. Hilda, whose face had lit up with hope, sagged back against Patrick. "Thank you," she whispered faintly, and they walked away to try the next clump of people.

After an hour they were the only people left within the gates except for the circus performers. Many of them seemed to have left, as well. Patrick hunted up the circus owner to ask where they might be.

"Went to stock up on groceries, most likely," said Mr. Bigelow. "Or to eat in town. They get tired of their own cooking after we've been on the road awhile."

"Do you know if the trapeze artists are on the grounds?" asked Patrick. "They're not in their wagon."

"Then they're likely not around. That's where they'd be. Say, why're you so interested in them, anyway? You're the second folks been around askin' about them."

"Today? Were the others asking today?"

"No. Let's see, last week, it would have been. We was up in Buchanan, and some man come around, wantin' to know if we had any new trapeze acts. Told 'im we did, and a good one, too. Name of Foster."

"The man who was asking?" Patrick put in.

"Naw, the artists. The Fantastic Fosters, they are, from back east somewhere. Pennsylvania, I think they said. Haven't got the name painted on their wagon yet, though. Said they bought the wagon, lock, stock, and barrel, from somebody gettin' out of the business."

Hilda's shoulders sagged again. So this wasn't the Shaw family after all, just some other group of trapeze artists using the wagon. Then she brightened a little. If that terrible Mr. Shaw wasn't around, the chance of Erik being in danger was less.

Patrick caught that point, too. His demeanor became less anxious and more angry.

"When I catch that young rapscallion," he muttered, "I'll make him wish he'd stayed away."

"So what d'you want with the Fosters?" Mr. Bigelow persisted.

"We think my little brother is trying to run away with them. He has been lost for an hour."

"Well, why didn't you say so in the first place? I'll get a couple of horses and get some of the clowns to help you. They haven't got much to do between acts, and you can see better from a horse."

For another hour they looked. That is, Patrick and the clowns looked. Hilda's headache had reached its peak. She had suffered the humiliation of being sick in a public place and gratefully accepted the ministrations of Mrs. Bigelow, who put her in a neat, compact bed in one of the band's wagons and put cold cloths on her head. Gradually Hilda's head began to feel better, but her heart grew colder and colder. Where was Erik?

At last it became obvious that there was no point in searching further. The second performance would not begin for another two hours, but the performers had already picked up their tempo of preparations. The clowns and the horses were needed elsewhere. Patrick returned to Hilda. One shake of his head told her what she already knew.

"We'll stop at the police station on our way to the train," he said quietly. "There's nothing more we can do here. He's off, or he's hiding. I've called till I'm hoarse. I think he's off."

Hilda was too exhausted and upset to do more than nod.

Patrick made her stay outside while he went in to report to the police. She was glad enough to leave the chore to him. She hated police stations.

"Are they going to do anything?" she asked when he came out again. There was little hope in her voice.

"Well—they didn't take it too seriously. Said lots of boys run off, and he'd come back when he was ready."

"I knew they would be that way. Patrick, we must go home and talk to Sergeant Wright."

Patrick made no protest. Now was not a time for teasing.

They didn't speak on their way back to South Bend. There was too much to say, too many recriminations and self-accusations to exchange, and none of it mattered. Nothing mattered except finding Erik.

When they got to the South Bend station, Patrick said, "Hilda, will you let me go to the police alone? You should rest."

"Yes, Patrick, you go, but I cannot rest. I—I must tell Mama."

Patrick looked down. He could not take on that unhappy duty for her, and accompanying her would only make matters worse. "Tell her—tell her I'm sorry, and I'll find him or die tryin'."

Hilda nodded miserably and turned south as Patrick headed north.

The moment when she had to confront her mother with the news that Erik was truly missing was one that gave Hilda nightmares for years to come. She said no word in her defense, only repeated over and over that she and Patrick would find Erik. She bowed her head under the storm of grief and wrath, saying almost nothing, until Sven finally took his mother away. "I will make her lie down," he said quietly to Hilda. "You must do the same. And we will all pray."

"Yes," said Hilda, and with unutterable weariness turned away and trudged back to Tippecanoe Place.

The sun was just dipping beneath the horizon when she stumbled down the basement steps, nearly falling. Mr. Williams, who had been waiting for her to come in before locking the door, started to snap at her, took a better look, and said instead, "What is it? Are you ill?" His voice held real alarm. Even in the midst of her worst headaches, he had never seen her look like this.

"Erik is missing. Do not lock the door yet; Patrick will want to tell me what Sergeant Wright is going to do." She turned toward the servants' room.

Mr. Williams was so startled that he did as Hilda asked, without protest.

When Patrick came, Mr. Williams let him in, again without protest. Patrick was too upset even to notice.

"I couldn't find him," he said as he dropped into a chair next to Hilda's. "I went to the police station. They said Wright's been off duty most of the day. So I made them give me his home address, but he's not there, either. I made the police take down the information, of course. Lefkowicz was there; he was good about it. But—" He broke off and shrugged despairingly.

"They will do nothing until Sergeant Wright comes back," said Hilda. There was no expression whatever in her voice. "There is nothing we can do until then, either."

"No, there's nothing you can do," said Patrick. If Hilda had been in full possession of her wits, she would have noticed the pronoun. "Go to bed, darlin'. Maybe he'll turn up by mornin'."

Hilda lifted her hands in a gesture of futility. She didn't follow Patrick to the door. If she had, and if she had accompanied him up the stairs, she might have noticed that he turned, not in the direction of his home or the firehouse, but toward the train station.

He had spent nearly all his money that afternoon. He was prepared to sneak or bully his way onto the train, but fortunately cousin Keith was still on duty. When he heard Patrick's story, he was happy enough to let him travel free. "And I'll keep me eye open for the boy meself," he promised. Patrick doubted whether Keith would be of any help, but the offer warmed him a little.

The evening performance was in full swing when Patrick arrived at the circus. Again he had to explain to get past the ticket taker, but once he had, the man not only let him in, but deputized one of the roustabouts to help him search. A lantern with a dark slide was procured, for night had now fallen, and the two set out.

"I'm thinkin' he was hidin' somewhere when we was lookin' for him before, see," Patrick explained. "If we're quiet, and only use the lantern when we have to, we may come across him before he knows we're there. Where would a boy hide?"

The roustabout knew all the places, of course. He was accustomed to finding boys and throwing them out. "In the bushes at the edge of the field, most likely. Or sometimes they go from one wagon to another, hiding at the back, see, and moving when you're not looking."

So they went back to where Erik had vanished, earlier, and began a methodical search of the area between the backs of the wagons and the trees and bushes behind them.

As they neared the end of the row, where the erstwhile Shaw wagon stood, the roustabout opened the lantern briefly to help Patrick get his bearings.

They both saw him at the same moment, a small figure in black pants and a white shirt, sprawled awkwardly on the ground, his head against a wagon wheel gaudily painted in white and gold. In the light from the lantern, they could clearly see the blood on the hub and the lower spokes, and on his head.

20

Today of past Regrets and future Fears . . .
—EDWARD FITZGERALD, *THE RUBÁIYÁT OF*
OMAR KHAYYÁM, TRANSLATED 1879

H E is dead," said the roustabout, at the same moment
that Patrick said, "It's not Erik."

They moved toward the pathetic, still figure, moving
as gently as if they might disturb him. But nothing would ever
disturb the child again. They could see that before they stood
over him, the lantern casting its bright but confusing light.

They could see that he had been struck a hard blow in his
face. A dark bruise showed under his left cheekbone. The right
side of his head, above the ear, was a mass of drying blood.

"Some bastard hit him," said the roustabout in a grim un-
dertone. "He fell and hit his head against the hub of the wheel.
Never had a chance, poor little kid."

"And look," said Patrick, who had dropped to his knees to
examine the boy closely and make quite sure he was not Erik.
He pointed to the boy's knickerbockers. They were disarranged
and torn.

The two men shook their heads in horrified disgust, and
Patrick made the sign of the cross, as though to ward off evil.

Then he stood. "When's the performance over?"

The roustabout cocked an ear toward the tent to listen to the music. "That's the elephants, now. A little over half an hour more."

"And the trapeze artists do a bit at the end, don't they?"

"An extra flourish or two, yeah."

"Then I'll stay here. You get the police, and a doctor. This was done by the same man who hurt that kid in South Bend three weeks or so ago, and he's one of your performers. I want to make sure he doesn't get away. Go, man!"

"Here." The roustabout pulled a wicked-looking knife out of his pocket and handed it to Patrick. "That's in case there's any trouble."

Patrick got back to his knees and said a quick prayer for the poor dead child, and then stood, knife in hand, ready for anything. Nothing happened. In less time than Patrick would have thought possible, the roustabout was back with a couple of uniformed policemen, a man in a black coat carrying a black bag, and the circus owner. "I took a horse into town," the roustabout explained. "Quicker."

The doctor knelt to examine the boy, while one of the policemen said to Patrick, "All right, now, tell me what you know."

Patrick had thought about the quickest way to tell the story. "I don't know the boy, but it looks as though someone tried to—interfere with him. When the kid fought back, the man hit him, and he fell against that wheel. The wagon belongs to the man who beat and abused the boy in South Bend. Fritz Schlager, you know?"

The policeman nodded. He was certainly familiar with the story of Fritz. "What makes you think it was the same man? And how do you come into it, anyway?"

"The man was—is—a circus performer named Shaw. This is his wagon. It's been painted over, but by daylight you can see. The people who are using it now claim to be different, say they bought the wagon, but I'd say this boy, here, proves different."

"Hmmm." The policeman scraped his jaw. "And you?"

"Fritz is a friend of a young friend of mine, the brother of the lady I hope to marry. We all came to the circus today, Miss Johansson and her brother Erik and I. Erik's gone missing and I came back to find him."

His voice began to shake and he stopped. For just one terrible, endless moment he had thought he *had* found Erik. He would not soon forget his fear.

The policeman seemed to understand. His face took on a more sympathetic cast. "Yes, I think I remember you reporting that earlier. I guess it's maybe more serious than we thought. We'll get some men out in a bit to help you look. The first thing is to get this villain under lock and key. Now, Mr. Bigelow—"

"Just a moment." The doctor stood and dusted off his hands. "Do I gather you're saying that this boy was killed by one of the circus performers?"

Patrick nodded. "One of the trapeze artists. And the sooner we get that man—"

The doctor ignored him. "And you, sir. You are the manager here?"

"The owner," said Mr. Bigelow. "We've never had any trouble before, and I can tell you, I never—"

"Then you can tell me when the show started."

"Eight o'clock sharp, the second show. We pride ourselves on—"

"And the performers would all be where, exactly, while the show was going on? They are not all performing at the same time, as I understand it. Do they wait at their wagons, or in a tent somewhere?"

"Depends on what act. The animals, now—"

"Please, Mr. Bigelow." The doctor puffed himself up. He was a person of importance, and the owner of a small circus was a person of no importance whatsoever. "We are not discussing animals, sir. We are discussing the trapeze artists, as I believe they call themselves."

"The Fantastic Fosters, yes. They're on almost all the time, one way and another. Never more than ten or fifteen minutes between their acts. They do the high-wire stuff, too, see, and then the trapeze, and then they're acrobats, too. Different costumes, of course, to make it look like they're different people. They stay in one of the dressing tents the whole time. They—"

"Look here," said the policeman who had done all the talking. "I'm not interested in the details of your circus. I'm interested in catching the murderer of this boy, and I want you to stop that damned circus right now!"

"There is no need, sir," said the doctor, looking at the policeman, "to stop the performance. If you are looking for the murderer of this child, you are not looking for one of the trapeze artists. It is now nearly ten o'clock. This boy has been dead for less than an hour. If what Mr.—er—Bigelow says is correct, he cannot have been killed by one of the—er—Fantastic Fosters."

For Patrick, the shock was devastating. If what the doctor said was true, then a murderer was still out there in the dark, somewhere.

And so was Erik.

"Are you sure?" said Patrick, the policeman, and Mr. Bigelow, more or less at the same time.

"I'm sure of the time of death, within fifteen minutes either way. If you knew anything about death at all, you'd know how soon the body cools, how soon rigor mortis sets in."

"Rigor which?" asked Patrick.

"Mortis. Latin for the—er—stiffening of the body after death. It sets in about two hours after death, give or take a little, as the body cools. This boy is still limp and quite warm. In my judgment he's been dead, at the very most, for forty-five minutes."

The policeman took that in and then shrugged. "Well, that's all very interesting, Doctor, but I reckon this Shaw or Foster or whoever he calls himself could have managed it if he was offstage or out of the ring or whatever for fifteen minutes. And there's the boy in South Bend to consider, the

Schlager child. I reckon the South Bend police would like to talk to your Shaw about that, too. So we'll just go on over to the tent, Mr. Bigelow, and catch these people as they leave. I guess we've got no cause to stop the show. People have paid good money for it, and it's almost over anyhow. But I don't intend to let Shaw get away this time."

Patrick was half-convinced. He wanted to be convinced. How could the doctor be so certain about when the boy died?

But if he was right, and Shaw didn't do it, then who did? And where was Erik?

"I'd be obliged," he said to the roustabout, "for the loan of your lantern. I've got to go and look for the boy who's goin' to be my brother one day."

"Take it and welcome," said Mr. Bigelow. "You don't need to bring it back. We'll be packing up and moving on after the show's over, or I'd send some of my men along to help. Good luck to you."

"Here, son, wait a while and I can send some of my men," said the policeman. "I can't spare my patrolman here until we've got this fellow where we want him."

"Thank you, sir, but I'll be on my way. If you can send out some men when you can, I'd be grateful. I'll let you know if I find him."

Patrick returned the unneeded knife to the roustabout, and started off hopefully. Erik was a country boy. He, Patrick, had been a country boy. He knew where a boy was likely to go and hide. He made for the nearest barn and started searching its hayloft.

Hayloft after hayloft he found and searched in vain. A few farmers, seeing the light, came out with a pitchfork or a shotgun in hand. When they heard Patrick's story, they joined in the search.

There were few haystacks left at this time of year, but Patrick searched those, too, shining his lantern around the base for telltale signs that someone had disturbed them. He found none. Erik was hiding in no sheds that Patrick could find, lying beneath no hedges, curled into no ditches. The night was growing chilly; the boy must have found shelter somewhere.

All night Patrick searched, in growing despair. When dawn began to break, he, too, was broken. A kindly farmer gave him a lift into town on a milk wagon and dropped him at the police station.

"Nothing?" he said as he staggered in and dropped down to the bench in front of the desk.

"Nothing," replied the patrolman, shaking his head sadly. He had been told the whole story.

"Shaw?"

"Says he didn't do anything. He's told the sergeant some story. I don't know if there's anything to it."

Patrick cast the problem away. "I have to get some rest before I go out again. Can you get a message to the boy's sister in South Bend?"

"I can send a wire. What shall I say?"

"Just—" Patrick tried to rouse his dull brain. "Just tell her I'll be looking till I find him, that's all." He had a sudden, chilling thought. "Do you know if anyone has told Erik's family about the boy who was killed?"

"Don't know."

"Can you find out? And if they haven't, tell them not to? It would make them wild with worry."

"Sure. I'll take care of it. Anything else?"

"Just—is there a cell I can sleep in for an hour or two? I'm dead on me feet."

"I can do better than that. I'm off duty in ten minutes. My wife'll put you up and happy to do it. We've got a boy about that age."

Patrick nodded dully, his head already sinking to his breast. He roused when the patrolman shook him a few minutes later and trudged by his side the short distance to his house.

"Have they found out who the other boy was, the one who was killed?" Patrick remembered to ask just before he fell into a bed.

"An orphan named Sam Reedy. A farm couple adopted him just a week or two ago when the orphan train came to South Bend. I've heard tell they was pretty strict with the boy, but they're mighty broken up about it, all the same. They never had no other kids."

Patrick didn't hear the last few words. He was asleep.

21

For this my son was dead, and is alive again;
he was lost, and is found.
—THE GOSPEL ACCORDING TO LUKE, 15:24

THE patrolman (whose name was Abbott) had told his
wife to let Patrick sleep as long as he could. But noon
was still hours away when Patrick woke with a start, a
terrible taste in his mouth and the memory of a terrible dream
in his mind. He had no idea where he was for a moment, and
when he remembered and the horror of the thing swept over
him, he thought for a moment he was going to be sick.

Someone had undressed him and had washed and ironed
his shirt and underthings, which lay neatly folded in a chair.
His pants and suit coat had been brushed as well as they could
be, though traces of the long night's search through mud and
hay and brambles still showed. He was attired in someone's
nightshirt. Shaking his head that he could have slept through
such things, he rose and dressed hastily.

"Mr. Cavanaugh!" said Mrs. Abbott when Patrick appeared in the kitchen of the tiny, spotlessly clean cottage.
"You should still be resting! Mr. Abbott said—"

"I'm all right," he said. "I thank you, ma'am, for looking after my clothes."

"They're not what I'd wish. They need a good cleaning, but I did the best I could. Now you sit down and have some breakfast."

"I must go, thank you, ma'am."

"Now you listen to me, young man." Mrs. Abbott, a substantial woman in her forties, moved with surprising speed and planted herself in the kitchen doorway. "It'll do nobody the least bit of good to run yourself down to a shadow. There's others out looking for your brother, and you can go out yourself in a bit, but first you're going to have some coffee and some bacon and eggs, and I'll have no argument about it. Sit down!"

Patrick sat. He ate and drank. He didn't bother to correct her version of Erik's relationship to himself. It would, he hoped, one day be true. If only he could *find* him . . .

He gulped a last swallow of very hot coffee, wiped his mouth, and stood.

"Thank you, ma'am, for everything. I feel a lot better, and I'm grateful to you, but I *must* go and look for Erik."

She nodded. "Stop by the police station first. No point in you going the same places they've already been."

The police had no news of any great importance. They had the trapeze artist in jail, but they weren't sure they could keep him there for long.

"He's Shaw, all right," said the patrolman on duty, a man Patrick had never seen before. "He's admitted it. He says he and his family got scared when there was all that to-do about the other boy. He admits the boy came to him after the circus in South Bend. Hid in the wagon, he says, and only came out when they were on the road. Tried to talk them into letting him join the act. Well, he—Shaw—says he tried the boy out when they were practicing one night, and he wasn't good enough, not by a long shot. So they told him they couldn't use him, but that they'd let him ride along with them to Fort Wayne, where he could get a train back home."

"And what about the shouts and screams the people in the other wagons heard?"

"Says it never happened, and he doesn't know what they're talking about. Says the boy just left, after they said they couldn't take him on, walked away when their backs were turned and didn't come back. But they read in the paper a couple of days later about the boy being found in such bad shape, and they figured Mr. Shaw'd be blamed."

"Why, if he hadn't done anything? Sounds mighty thin to me."

"He says circus people are always blamed for everything. Everybody likes to come and see them, he says, but they're treated like scum."

"Well, I suppose they'll get to the bottom of it one way or another," said Patrick. Shaw's guilt or innocence was, just now, of secondary importance. "I'm off to look for Erik. I'll check in now and again."

All through that long morning, searchers looked for Erik, in the town and in the country. The police knocked on doors in Niles, in South Bend, in surrounding areas. Wires flew back and forth between the police forces, but all said the same thing: "No trace so far." At Tippecanoe Place Mr. Williams had taken pity on Hilda and told her she could keep to her bed. She went to Sven's house instead, to help her family search. Mama stayed home, weeping and praying and hoping every minute that her son, tired and dirty, would walk in the door.

The first hint of anything out of the ordinary came outside Niles, just before noon. Patrick, plodding from one farmhouse near Niles to the next, encountered one farmer who had scant sympathy to spare for a lost boy.

"Boy! What about my horse? Since morning he's been gone, and what are the police doing about it? Nothing, that's what. Wasting all their time looking for some worthless runaway boy, and how am I to do my work today without a horse, tell me that, eh?"

Patrick was on the alert at once. "What does the horse look like, sir?"

"A roan, a little over fifteen hands, four years old, and the best piece of horseflesh I've ever owned. I've *told* the police all this."

"Yes, and when did you say he went missing?"

"I went to the barn this morning to feed him, and he was gone."

"Is there any chance he could have run away by himself?"

"Not unless he could fly through the barn window, there isn't! The door was shut and latched when I went to the barn. And there's a bridle gone, too. I suppose you think he took that in his teeth!"

"Saddle?"

"No. Both saddles still here, and the one is new, too. Stupid thief, if you ask me, taking a horse and no saddle."

"Stupid, or good at riding bareback."

"One of them circus people!" said the farmer excitedly. "I always said they was no good."

"It could be, sir. I'll keep a lookout for your horse, I promise you."

Patrick left before the farmer could make the connection between a missing horse and a missing boy who could ride anything on four feet.

He wasn't so far from town, and he half-ran most of the way. As he went, he thought hard.

There were two possibilities, only two, really. One was that Erik had been abducted, most likely by the same man who had killed the orphan boy Sam. Patrick was still not entirely convinced that Shaw was not that man, but if he was, he certainly didn't have Erik. And if Shaw wasn't the man, then he, Patrick, had no idea who was. So he would have to abandon that possibility for now. Urgent and terrifying though it was, it simply couldn't be dealt with until he or the police had some idea of who the killer was.

The other possibility, of course, was that Erik had gone off on his own, for some reason of his own. The stolen horse gave credit to that speculation. If Erik had wanted to get somewhere in a hurry, his first thought would have been a horse.

But Erik was not a thief. A mischievous boy, yes, but one who had been well brought up, and who knew right from wrong. If he had stolen that horse, it was because he needed it so badly that other considerations went by the board.

And that led Patrick to another big question, one that had bothered him all along. If Erik had left of his own free will, why?

Knowing all he did of Erik, and adding in the matter of the horse, Patrick could think of only one answer to that question. He had left because he was afraid, and he was afraid because he knew something.

Had he seen little Sam being killed?

It was a thin thread of speculation, but it was all Patrick had, and he clung to it like a lifeline. When he reached the police station, he gasped it all out for the benefit of Patrolman Abbott, who had just come in.

The policeman nodded thoughtfully. "Makes a certain amount of sense, I suppose. He could have gotten quite a ways away by now on a good horse. Any idea where he might have gone?"

"I'd have thought he'd head straight for home. But he hasn't been there, you say."

"Not by the last wire, just half an hour ago."

"Then he could be anywhere. One thing's pretty sure: There's not much point anymore in lookin' for him on foot. How many horses do you think we can scare up?"

The Niles police department was small, as the town was small. They had only two horses of their own, but they were able to borrow two more from wealthy men of the town who kept them for their carriages and said they didn't need them for a time. So Patrick and three policemen rode out, each in a different direction. Patrolman Abbott went south, toward South Bend, still on the assumption that Erik would eventually head for home. The two other policemen took to the east and west and Patrick, for no particular reason except that he hadn't tried that way yet, went north.

There weren't so many farmhouses here. Much of the countryside was forested, and the land, where it was cultivated, was in apple and cherry orchards, their blossoms almost gone now, and the fruit beginning to set. Here and there a railroad line crossed the dirt lanes, and once Patrick saw, in a little hollow off to the side of the road, a small group of hoboes cooking something over a fire. It smelled good. Patrick remembered he had had no lunch.

His search ended abruptly, and easily. It was a piece of amazing luck, or the answer to prayer. He never afterward stopped to analyze which.

He saw the horse first, or rather, his mount did. He was on a pretty little gray mare. She was walking slowly and delicately through a small wood when she lifted her nose and whinnied softly. Patrick loosened the reins and let the mare follow her nose. When she saw the roan, she stopped, testing the air for friend or foe. Patrick swung himself out of the saddle as silently as he could, tethered the mare to a small tree (as the roan, a few yards away, was tethered), and walked noiselessly on the deep carpet of leaves and moss.

He might have searched for a long time if he had not happened to step on a twig. The leaves nearby quivered and heaved, a human shape emerged, trembling, and Erik would have been running if Patrick had not thrust out a long leg and tripped him. In another moment he had the boy in his arms, holding him tight as he struggled.

"It's all right," he said over and over. "Ow! Don't bite me, you great gomerel, it's me. It's Patrick. You're all right now."

And Erik, for all his twelve years, broke down and clung to Patrick and sobbed.

22

*. . . whence this secret dread, and inward
horror . . . ?*

—JOSEPH ADDISON, *CATO,* 1713

W HEN he was sure Erik wasn't going to run, Patrick
stood, set him on his feet, and loosed the roan horse,
which had been twitching uneasily at the commotion.
Erik made a small noise of protest.

"Never mind, it's all right. I've got me own horse—well, a
borrowed one—and if we let this fellow go, he'll find his way
back home. There's a law against horse thievery, you know,
me boy, and they'd not treat you kindly if it was known you
stole this one."

"I borrowed him," said Erik in a very small voice. "I would
have taken him back."

"I'd not like to see you have to prove that in a court of
law. Now don't worry about it anymore. I know you thought
you were only doin' what you had to, but remember in
future that takin' without askin' is stealin', and no two ways
about it. Now we've got to get you back to the police station—"

"No!"

If Patrick had not had his arm around Erik, holding him

close, he would have bolted. Patrick tightened his grip and looked at him hard. "I'll not tell them about the horse, you know."

"It isn't the horse. I—" He shut his mouth firmly.

"What are you afraid of, boy?"

Erik looked at the ground.

Patrick drew a few conclusions. "I found a boy last night, Erik. For one awful minute I thought it was you. You'll know something about that, will you?"

The boy turned even paler. Patrick thought Erik was going to vomit or faint, but he simply stood silent and rigid.

Patrick raised his eyes to heaven. "If you're not as stubborn as your sister, then! But if you won't tell me, you won't. I'll just let you tell it to the police—"

Again Erik tried to break free.

Patrick held on tight and sighed. "All right. No police. We'll just take you home, though how, with no money for the train—"

"I don't want to go home." Erik was crying again.

"But they're scared stiff about you! And you're tired, and wet through, and likely you'll catch cold—"

"Please!" Erik lifted his face to Patrick's. Tears had made tracks through the dirt on his face. He lifted a fist to wipe away the tears and made matters much worse. "Please don't make me go home. I can't tell you why, but *please!*"

"Well—what *are* we to do with you, then?"

"Take me to Hilda. She'll think of something. She always does. Only don't tell anybody where I am!"

Patrick sighed. "I'll try. But I don't know how I'm to get you there with no money in me pocket, and tellin' nobody. And, Erik, I have to tell the police you've been found. They've got men out lookin' for you, have had all night."

A long shudder went through Erik's thin body. "I know. Couldn't you—couldn't you say you found me, but I ran away again?"

Patrick was beginning to understand Hilda's headache of

yesterday. "They'd still be out lookin'. We can't let 'em waste their time that way, Erik. It's not fair."

"Well, then—say you found me and—and sent me off with your cousin Kevin to—to a farm where I maybe couldn't get into more trouble! They'd believe that, wouldn't they?"

Patrick sighed yet once more and went to untie the mare. "I suppose, maybe. You an' your sister can come up with more lies than any Irishman I ever knew, and take it from me, that's an accomplishment. Now have you also worked out how I'm to get you home? Were you thinkin' of ridin' double all the way?"

"No," said Erik, a trace of spirit back in his voice. "It's too far for a horse to carry two. You'll think of something." He yawned mightily.

"Here, don't fall asleep on me. We've got to get you on that horse. Lucky you're a wiry one, and I'm not so fat meself. Reckon Dolly here can get us as far as town—"

"*Not* town. Not where anyone can see me."

Patrick shook his head, but climbed up on Dolly's broad back. Erik hoisted himself behind, grasped Patrick's waist, and was asleep before they got out of the wood, his head lolling against Patrick's back.

He headed Dolly absently back toward town, trying wearily to think of a way to meet Erik's demands. They seemed unreasonable, and Erik was not an unreasonable boy. There was something here Patrick didn't understand. Why wouldn't Erik tell him what he was so afraid of? Why was he so anxious that no one know where he was?

So tired he scarcely knew where he was going, he looked up suddenly when Dolly stumbled and found himself looking at the solution to one of his problems, at least. He had arrived at the hoboes' camp, and they were still there.

He looked more closely. No, there was a group of men there still, but Patrick thought they were different from the men he'd seen before.

He directed Dolly down the slope and stopped. "Erik. Get down. This is where you get off."

Erik was hard to wake, and one of the hoboes stood laboriously and came over to them, looking with sharp curiosity at the combination of a man and a sleeping boy, both looking as if they'd slept in their clothes, and a fine, well-fed and well-groomed horse. "What's up, mate? Some kind of trouble?"

Patrick thanked his stars that both he and Erik looked so disreputable the other men felt no fear. "If you can help me get the boy down, I'll explain."

Between the two of them they managed to get Erik safely off the horse. He stood for a moment, looking about stupidly, and then went over to the fire, lay down in the dirt like a tired dog, and went to sleep again.

"Been here long?" asked Patrick in what he hoped was a casual manner.

One of the men laughed gleefully. "Never stay anywhere long, son. The likes of us, we keep on the move. We dropped off the freight an hour or so ago. Been out west, but it got a mite hot out there, so we thought we'd try our summer place." He gestured around the scrubby clearing as though showing off a palace. "How about yourself?"

The men were bronze-skinned, as if they'd been spending time in the hot sun. One of the crates they were sitting on had pictures of oranges on it. Patrick took a deep breath and made his decision. "Well, your friend was right. We're in a spot of trouble." Briefly he explained the situation. He didn't have to go into details; the hoboes saw nothing unusual in being penniless and wanting to avoid attention. "So do you know this line? Could you get him on a freight train headed for South Bend? After dark?"

"Easy, mate. Jake, here, is from these parts. He knows all the trains. One of us'll go with the boy. Maybe all of us. Tired as he is, he'd sleep right on till he got to Chicago, and our time, as you might say, is our own."

"I'm sorry I can't give you anything for your trouble, but the truth is, I've not got a penny to me name just now."

One of the men laughed. "Don't matter. Money's not

much good to us, anyway. We mostly live by our wits. Now don't you worry. We'll feed the boy if he wakes up, and we'll take him to South Bend for you. He'll know what to do when he gets there?"

Patrick certainly hoped so. At least Erik was safe for now, and as soon as he, Patrick, got back home himself, he'd check on the boy. "I'll likely get there before he will. Where will you put him off the train?"

Jake explained exactly where the freights on that line slowed at a curve on the west side of town. Patrick knew the spot. "If I can," he told them, "I'll be waiting for him there. If I'm not there, tell him to hide and not come out till he sees me. I'll be off now. I'm much obliged to you all, and I hope we meet again someday."

The hoboes doffed their crownless hats and bowed graciously, and then went serenely back to their stew and their corncob pipes as Patrick made his way back to the Niles police station.

Patrick gave the police a story along the lines Erik had suggested. It was evidently convincing, because it didn't seem very long before they had taken Dolly and fed her, taken Patrick and fed him, called off the search, and put Patrick on the train back to South Bend. Patrolman Abbott paid the fare, "For you've had enough problems for one day."

"I'll pay you back, but I can never pay you back for all the kindness you've—"

"Ahh! A pleasure. Just glad it worked out all right. You get some good rest tonight, now."

Patrick thought he'd fall asleep the minute he sat down in the train, but instead he sat there fretting, tortured by doubt. Would Erik be all right? Was he a fool for entrusting Hilda's precious brother to a bunch of bums and layabouts? They seemed nice enough, but would they keep their word?

At least they wouldn't tell anybody what they were up to, or nobody but other tramps like themselves. Of that he could be sure. They had good reason to distrust authority. And he was pretty sure they'd been telling the truth about just arriving in the area. That meant they couldn't have any connection with the murderer.

Or at least he hoped it meant that. What with worry and fear and little sleep, he wasn't sure his brain was working very well. He didn't see what else he could have done, but still . . .

Gnawing on a fingernail, he worried all the way to South Bend, and when he got off the train, he ran most of the way to the place where the rails curved and the freight trains had to slow. There were signs that this, too, was a hobo camp, but no one was there now.

Daylight still lingered in the western sky, but night was fast approaching. Patrick looked for Erik and called softly, but he didn't expect to see him there yet. He'd told the men to wait until after dark.

He paced, chewing on the fingernail until he drew blood. He knelt by the rails now and then and put his ear to them, hoping he could hear the hum that meant a train arriving soon.

The first train that came through was all coal cars, bound for Studebaker's, Patrick thought. He didn't expect the hoboes to be on that one, and sure enough, no one jumped out when the train slowed for the curve.

The evening was well advanced, the daylight long gone and the moon high in the sky, and Patrick was nearly out of his mind with worry when the next train came along. This one had several boxcars and sounded lighter on the track, as though some of the cars were empty. The almost full moon allowed him to see a little, but the shadows were deceptive. He heard a rasping noise. A car door being pushed aside? Then there was a thump, followed by one or two more. When the train had passed, he waited a moment, his heart in his mouth, and then hissed softly, "Psst! Over here."

"Keep talking, friend, and we'll find you."

Patrick risked lighting a match. He heard running feet,

and then just before the match burned his fingers, Erik was at his side.

"Okay, friend?" It was one of the hoboes, which one he didn't know. Patrick wished the man were nearer, so he could shake his hand.

"Okay. And thanks." Patrick let out a long breath and took Erik's hand. "Let's go find your sister, shall we?"

23

How much better it is to weep at joy than to joy at weeping.

—WILLIAM SHAKESPEARE,
MUCH ADO ABOUT NOTHING, 1600

ILDA had spent the day with her family, searching and worrying and weeping until she thought she would lose her mind. Sven sent her back to Tippecanoe Place as evening approached. "I will rest for a little and then search some more. We have much help, Hilda, the church people and the neighbors and the police. You must rest."

Dully she obeyed him, too weary to protest. Her head was pounding relentlessly, and she hoped she would not be sick, for there was nothing in her stomach except endless cups of coffee. Too much coffee, she knew, for her nerves were stretched tight and her stomach roiled. She had been too upset all day to eat.

Mr. Williams was waiting for her when she came in. For once he had no word of blame. "Any news?" he asked.

Hilda simply shook her head and turned toward the stairs, the endless stairs, to her room.

Mrs. Sullivan intercepted her. "You're to come and sit down and have something to eat."

"Thank you, Mrs. Sullivan, but I couldn't. My stomach is upset."

"Your stomach is empty, that's what. I've made some baked custard, and you're to eat it. Mrs. Clem said so. And Mrs. George gave me some headache powders. She reckoned you'd be feeling poorly."

Again she had lost the will to resist. She allowed the cook to seat her at the kitchen table. She ate the custard and took the headache powder. She accepted a piece of hot buttered toast and ate it mechanically. Nothing had any taste, but she discovered after a time that she was feeling better.

"That's better," said Mrs. Sullivan, who had been watching her closely. "There's a little color in those cheeks now. When you come in, you was as white as my apron. Now, you're to go up and see Mrs. Clem. She's in her sitting room and she said I was to tell you she wanted special to talk to you."

Hilda was past feeling alarm at the unusual order. She was, she thought vaguely, past feeling anything. She stood. "Thank you, Mrs. Sullivan," she said politely, and went up the stairs to the family bedroom floor.

Mrs. Clem's sitting room adjoined her bedroom. The door was ajar. Hilda tapped on it, went in, and curtsied. "You wanted to see me, madam?"

Mrs. Clem had been reading. She put her book down, stood, and went to Hilda. "You poor child!" She patted her lightly on the shoulder. "Sit down, my dear, before you fall down."

"I am all right, madam," said Hilda. It was a rare thing for her to sit in the presence of her employers, and now she sat for the second time in just a few days. The chair was soft and comfortable.

"You've eaten? I told Mrs. Sullivan to make sure you did."

"Yes, thank you, madam."

"Good. Now, I don't want to keep you. You must go straight to bed. But I couldn't have you worrying about your work, not with everything else on your mind. You're not to give a thought to us here until your brother is found. And if there's anything we can do to help with the search, you're to tell me. George is ready to send out men from Studebaker's to help if necessary. All right?"

The unexpected kindness touched Hilda as nothing else had for hours. She felt her lip quiver. "I—it is very good of you, madam. I am sorry to be such a trouble to you."

"Nonsense. Have you never done anything for us, child? Now you get some rest, and if there's any word, I've told Williams to let you know at once."

Hilda curtsied and fled before she could disgrace herself by bursting into tears.

Once she reached her bed, she lay down fully dressed, too utterly drained even to take off her boots, but she could not sleep. She wept for a while, and it did her good. Some of the tension left her, but still she could not sleep. Too much coffee, too many thoughts.

If only they had never taken Erik to the circus. If only they had kept a closer watch on him. If only Sergeant Wright had been more diligent in looking for small circuses.

He was being diligent now, she thought bitterly, now that it was too late. All day he, himself, had searched, and had driven his men hard. He had reported back to her from time to time, always to say he had found nothing, always to reassure her that they were doing all they could, that Erik would surely be found soon.

There's that other boy, she kept thinking. The one who was never found. What if Erik were never found? What if she had to watch Mama, week after week, month after month, worrying, hoping, losing hope, growing older with her grief . . .

Round and round the thoughts raced in her mind, giving her no chance for rest.

When the tap came at the door, she sprang up, her heart pounding. News!

It was Mr. Williams, knocking on her door in the middle of the night. He was dressed in his pajamas and bathrobe, and his hair was sticking up on one side. Hilda had never before seen him in any other than perfect order.

"Hilda, Mr. Cavanaugh is downstairs. Erik has been found."

She fainted, falling to the floor like a stone.

When she opened her eyes, she was lying on her bed. The gas had been lit, and she could see Norah sitting on the bed, a damp cloth in her hand.

"Ah, that's better, now." Norah passed the cloth once more over Hilda's forehead, and applied it to her wrists. It was cool and refreshing. Hilda's eyes focused. She looked vaguely around the room, sensing another presence. All was as usual except that in the shadowy doorway stood . . .

"Patrick?"

"The same," came his subdued voice.

Hilda sat up, the mists dispersing a little. "Norah, I am all right. Patrick, they let you come up here? Where is Mr. Williams?"

"He's gone to tell Mrs. Clem the good news. When you passed out on him that way, he sent Norah down for me, to help get you to bed. He'll be back any minute. He doesn't trust me."

"But Erik, Patrick! Where is Erik?"

Norah grinned a little and moved to the door. "You come along in, Patrick. I'll keep watch for Himself."

Patrick pulled the chair up to the side of the bed and began to whisper. "This is for your ears, and yours alone, mind. Norah knows. Nobody else. Erik's down in the cellar, and there he's to stay for a bit."

"But—"

"Hush! Listen, there's no time for questions. I found Erik, but he's scared blue about somethin' or other. He won't tell me a thing, only that he doesn't want to go home, and he won't talk to the police. He made up a story about how I could say I'd sent him off with me cousin to a farm somewhere, a place where he couldn't get in any more trouble. It's a good enough story. He's near as good a liar as you. But all he wanted to do was come to you; he said you'd think out a way to help. So I've come, and he's in the cellar where you hid that Chinaman once. Norah says nobody ever goes there."

Hilda took a deep breath and tried to make some sense of what she had been told. "Why will he not talk to you?"

"Search me. I even had to sneak him home. Put him on a freight train with some hoboes."

"Patrick! What if—"

"And do you think I wasn't thinkin' the same thing? But it worked out okay. He's fine, and he's havin' his supper right now. Norah found some food she thought she could get away with pinchin', when she was downstairs supposed to be get-tin' the cool cloths for your head."

"He's comin'," said Norah in an urgent whisper from the doorway. The faint sound of the elevator came to them, the butler being the only servant privileged to use it.

"What does he know?" Hilda's whisper was also urgent.

"Only Patrick's tale—that Erik's been sent away."

Patrick had time for no more. Mr. Williams had arrived. He made a faint grimace when he saw Patrick in the room, but with Norah there, and Hilda fully clothed, the impropri-ety was not as great as it might have been.

"Thank you, Mr. Cavanaugh, for bringing us the welcome news. Mrs. Studebaker was greatly relieved to hear it. I trust, Hilda, that you are feeling better?"

"Yes, sir," she said demurely. "Thank you for your kindness, sir."

"Then I suggest, since it is now well past two o'clock, that you should be on your way home, Mr. Cavanaugh, and that the rest of us retire. You, Hilda and Norah, may sleep somewhat later tomorrow morning, in view of your dis-turbed night. I will have one of the underhousemaids wake you. Good night."

He bowed in a chilly manner to Patrick.

"Oh, but—please, Patrick, will you go to my family and tell them the news?"

"It's late," Patrick said. In his eyes was the thought that the news he would be bringing would not be entirely welcome. Erik was found, but he was not coming home. He, Patrick, had taken it upon himself to send him away. Oh, no, that was not news the Johansson family would greet with cries of joy.

Hilda saw the problem. She thought frantically, not only about what to say, but how to say it in front of the butler. "You should maybe not tell them quite the truth. Tell them—tell them you brought him to me, and it was I who sent him away. Tell them I thought it would be for the best. Tell them he refused to go home. Oh, Patrick, tell them anything, but please do not let them go through the night not knowing he is safe! And say I will try to go to them tomorrow."

She looked at Mr. Williams, who made the sort of face that means, "We'll see," and bowed again to Patrick, this time waving a hand toward the door. Patrick bowed back, very properly, and only Hilda saw the little nod he gave her as he went out the door. Mr. Williams followed him downstairs to let him out and make sure the back door was properly locked.

The moment he was out of earshot Hilda swung her feet over the edge of the bed. "I must go to Erik," she said, her eyes shining.

Norah gave her a little push. "Mornin's time enough for that. He'll be asleep, you know. He could barely keep his eyes open when I took him his food, hungry though he was. I'll see you get time tomorrow to look after him, but for now it's time you got some sleep yourself."

"But, Norah, I must talk to him! I do not understand why he is so afraid. I do not understand—anything."

"Nor me, neither, but it'll all keep till the mornin'. Things'll be better then. They always are."

And with that piece of homely advice she gave Hilda a hug and went off to her own bed.

Hilda, suddenly overwhelmed with exhaustion, pulled off her boots, managed somehow to rid herself of her outer garments, and went to sleep in her camisole and petticoats.

24

Work brings its own relief; He who most idle is/Has most of grief.
          —EUGENE FITCH WARE ("IRONQUILL"),
                              DATE UNKNOWN

S HE slept deeply, but not restfully. Terrors chased her
through the night; she tossed in her narrow bed and
cried out now and again. Toward morning she fell into a
more refreshing sleep and was still in it when Janecska, the
new daily, woke her. "Please, miss, I'm sorry, miss, but Mr.
Williams, he said you should get up now. And Norah, she's already up, and she said to tell you she needs your help in the
dining room when you can do it, miss."

Hilda sat up groggily. Her head ached. She felt as though
she had slept for five minutes, but the alarm clock by her bed
said it was nearly eight o'clock. Eight! Mid-morning! Mr.
Williams had certainly indulged her.

And if Norah wanted her, she thought more coherently, it
was almost certainly something to do with Erik.

"Thank you, Janecska," she said, stumbling a little over the
name. "If you will help me with my back buttons, I can be
ready very soon."

Hilda dressed with record speed in yesterday's rumpled

and unwashed clothes, washed her face sketchily, and pinned up her braids. They needed to be taken down, brushed, and rebraided to look proper, but that, thought Hilda, was what caps were for. She pinned hers on with vicious jabs of the pins and ran down the stairs.

Mr. Williams had been unusually kind and thoughtful throughout the Erik episode, but now that he thought it was over, Hilda felt she dared take no chances. So the first thing she did was hunt him down in the butler's pantry and ask for his orders.

"There is nothing special for the day. Colonel and Mrs. George are going out to dine, and Mrs. Clem has asked for a tray in her room, so it will be an easy day. She asked me to say, Hilda, that she is happy for you that your brother has been found, and that if you wish to take a little time today to talk with your family, you may do so."

"She is a kindhearted, Christian lady, and I will thank her if I see her," said Hilda, "but I am not sure where I can find my family today. I suppose that they, too, will be back at work."

"You have my permission to go early in the evening, Hilda, after our supper, since there is no dinner to speak of."

This was such an unheard-of concession that Hilda blinked and found herself without a response.

Mr. Williams looked at the teapot he was polishing and said, almost to himself, "I had a small brother once."

Hilda could hardly believe what she had heard. The butler raised his eyes, looked at Hilda coldly, and said, "That is all, Hilda. If you have had your breakfast, Norah requires your help in the dining room."

Hilda blinked again and went to the kitchen to beg some bread and ham from the cook, whose temper was back to its usual state and who snarled at Hilda accordingly.

"So it's the fine lady you are, gettin' up anytime you please! Well, there's some of us as has to work, so I'll thank you to get out of my kitchen."

Hilda rolled her eyes and cut the bread and ham herself.

Stuffing a sandwich in her apron pocket, she fled, the cook's invective following her all the way to the dining room.

Norah did not, as Hilda had suspected, need any help. With no entertaining today, Norah's work would all be in the family dining room and the kitchen. She was in front of the great sideboard fussing with the silver knives in the drawer when Hilda came into the room.

"What are you doing?"

"Checkin' the silver, I told *him*." Norah nodded toward the butler's pantry two rooms away. "I said Mrs. George said some of it needed cleanin' and I was to check it over. Because I wanted to get you where I could talk to you."

"Yes." Hilda opened the next drawer and cast a critical eye over the forks. They all gleamed brightly. "Erik?"

"Erik's all right. I snuck him to the toilet, and he's cleaned up a little, but his clothes . . ." Norah shook her head and made a tut-tutting sound. "He's bored, but I found some old books for him to read. Baby stuff from when George Junior was little, 'cause I know reading English is still hard for him. He wants to talk to you right away."

"I want to talk to him. What has he told you?"

"Not a durned thing. I asked him what happened, how come he ran away. Not a word would he say."

Hilda furrowed her brows. "Is he afraid?"

Norah shrugged. "Not now, I don't think. But he doesn't like it much down there in the cellar."

"He did not like closed-in places when he was a little boy. He likes to be out-of-doors."

"But there's a little window in that room, high up, so he isn't in the dark. He's just—jumpy, like. Not knowin' what to do next, I'd say."

Hilda bit her lip. She was not all that sure what to do next, either. "I must talk to him."

"You'd better not let Himself catch you."

"No. No, I must not, because then he would know that

Erik is here. Norah, I do not know why Erik thinks it must be so secret, but he is smart. It will be a good reason."

"Meself, I'd say wait till your rest time, when you can do anything you like. Sneak down there then."

Hilda didn't like it, but Norah was right. It was the only safe way.

She pushed the morning along. As usual, when she wanted time to fly, it plodded. The underhousemaids had taken over most of her work and were doing it quite competently, so Hilda had time on her hands. She ate her sandwich breakfast on the back porch, catching the crumbs in her apron and throwing them to the birds. She polished the state dining table, which was not in the slightest need of polishing. She blacked her own boots, which was the footman's job, and ironed her own dress, which was the laundress's job, thus offending both of them.

At last, at last, luncheon for the family and the servants had been served and cleaned up. Hilda made sure to tell Mr. Williams she was going to her bed to rest, and she did indeed go up the stairs and close her door.

After a few minutes, when she was reasonably sure the butler was settled in his special chair and snoring, she took off her boots and crept down the stairs. Her heart in her mouth, she crossed in front of the kitchen door to the cellar door.

It was very dark going down the stairs. Hilda hadn't dared filch a candle from the kitchen. She felt her way slowly, boots in hand, and when she came to the bottom, she very softly called Erik's name.

"It's me, Erik. Hilda. Be very quiet, but open your door so I can see where you are."

A tiny crack of light appeared. It seemed bright in the total darkness. Hilda moved toward it, eased her way into the room, and gathered her brother into her arms.

She had intended to scold him soundly for frightening everyone. She had intended to question him closely about everything. She did none of those things. She held him tight as both of them wept.

"I can't breathe," came a muffled whisper from somewhere around her collarbone.

She released him from her tight embrace, but held him at arm's length and looked at him.

Even in the dim light from the narrow window up next to the ceiling, she could see that his clothes were beyond hope. What with the rips and tears and stains, they were fit, really, only for the rag bag. His boots—she averted her eyes from his boots.

The boy inside the ruined clothes seemed to be in somewhat better shape. His washing had been perfunctory, and he smelled a bit, but though there were still smudges here and there, she could see no bruises on his face. His arms and legs were a trifle scratched—she would have to tend to those scratches—but they were otherwise intact. His face still showed the tracks of tears, and it was very, very solemn.

She took a breath and then let it out again. None of the things she wanted to say were right for that grave and stoic face. She sat down on the old bed in the corner of the crowded room and gestured to the abandoned rocking horse for Erik.

"Tell me," she said simply.

"You won't tell anybody? Nobody at all, Hilda, you have to promise."

"I will not promise not to tell Patrick. No one else, though."

"But he might tell!"

"He will not, if I say he must not. If you trust me, my little one, you must trust him."

Erik glared at her. She waited, saying nothing.

"Well—but you've got to be *sure!*"

"I am sure."

"This isn't just a game, you know!" he said hotly. "I'm not a little boy anymore. This is serious, and it's bad."

"Hush! You must not speak so loudly. Mr. Williams is up-

stairs, and he must not hear. To me you will always be my little one, but I know you are nearly grown, and I know there is
something bad, or you would not be afraid. You are brave.
Even when you were very small, you dared to do more things,
harder things, than the others. Now you must be brave
enough to trust Patrick and me or we cannot help."

Erik thought about that, chewing his lip. "Okay," he said
at last. "I couldn't tell anybody before because I saw what
happened."

Hilda's heart contracted. "You saw what happened to
Fritz?"

"No. To the other boy. The one who was killed."

Hilda put out a hand to steady herself on the bed. "I do
not know what you are talking about. What boy?"

"Nobody's told you? A boy was killed"—he stopped, and
swallowed hard—"was killed at that circus. And I—I saw it
happen."

"Erik!" He could have been killed himself! He could have
. . . the room seemed to darken. Hilda's head swam, but she
took several deep breaths and forced herself to focus. She
must not faint.

Erik was talking. ". . . my fault, I know, but I couldn't
think what to do. If I had only tried to stop him, maybe—"

"*What are you saying?* If you had tried to stop him, you
would have maybe . . ." She couldn't say it. She couldn't think
it. She tried to make her mind work again. "Is that why you
were afraid to go to the police? You thought they would blame
you?"

"Partly." A tear slipped down his cheek.

"Foolish boy! Of course they will not blame you! We will
go to the police right now, and you can tell them what you
know, and—"

"*No!*" It was an anguished whisper. "You promised!"

"Yes, but Erik—"

"I think maybe I know the person who did it," he said
fiercely.

"But, Erik, if you know, you must tell!"

"No! You don't understand!" He nearly wept with frustration. "I don't mean I can tell a name. I'm maybe even wrong. I just think it was someone I know, but I'm not sure who!"

Hilda was confused, but she did her best to soothe. "It's all right, little one. We will go to the police with what you know, what you remember, and they will help find—"

"No, don't you *see?*" he wailed. "If I know him, he knows me. And it could be anyone, anyone at all. We can't tell anybody!"

25

You will wake, and remember, and understand.
—ROBERT BROWNING, "EVELYN HOPE," 1846

HILDA tried to pull herself out of her fear and confusion. "You mean," she said slowly, "that you recognized something about this man, but that it could be one of several people?"

"No, not like that. It's—I can't tell you, because I don't know. For a minute there was something about him, something that made me think it was someone I knew. And then before I could even think about it, the boy was—was hurt—and the thing I maybe knew was gone, and now I don't know what it was, and, Hilda, I'm so scared!"

There he sat, on the rocking horse, his legs so long they touched the floor, a child-man looking now very much a child. She put her hand on his.

"You must try to think. Was it his voice, the way he talked, something about—oh, his shoes or something else you could see?"

"I have thought. I have tried to remember. I can't," he said with the flatness of exhaustion.

She let out a long breath, trying to find a way to cope. "All right," she said at last. "Tell me what you do know, what you do remember. Tell me everything that has happened, and I will think of a way to—to make things right."

"How?" The question was bleak, despairing.

"I do not know, but I will, somehow, because I must. Tell me, Erik."

"Well—where shall I start?"

"Start with when you ran away from us at the circus."

So he told his terrible little story.

"I saw the wagon when you did, and all I could think of was about that man, and what I thought he'd done to Fritz. I know what happened to Fritz, Hilda. His brothers told me. I didn't want to talk to you about it, because . . ." Even in his distress, he was embarrassed.

"I know." Hilda felt her own face turning red. "I did not want you to learn of it, because it is terrible. We will not speak of it. Go on."

"Well, so I went to the wagon and nobody was there. And I knew you'd be looking for me, and I knew I should go back to you, but I was so mad about Fritz! You know he just lies curled up in a ball most of the day and cries? He won't talk to anyone. And I thought of someone—doing that—to him, and I just wanted to get the man and—I don't know what then, I guess. But I hid from you and Patrick so you wouldn't find me and make me go home."

Hilda shuddered at the memory, at what might have happened. She said nothing.

"I'm sorry I scared everybody so much. Do you think Mama will make Sven whip me?"

"I don't think so, Erik. Not when they know everything. Go on."

"Well, so I decided to wait for them to come back. I knew they had to come back pretty soon, because they had the next show to get ready for. I waited a long time, and—well, the longer I waited, the scareder I got. I started to think what everybody'd do to me when I got home, and what might happen if I did talk to that man, or try to fight him, or anything. And I lost my nerve.

"I was going to leave when I heard them coming back, and then I got *really* scared. I was hiding in one of the cupboards in the wagon, but it had stuff in it I thought they'd need for the act, and they'd find me. So I got out of the cupboard, real fast, and got out of the wagon, but they were real close, then, and I had to duck under the wagon or they'd have caught me, for sure.

"So pretty soon I heard the music start for the beginning of the circus and they all left, and I figured I could go to the train station and maybe Patrick's cousin would let me sneak onboard a train back home. And I was just about to crawl out from under the wagon when I heard voices, real close. A boy's voice and a man's."

Erik's own voice broke. The light in the small room was dim, but Hilda could see that Erik's face was pale.

"Little one," she said gently in Swedish, "I know it is hard. I am sorry. I do not want you to have to remember, but if you can, it is important."

He made a sound that was half sob, half hiccup. "I *want* to tell you. It—somebody has to know."

Hilda wasn't at all sure she wanted to know, but she smoothed back the lock of hair that had fallen over Erik's forehead and waited.

"He was talking funny to the boy. Kind of like a man talks to his lady friend, you know? And I didn't like it. It made me feel funny. I didn't *like* it," he repeated. "So he was talking to this boy that way. I don't know who the boy was, but I could tell he was sort of scared, so I kind of scrunched out a little so I could see."

Hilda shuddered at that. "Erik! Suppose the man had seen you!"

"I know. But it was pretty dark by then, and anyway, I didn't know what was going to happen. I thought maybe I could do something to make him stop talking that way, because he was scaring the boy.

"And then I saw he was touching the boy, too, sort of soft, like, and I started to get scared. I don't know why, but I did. I tried to see if I knew the boy, but it was pretty dark and he had his face down, so I couldn't tell. And then—"

Erik swallowed hard. Hilda waited.

Erik took a long, shuddering breath. "He tried to make the boy take his pants off. He—he had ahold of him by one arm, and with the other he—he was trying to unbutton—"

"Yes," said Hilda. "You do not have to tell that part."

"And the boy got real scared. He hollered, but the circus music was real loud just then, and I don't think anybody could hear. And then he tried really hard to get away, and the man hit him, and he fell. And he didn't get up."

Hilda discovered she had been holding her breath. She released it.

"I scrunched back under the wagon then, just as quiet as I could. Hilda, I was scared so bad!"

His face crumpled. He buried his face in Hilda's shoulder and sobbed like the little boy she had known all those years ago, back in Sweden. She murmured soothing noises, phrases in Swedish, and let him cry. It was what he needed. He had told the worst of his story, had gotten it out of his system. Now he could relax a little.

When the sobs had diminished a bit and were turning to sniffles, she reached in her pocket for a clean handkerchief and handed it to him.

"I have one," he said, struggling to regain his dignity. He reached in his pocket. "Oh. I guess I don't. I must have lost it."

"I always carry two," said Hilda. She would have liked to wipe the tears from his face, but he was eager to distance himself from that crybaby of a moment ago. She let him make the necessary ablutions himself.

He showed no inclination to continue with his story, so

Hilda continued for him. "When did you think there was something about the man that you recognized?"

"I think it was when he first started talking to the boy, because I started getting scared right after that, and I think I wouldn't have noticed anything much then."

"And after the boy fell, the man was frightened and ran away, and when you came out, you saw there was nothing to be done for the boy, *ja?*"

Erik nodded drearily. "He'd hit his head on the hub of the wheel, it looked like. And all I could think of, over and over, was that I should have done something. But then I started to wonder if the man knew I was there, and if he'd come after me, and I knew I had to run away as far as I could get."

"Where did you go? Everyone was looking for you."

"I just ran out into the country as far as I could. I really ran, ran fast, and when I couldn't run any farther I saw I was at a farm. There was a horse; I could smell the stable. So I—well—I stole it, Hilda. I told Patrick I borrowed it, and I really did mean to take it back, but Patrick says taking something without asking is stealing."

"Patrick is right, but this time I think maybe you are not too much to blame. Where is the horse now?"

"When Patrick found me he untied it and sent it home."

"Good, then that is all right. So you rode farther?"

"I rode all night, until I was almost falling off. I didn't know where to go, so I followed the Polstjärnan—what is that in English?"

"The North Star."

"Yes, because I knew south would be back to South Bend and that was where he would go."

Hilda didn't have to ask who "he" was.

"By the time it was getting light and I couldn't see the star anymore, I'd come to some woods. I don't like woods."

Hilda nodded. The old Norse fear of forests and the spirits that might inhabit them died hard.

"But I couldn't ride anymore, so I tied the horse to a tree

and hid myself under some leaves and went to sleep. And Patrick found me there."

"How did he know to look for you there? And how was he able to go so far?"

"He knew about the dead boy. He found him."

Hilda drew in her breath.

"He reckoned I'd run as far as I could. And he knew the horse had been—had been stolen, so he thought I'd done it. So he got a horse himself, to look for me farther away."

"And he found you, and put you on a freight train to come to me."

"Yes. They were nice to me, the men on the train. They didn't ask any questions, just helped me." Erik yawned. He was exhausted. The telling of his terrible story had been hard. He sighed deeply. "And now what are we going to do?"

That was the question, wasn't it? Hilda sat back and tried to organize her mind. She had been battered by too many emotions to think at all clearly, and she was physically exhausted, as well. But something had to be done, and quickly. Erik wouldn't be safe here for very long, and he wouldn't be safe anywhere until the man was captured.

The man who would certainly kill him if he found him. She shuddered and tried to pull herself together.

"Erik, I do not know what to do," she said at last. "What you have told me changes everything. You are right. We can tell the police nothing, or nothing of the truth, anyway. They might tell the wrong person. And you cannot be seen, not until we have worked out a way to try to learn who did this."

She thought a little more. "Of course, the police are trying to catch him, too. Maybe they will."

Erik shook his head. "They think it was someone from the circus. It wasn't. I don't know any of them, and anyway, they were all doing their acts when it happened."

"Is there—Erik, I do not try to badger you, but is there anyone else it could *not* be? You know many men."

Erik tried his best, bringing his weary mind to bear with visible effort. "He sounded like an American, not a Pole or a Swede or anyone like that."

Well, that wasn't much help, but it was some. It eliminated anyone from their church, and most of the people from their neighborhood. It eliminated some of the people who had worked at the various places where Erik had held jobs. Many of them were immigrants. Many, however, were not.

It didn't solve the problem.

There was a grim little silence, broken finally by Erik.

"Maybe I should really do what I told Patrick to say I'd done. Go away somewhere, maybe to another town." He sounded forlorn.

"No, my little one, I could not bear it if I did not know where you were. I would think always that maybe something bad was happening to you. No, I must find a place for you, and a way to make you safe."

"How?"

"I do not know," she said again with a deep sigh. "But, Erik, I will see Patrick later today, and I go to see Sven and Mama and the others this evening, and we—"

"You can't tell them!"

Hilda shook her head and stood up. "I do not know what I will say. You must trust me. Silence is not always best, little one. Patrick and I will talk, and we will think what to do. You must trust me, and Patrick, and the Herre Gud. And you must promise to stay here until I come back. It is not safe for you to go anywhere alone."

He looked both frightened and rebellious. Hilda frowned and put her hands on her hips.

"Erik, if you will not promise, I must lock you in. I do not want to do that, but there is a good lock on this door and I will use it if you do not promise. This minute, Erik! I must go back to work, and if I leave before you promise, I will use the lock."

If there had been a mirror in the room, it would have

shown the two faces set in identical expressions of stubborn resolve. Hilda stood a moment or two longer and then turned to leave.

"Oh, all right. I promise." He spoke in English. Hilda realized only then that much of the conversation had been conducted in the Swedish Erik usually scorned. He was feeling better then.

He also sounded sulky in the extreme, but Hilda thought she could trust him. He had never broken a promise to her, not when he was little, anyway. She relaxed and ruffled his hair.

"I do not know when I will be back, but if I cannot come soon, Norah will bring you some food and something to drink."

"What if I have to . . ."

Hilda pointed eloquently at the chipped chamber pot in the corner, and closed the door behind her.

She looked at the padlock and hasp for a moment, tightened her lips, and went back up the stairs leaving the door unlocked. She, too, had promised.

26

The bow too tensely strung is easily broken.
—PUBLIUS SYRUS, CIRCA 42 B.C.

S HE was weary to the bone, but her afternoon rest time
was over and she knew she would not have been able
to sleep, in any case. Too much lay on her shoulders,
too much had to be done before she could even think about
rest.

She and Norah avoided each other the rest of the afternoon, fearful that their shared secret would somehow show in
their faces. Hilda was fearful, as well, that Norah would somehow worm out of her something that would put Erik in jeop-
ardy. At this point, the fewer people who knew anything at all,
the safer Erik was likely to be.

At five o'clock she slipped out for a moment to talk to
Patrick. They went to sit on their favorite bench, close to the
carriage house.

"Will John hear?" asked Hilda anxiously.

"He's out, exercising the horses I'd guess," Patrick said. "I
looked."

"Good. Patrick, what must we do with Erik? He cannot
stay here for long."

"You couldn't talk him into going home?"

Hilda gave a long, shuddering sigh. "He cannot go home. He cannot go to the police. He saw some of what happened when the little boy died, Patrick."

Very quickly, she told the terrible story. "So you see . . ."

Patrick saw. He stood and paced in frustration. "But it could be anybody!"

"Anybody except the circus people. Erik does not know them."

"But wait a minute! What about that person I overheard at the fire talking about Shaw?"

"Maybe it does not mean anything. Maybe it was about someone else. It is a common name, Shaw. And he is probably far away, anyway."

"No, I forgot to tell you. The trapeze people at the circus, they were the Shaws, all right. And the police have Shaw in jail. But they don't really think he could have killed the boy, and neither do I, to tell the truth."

"And neither does Erik."

"It would be a lot easier," said Patrick glumly, "if Erik could tell what he knows. He can't remember anything more?"

"Oh, Patrick, I could not try to make him remember. He is so afraid, and so tired, and it is all so horrible! Later maybe something will come to him, but we must keep him safe until then. What are we to do? I must go in soon, and I promised him we would make a plan."

Patrick didn't have to think twice. He had been thinking about the problem all day. "First off, I take him to me uncle Dan's house. No one'll ever think to look for him there, and you know Aunt Molly thinks the sun rises on your head. She'd do anything for you, and it's a big house. Nobody'll know but Uncle Dan and Aunt Molly."

Patrick's aunt and uncle were the only members of his family who truly loved Hilda, for she had saved Daniel Malloy's political career, and perhaps his life, less than a year past, at considerable risk to her own well-being. Patrick was right. That family would do anything for Hilda.

She nodded. "Yes! I do not know why I could not think of that."

"Because you're about to drop dead from worry and lack of sleep, that's what. You need to get some rest."

"Yes, but I cannot. Not yet. We must get Erik to safety, and I must talk to my family. I do not yet know what I will tell them."

"Well, anyway, you let me take care of Erik. Tell Norah to expect me—when? When's old Williams out of the way of an evenin'?"

"He has said I might go to see my family after our supper, when my chores are done. There is no dinner for the family tonight, only a tray for Mrs. Clem. After I go, about six-thirty or seven, I suppose, he will probably go to his chair in the servants' room and read the newspapers until I come home. Unless Mrs. Clem rings for him, he will stay there, and she will not ring. She never does."

"All right, then, tell Norah as soon as it's dark. I'll meet her at the back door and between us we can smuggle the boy out. Then I'll take him to me uncle's house, and then I'll go and fetch you home. I don't want you walkin' the streets after dark. I'm none too happy about you bein' out in the daylight, if you want to know the truth."

"I will be careful, but I will be happy if you can see me home. Only—do you not have to work tonight?"

"I do, but I've told 'em I've business to attend to. It's me best mates that're on duty with me tonight. They'll never tell the chief. Don't worry about me losin' me job, darlin'. You've enough to worry you without that."

"I am not so worried anymore, Patrick. You are—you have—" Her chin, and her voice, trembled.

"It's all right, darlin' girl. When this is all over, you can cry all you want. Meantime, just keep on bein' brave. We'll see it through, you an' me together." He ran one finger gently down her cheek and then strode down the back drive.

Hilda touched her cheek and for one brief moment felt a little better.

Her work for the day was soon done. When the servants' supper had been eaten and cleared away, and the sun was beginning to look big and golden, she took off her cap and apron and started for Sven's house.

She could not clear her mind enough to decide what she was going to say. A mixed bag of fears, lists of things she must do, and ideas tumbled through her weary brain, nothing staying at the forefront long enough for her to fix on it. She plodded along, trying to think of nothing except keeping an eye out for possible danger. It was fortunate that no one and nothing seemed to lie in wait for her. She might not, this time, have had the wit to avoid trouble.

Her family was surprised to see her, and none too pleased. Mama, in particular, was frigid. She looked up as Hilda entered and then turned her attention back to the sock she was darning. The others nodded and spoke a word or two, but they were clearly angry.

Hilda couldn't bear it. She leaned back against the door jamb and began to cry.

"So you are sorry for what you have done, you and that person you think is so wonderful? Maybe now you know what we feel." Mama threw the Swedish words like darts at Hilda, and like darts they stabbed her to the quick. She lost whatever resolve she had had.

"No! No, it is not the way you think! Please, you must *listen* to me!"

The passion in her voice got their attention, if they were not yet quite ready to credit what she said.

"Sven, is there another chair?" Hilda felt that if she did not sit down, she would fall down, and she had no wish to show any further weakness. She wanted their cooperation, not their sympathy.

Wordlessly Sven fetched a chair from the dining table. Hilda sat on it and gathered her scattered wits. There was only one thing to do. She hoped it was the right thing.

"Sven, close the door, please. And the windows."

"It is very warm in the house, Hilda," said Gudrun with a sniff. "Do you want us all to suffocate?"

"No. I want to tell you a story, and I want to make sure no one else hears." She said it in a whisper.

Sven looked at her, frowned, and did as she asked.

She took a deep breath and began, in Swedish. "Before I say anything more, I must ask you to promise you will tell no one. No one at all who is not in this room." She looked at the two youngest. "Birgit, Elsa, do you understand? *No one* must know."

The girls nodded. Mama and the older siblings looked stubborn. Hilda sent up a small prayer that the story itself would convince them.

"Then I will tell you that Erik has not gone away. He is here, in South Bend, but he cannot come home for a time. Not until he is safe."

There was an immediate babble of protest. Hilda shook her head violently. "No, do not ask questions, do not complain, not yet. And please speak Swedish, all of you. It is safer. Understand, we are all in danger, but Erik most especially. In danger of his life!"

The family was instantly silent, except for the shocked sound of indrawn breaths.

"There is something you do not know, maybe, unless you have read the newspapers this evening. I have not seen them; I do not know what they say. But a boy was found dead at that circus in Niles. Patrick found him. That is why he spent all night looking for Erik. Now Erik has told me that he saw it happen. It was maybe an accident, maybe not, but there was a man there, who ran away."

She drew a deep breath. "This is the bad part. Erik thinks that he knows that man. There was something about him that was familiar. He cannot yet remember what it was, and cannot put a name to the man, but the man does not know that. If he thinks Erik knows what happened and who he is, he will kill Erik, too. And the man could be almost anyone Erik knows."

Mama was crying, slow, silent tears that dripped, unnoticed, on the work in her lap. The others sat in shocked silence. The two youngest were frozen in what looked like sheer terror. Hilda looked at them uneasily.

"Elsa, Birgit, I am sorry you must hear this. It is not a good thing, but life is not always good. You must know, so that you understand that you can say nothing. It would be better if you thought Erik was far away. Do you think you can pretend that is so? No matter who talks to you?"

They nodded solemnly, but her uneasiness persisted. Elsa would be all right, maybe. She had an imagination and had been able, when she was a little girl, to tell believable tales of trolls and tomtes that had entertained the two smallest children. She would lie with great goodwill if she was questioned about Erik.

But Birgit? Precise, literal Birgit? Oh, she would certainly obey. If asked, by anyone, she would repeat whatever story she had been told to tell. The trouble was that she would tell it with all the dramatic flair of a lump of clay. She wouldn't convince a two-year-old.

It would have been better to keep the family in ignorance, but Hilda hadn't been able to do that. Weary and troubled, she had told the truth to escape their accusations. Well, now she had to live with it.

"It is your fault, you and that Irishman!" Mama's bitterness had gone beyond tears to fury. "If you had not taken him to that circus, against my wishes—"

"I know, Mama. You have told me enough times, last night, tonight. But I cannot undo that now, and Erik is safe. All I can do is to make sure he stays safe."

Summoning up one last bit of energy, she faced the last hurdle.

"You see now why you must stay quiet about all these things. And to help you not to talk, there is something that I will not tell you. You will not like this, but it is better, safer, that you not know. I will not tell you where Erik is, only that he is not with me, and he is safe."

A wave of protest arose, broke, dashed against Hilda. She sat in her chair, head bowed, and let the turmoil rage around her. She had done what she had to do, and she would not let the rage of her family undermine her resolve.

A knock, almost inaudible in the uproar, came at the door. Hilda heard it because she was waiting for it. She made quite sure it was Patrick before she opened the door and stepped out into the warm, muggy May evening.

27

*. . . the native hue of resolution/Is sicklied o'er
with the pale cast of thought . . .*
—WILLIAM SHAKESPEARE, *HAMLET,* 1601

PATRICK took her hand, tucked it away on his arm, and led her away before saying quietly, "I have bad news."

Hilda had thought she was too tired to feel anything. She had been wrong. She clutched Patrick's arm. "What? Is Erik—?"

"Quiet, now. We don't know who might be out there." He put his mouth close to Hilda's ear and said, "He's gone."

"What do you mean, gone?" It was an agonized whisper. Surely Patrick didn't mean what she thought he meant.

"He wasn't in the cellar. Norah couldn't find him anywhere. You left the door unlocked?"

"Yes, I remembered what it was like to be a prisoner behind a locked door. I could not do that to him. He promised he would not try to go away, and, Patrick, he has *never* broken a promise to me."

"He did this time. Norah found a note, but it isn't in English. Swedish, I suppose."

"Show it to me!"

"It's too dark. Wait until we get back. It isn't safe to stop under a lamppost."

He didn't have to tell Hilda to hurry. Indeed she pulled him along so fast he had to hold her back. "Don't run," he cautioned. "It's too noisy and it draws attention."

When they reached Tippecanoe Place, Hilda ran down the back stairs and led Patrick inside without any hesitation. Mr. Williams, who had been waiting to lock the door, bustled up at the sound of their voices and frowned at them.

"Hilda, you are very late! It is after eight-thirty! I trusted you not to abuse this special privilege, but you have done so. You and your family have caused quite enough disruption in this household—it must cease! Furthermore, Mr. Cavanaugh must leave at once. It is far too late for you even to think about entertaining a caller. The idea! You know the rules."

Hilda opened her mouth for an angry reply, but Patrick forestalled her. "This is an emergency, sir. I have had word that Erik is missing again. I will stay for only a few minutes, but Miss Johansson and I must talk about this before I leave."

Patrick was taller than Mr. Williams, and younger, and built more sturdily. The butler capitulated. "It is most irregular, young man, but talk, then, and be quick about it." He folded his arms and glared at them.

"We must talk privately, sir. We can go to the servants' room—"

"You most certainly cannot, not at this time of night!"

"Then we'll stay here, and you can go back to your reading. Hilda can lock up."

Mr. Williams had his faults, but stupidity was not one of them. Recognizing an immovable object, he threw up his hands. "I'll wait in my pantry. Five minutes!"

The moment he was out of sight, Patrick produced the note from his breast pocket and handed it to Hilda.

She scanned it. There were only a few words in Swedish, scrawled rapidly in a childish hand. "I am sorry. I must go. Someone came here, looking for me."

Her mouth dry, Hilda translated for Patrick, who cursed under his breath.

"The little fool! He would have been safe here!"

"Yes, perhaps, but he is only twelve, Patrick. He must have been very afraid." Her voice, oddly devoid of emotion, had taken on a pronounced Swedish lilt.

Patrick studied her face, found no clues there, and heaved a sigh. "Then I've got to go looking for him again. I guess I can't tell anybody, get any help?"

"No." Still that flat, dull voice. "Patrick, I must t'ink."

"Look here, are you all right? You sound peculiar, like."

"I feel peculiar, but I must t'ink only, now. Not talk, not feel, not at all." She closed her mouth tightly, and Patrick saw that her fists were clenched. She was keeping herself under control only with desperate effort.

"I'll go, then," he said when Hilda made no further comment. "I'll have to go to the firehouse first and tell me mates I won't be comin' in at all tonight. I don't s'pose you've got any idea where he might have gone to?"

"Not yet. I will t'ink. You could see if he has taken a horse. I do not t'ink he would, not a Studebaker horse, but it is possible. But, Patrick, come back in"—she glanced into the kitchen at the eight-day clock on the wall—"in two hours. Colonel and Mrs. George will be home, and Mr. Williams will be in bed, by dat hour. I will let you in. Maybe den I will have an idea."

Patrick didn't like to think about what would happen to her if she were caught admitting him to the house in violation of every rule, not only of the household, but of propriety. Now was not the time to mention it. Nor did he dare touch her. A caress might shatter her iron control, and she would never forgive him. He sketched a salute and let himself out the door.

She locked it and went up the stairs to her room. Let Mr. Williams discover for himself that Patrick had left. She had matters of life and death on her mind.

She didn't light the gas, nor did she undress. She sat on her bed and tried to force her brain into action. Precious minutes passed. No coherent ideas formed in her mind. She heard Norah come upstairs and go to bed early, but she made no effort to talk to her. She was so tired, so afraid, but she must make herself think.

Where would a boy go, a terrified boy who dared not go to anyone in authority?

And who had come inquiring for him?

Whoever it was, he had not believed the story about Erik going away to Patrick's relations.

He had come here! Oh, Herre Gud, what had Norah said to him? Had she told him the truth?

She left her room, went next door to Norah's, and shook her friend.

"Norah! Norah, you must wake up!" Norah was deep in her first sleep. Getting only a mumbled response, Hilda fumbled in the dark, found the jug of water, wet a towel, and applied it to Norah's face, none too gently.

Norah came to wakefulness with a scream that Hilda cut off with the towel before more than a squeak could emerge. "Hush! It is only me. Are you awake?"

She was. She wasn't happy about it, as a few muttered words made clear when Hilda removed the towel.

Hilda ignored them. "I must know, Norah. Who came to the house looking for Erik, and what did you tell him?"

Her urgency cut through the fog. Norah sat up. "How did you know anybody was here?"

"Erik's note. Who was it, and what did you tell him?"

"There was more than one." Norah ran a hand through her disheveled hair, perhaps trying to get her mind in order. "Regular three-ring circus it was around here tonight. And you ought to have seen His Nibs. I thought he'd have a stroke, for sure . . . First there was a boy, Andy somethin'. A good-for-nothin', I'd say, ragged and dirty. *He* got sent away with a flea in his ear, I can tell you. Then that Sergeant Wright come around with another policeman, Erik's boss at the stables, I guess. They wanted to talk to you. Said he hoped you'd all let Erik come back home soon, 'cause he was good at his job. An' Mr. Hibberd come, too. Wanted to say Erik could have his job back if he liked. I tell you, I got tired talkin' to all of 'em."

"But what did you tell dem, Norah?" Hilda's voice was anguished.

"Nothin'. Just told 'em all you was off lettin' your family know what had happened, and I'd let you know what they said."

"You did not tell dem Erik was here?"

"Not me. I might've told the police, to tell you the truth, if they'd sent somebody else. I think it's daft, listenin' to a kid that age and not tellin' the police nothin'. But I don't like that Wright. Oh, he's good-lookin' and all, but he's smarmy. So I told him we none of us knew nothin' except that Erik was a good ways away, with some of me distant cousins out in the country, and I thought I might hear from 'em in a week or two."

Hilda breathed again. "Where were you when you talked to dem?"

"Outside. Williams wouldn't let none of 'em in. We was just by—oh, so that's how Erik knew somebody was here! We was just outside the window to that cellar room."

"Yes. Erik saw t'rough de window, I t'ink, or heard de talk." Hilda made a decision. "Norah, I did not tell you before, but now I must. You were right not to tell anyone anyt'ing. We must be silent, because Erik saw and heard part of what happened when the boy died, in Niles, and he t'inks de killer is someone he knows. So maybe de killer is looking for Erik, maybe to kill him." She had to clench her fists hard then, dig her fingernails in and think strenuously about how much it hurt, to keep from breaking down.

Norah began to speak, words of shocked horror and attempted comfort, but Hilda stood up. "No. T'ank you, Norah, but now I cannot talk. I must t'ink. I am glad you told dem nodding. Good night."

Leaving Norah with an open mouth, she went back to her room, closed and locked the door, and sat down to think some more.

Norah had told no one that Erik had been at Tippecanoe Place. The killer, if he was one of those who had come to ask, could only guess about that, and guess, also, where the boy might be now. That was not much comfort, because she, Hilda, could also only guess. She knew Erik better than any of them, of course, but she had not spent a great deal of time with him in this country. She had not, for example, known that he liked to fish in Howard Park.

It was Andy who had told her that. Andy. He had come as a friend, worried about Erik. Hadn't he?

Hilda had thought of him as a boy, but he was as big as a man. Fifteen, perhaps. Surely he couldn't have done any of these dreadful things! But he knew Fritz well.

Could Fritz be lying about who had abused him because he was afraid of Andy? Or could Andy know something he had wanted to pass along to Hilda?

What about Mr. Hibberd? Why had he offered Erik his job back? Erik had said nobody at the print shop had liked him or the way he worked. So why would the owner of the shop come to ask questions? Why did he want to know where Erik was?

The police—why were the police still looking for Erik? Did they want to question him about what he might know? Did they—oh, Herre Gud, could they possibly think he had anything to do with the boy's death?

Perhaps they simply wanted him back on the job. Perhaps Sergeant Wright simply wanted an excuse to talk to Hilda. Perhaps they were simply being kind. How dreadful to be afraid even of kindness!

Erik must be found, and soon. Others might be looking for him, too. Certainly the killer was looking for him, and the killer, she reminded herself, could be almost anyone.

What did she know about Erik that might help her to find him?

She knew that he loved horses and they loved him. But many people knew that. Erik was unlikely, then, to seek haven in a stable.

He did not like woods. Very few people knew that. That fear was buried deep in the Nordic soul. Erik had told Hilda because she already knew and understood. It wasn't likely he would tell anyone else. He would be ashamed of such an Old World, old-fashioned superstition.

So he would not seek out a forest as his first choice of shelter. That was no help at all. There were few deep forests within miles. Most of the outlying countryside was laid out in farms, with maybe a small wood here and there, but no good place to hide.

So where, where, where? She had to guess. The killer had to guess. Maybe the killer believed the story about Erik being far away. Maybe he did not. He could not afford to be wrong. He had to guess, just like Hilda.

But she must guess right, and first.

She forced her thoughts to remain coherent. She thought about everything Erik had said to her in the last few weeks and especially the last few days. She made pictures in her mind and rejected them, feeling more frantic with each passing moment.

At last the alarm clock by her bed told her she had been there nearly two hours. It was time to talk to Patrick, and she had no idea what to tell him.

Too weary even to move quietly, she plodded down the back stairs. If Mr. Williams was not yet asleep, he would hear her. What did it matter?

She didn't hold up the back of her skirt, as she normally did. It was already filthy, she thought drearily. What did it matter if the hem got a little dustier? No doubt she looked, and smelled, as bad as Erik. Well, nearly as bad. Her clothing was not yet torn, and her boots were clean. She had seen tramps with boots that looked better than Erik's.

The thought struck her with such force she nearly fell down the last few steps. Catching herself on the railing, she ran to the back door and opened it.

Patrick was there. The outside stairwell caught a little of the light from the corner street lamp, and she saw him shake his head.

"Nothing," he said.

"Come in quick." She pulled him inside and locked the door again. "Where have you looked?"

He detailed a search of nearby stables, the neighborhood where the Johanssons lived, including the Schlager house, the Wilson Shirt Factory. "I don't know what I thought he'd be doin' there, but it was all I could think of. It's hopeless, Hilda. This is a big city, and there's too many places for one person to look in."

"Yes. But there is one place you have not looked, and I t'ink—I *think*—it is where you will find him. You did not try the place where the hoboes camp."

28

It is a bad plan that admits of no modification.
—PUBLIUS SYRUS, CIRCA 42 B.C.

HILDA'S accent was back to something resembling her normal speech. That, to Patrick, meant she was more nearly in command of herself. He drew breath to argue with her, to question her idea.

She spoke before he could. "It is not time to talk, Patrick. It is time to think. I have only, this minute, had this idea, and we must think what to do."

They were whispering, even though they were three floors away from Mr. Williams's bedroom, but now Patrick's voice rose. "What to do! What do you mean, what to do? We go and see where he is, that's what—"

"Hush! Come into the kitchen. We can light the gas there and talk properly."

Patrick muttered under his breath, but he followed her.

Hilda closed the kitchen door and lit one of the gas fixtures on the wall. Even with the flame turned down low, they could see each other, at least. She also lit one of the burners on the small gas stove, filled a pot with coffee and water, and set it to heat.

"Seems to me you're mighty calm about this," said Patrick. "I've been tearin' around town for the last two hours lookin' for your little brother, and here you're makin' coffee like it's a party."

"Patrick, do not be angry. I am sorry you have worked so hard for nothing, and I know you are tired. So am I. Coffee will help us think. And we must think well, for Erik's life is in our hands."

That sobered him. He sat down at the kitchen table, and Hilda sat with him, waiting for the coffee to boil. "You see, Patrick, I am right about Erik being with the hoboes, or I am wrong. If I am right, he is safe for a little while, because no one knows about them. I mean, everyone knows there are hoboes, but they do not know about Erik knowing them. If I am wrong, then he could be anywhere and we could waste much time looking.

"But what we must think about is what to do now. Yes, we could go and get him. But, Patrick, what then? Take him to your uncle's?" Hilda shook her head. "He cannot hide all his life."

Patrick thought about that. "No, I s'pose not. But he could hide for now while we think of a way to figure out who this villain is. With him in jail, Erik would be safe."

"Yes." Hilda nodded decisively. "So we must use our minds, hard. We must know who this man is, and then we must work out a way to capture him."

"Hmmm." Patrick, looking unhappy, sat with his chin in his hands. Hilda stood up and began to pace.

The coffee came to a boil. Hilda adjusted the gas. When it had brewed for a sufficient time, she turned off the heat, took an egg from the larder, and broke it into the coffee to clear it. Neither of them had spoken a word. She poured out the coffee, put spoons and the kitchen sugar bowl on the table, and sat down.

They didn't drink the coffee immediately. It was much too hot. Hilda looked at Patrick, her eyes heavy with the need for sleep, her mouth set unhappily.

They were too weary to talk, almost too weary to think. But think they must. The coffee cooled. They sat and sipped it. Patrick put his hand comfortingly over Hilda's, but neither spoke for a long time.

At last she raised her head and looked at Patrick. "There is only one way," she said.

"Yes," said Patrick.

Neither of them wanted to say it, but after a moment Hilda, fortified with the last of the strong black coffee, took a deep breath. "A trap."

"Yes," said Patrick again. "And with Erik as bait. I don't like it, Hilda."

"No, but it is the only way he will ever be safe. We can make sure he will not be hurt."

"We can try. Anything could go wrong, you know."

She knew. There was no point in talking about it. "Your uncle will help?"

"We can have all the help we want from me family. Do you think Sven . . . ?"

Hilda considered. "No. I think if we tell him, he might say we must not do it. And Mama would not allow it. This I think we must do without telling them."

"And Erik? Do we tell him what he's risking?"

"Oh, Patrick, that is the hardest part. I do not know! If we tell him, he might act so that the killer would know something was wrong. If we do not tell him, he might run away and be in worse danger."

Patrick hesitated, and then took the plunge. "Hilda, he's your brother, and you've got to be the one to decide. But— well, one day I hope he'll be my brother, too, and if he *were* mine, I'd tell him. He's a brave kid, and he's smart, and I think he deserves to know."

Hilda nodded slowly. It was a terrible thing they were proposing to do, but she could think of no other way. "Yes," she said. "And we must tell him now, *ja?*"

"The sooner the better."

They discussed the details, worked out their plan. "I would feel safer if we waited until morning, and it would be easier to find everyone." Hilda shivered a little.

"Yes, and the man we want, whoever he is, curse him, wouldn't feel near so safe. No, it has to be at night, Hilda. Tonight, or tomorrow."

She swallowed hard. "You are right. I must be brave."

"You are brave, darlin'. You know you are. You've done hard things before."

"Yes, but then it was only me at risk, myself. Now . . ." Her voice faded, then resumed as she stood, heavily. "Let us go *now*, Patrick. If I think too much, I might lose my courage, and I must not show Erik that I am afraid."

Hilda left the Yale lock on the latch. She might not have time, when she got back to the house, to wiggle in through a kitchen window as she had done once or twice before. The major sin of leaving the house open to intruders bothered her conscience, but it was necessary. If she were caught, she would be dismissed anyway. There was no time to worry about it.

She and Patrick hurried through the dark night. The air was warm, was soft with the promise of rain later. They paid little attention. Rain would complicate their plans a little, but getting wet was the least of their worries.

Patrick was uneasy about taking Hilda to the hobo camp at the curve of the tracks. It was no place for a lady. The way led through dark streets, past looming Studebaker warehouses, along train tracks. They had brought no lantern, in part because they felt safer unseen, but there was no moon and very little streetlighting in this part of town. As they made their way as carefully and silently as they could, every night sound seemed a threat. Hilda clung to Patrick's arm, her eyes searching the gloom, aching with the effort to see.

They rounded the corner of a train shed, and a faint, fitful light showed itself, low to the ground. "Their campfire," Patrick whispered. "It isn't far, now."

Hilda gripped his arm even more tightly.

They had to go carefully, lest they trip over sleeping men. "I hope none of them have dogs," Patrick whispered grimly. Hilda hoped so, too. A dog might well resent their presence; it would certainly announce them to the world.

But there were no dogs at the camp that night, only a fair number of men, sleeping as best they could on the bare ground or huddled by the campfire, drinking coffee and talking. Patrick's foot crunched some gravel; the wakeful men looked up, alert and wary.

By the wavering light of the fire, Patrick could not see if any of the hoboes were the men he had met. He stepped up closer, Hilda still on his arm, and cleared his throat nervously. "Gentlemen, please don't worry yourselves. I've come here with a lady who's lost her little brother. We thought he might be here."

As the men saw Hilda, they struggled to their feet and pulled off their caps in awkward respect. She looked around anxiously. She could see no small form among the shadowy figures, but then, she remembered, Erik was no longer very small.

"Please," she said. Her voice broke. "Please, my brother's name is Erik. He is twelve. Some of you helped him last night. I thought he might come back to you."

The tallest man spoke, and Patrick recognized his voice as belonging to the man who had taken charge in Niles. "Well, now, ma'am, he's pretty tired and pretty scared. Just what did you want with him?"

Hilda nearly fainted with relief. "Then—he is here?"

"Reckon he is, if he's tall for his age, and skinny, and yellow-haired. Sound asleep over by the shed. Told us he wanted to go on the road with us. It ain't a bad life, you know. He's run away from you twice now, ma'am, and I don't reckon I'd want to make him go back with you, not if he doesn't want to. We look after our own, you know."

The man sounded kind, but firm. Hilda wished she could see his face better. "I would like to talk to him," she said, her voice shaking. "I will not make him do anything he does not want to do."

The man ran a hand across his bushy, unkempt whiskers. "Well, now, I s'pose you could do that. Over here, he is. Watch your step." He lit a long piece of wood from the fire and carried it as a sort of torch to light the way.

Erik lay wrapped in a thick, heavy coat, no doubt one lent him by the hoboes. He looked very young, very fragile. Hilda knelt beside him, oblivious to the dirt and gravel, and put her hand on his face. He woke at once and turned a frightened face toward her.

"It is all right, little one," she said in Swedish.

"I'd be obliged if you'd speak English, ma'am," said the big hobo. He had apparently taken on the role of Erik's guardian, and Hilda's heart warmed to him.

"English, yes," she agreed, and turned back to Erik. "I am sorry to wake you, but it is very, very important. Erik, I have a plan to catch the bad man, the man who hurt Fritz and let the other boy die, but you must help. Or no, not 'must.' This you will decide for yourself, Erik. This I cannot tell you to do."

She took a deep breath. "You can do two things. No, three. The first thing is, you can go and hide in the house of Patrick's uncle. He is rich, and a good man. He will take good care of you and tell no one, but you will not be safe when you leave. The second is, you can run away with the hoboes. That is not what I want you to do, and it would make your family very sad, but I will not try to stop you. The third thing is what I would like you to do. You can be very brave, and stay here, and we can catch this terrible man. If you do that, it will be very frightening for you, but you will be in no danger."

She paused for a moment, and then went on. "I *think* you

will be in no danger. We will do everything we can to make sure, me and Patrick and his family, but I cannot promise you nothing will go wrong. It is fair that I tell you that."

Then she waited. Erik sat up, rubbed the sleep out of his eyes, and for a little while said nothing. Then, in a very small voice, he asked, "What do I have to do?"

29

Hurry, hurry, hurry—Aye, to the devil . . .
                          —CYRIL TOURNEUR,
       THE REVENGER'S TRAGEDY, CIRCA 1607

ILDA swallowed hard. "We will lay a trap, Erik. Patrick will tell everyone we can think of that you did not like it where he sent you, and you ran away again, but he has found you. He will tell all the men we think might be the one who has done all these terrible things. And we will tell them that I go to you, to bring you home. We think one of them will follow me, to try to find you. That one will be the man we want."

"And I must stay here and let him come?"

The quaver in Erik's voice told Hilda he had understood exactly what was required of him. She steeled herself. "You must decide whether you will do it. If you do, I will be here, and Patrick will be hidden nearby, and some of his brothers and cousins, and some of the police. They will be here to watch what happens, and also to catch the man. All you will need to do is stay here, and try not to be afraid, and act surprised when the man comes. Can you do that?"

It seemed to Hilda that the small sounds of the night magnified themselves as she waited for his answer. A log settled in the hoboes' fire. The hoot of an owl was answered by another. Somewhere in the distance a train uttered its mournful whistle.

"Will my friends be here, too?"

"You betcha we will, son," said the hobo. "Couldn't keep us away."

That was a complication Hilda hadn't thought about. "But you must be hidden," she said anxiously. "The man will not come to Erik if he knows anyone else can see him."

"Ma'am," said the hobo with dignity, "we're right accustomed to makin' ourselves scarce. Don't you worry none. We want this feller caught just as bad as you do. T'won't be long, you see, before folks get to sayin' it must be some tramp doin' all those things. Well, I reckon you can guess we don't want that kind of talk. 'Sides," he added, "we've gotten right fond of the boy, here." He patted Erik's shoulder. "We don't want nothin' to happen to him."

There was another long pause, and then Erik, with sturdy nonchalance, said, "Okay. I'll do it. When?"

"It must be at night. It is, tonight, a little bit late, but I do not know if it is safe to leave you for a whole day."

"Don't you worry," said the hobo again. "We'll make sure he gets fed and hid and looked after till tomorrow night, if you think that's best. There's not a man of us doesn't know how to melt into shadows when we has to, and we'll make sure the boy sticks with us."

"Tomorrow night, then, Erik. Soon after nightfall, I think."

"Okay with me." Erik sounded somewhat happier, and Hilda remembered that a day, to someone his age, was a very long time.

"I will go now, little one. Try to sleep. Do you need anything?"

"Nope." Erik yawned. Hilda gave him a hug and then, without looking back, she returned to where Patrick was waiting.

No one had broken into Tippecanoe Place, Hilda was relieved to discover when they got back to the great mansion.

No one had awakened and found her missing. The house lay curled in slumber. Hilda kissed Patrick good night, locked the back door after him, and crept silently up to her room. To her surprise, she fell at once into exhausted sleep and had to be shaken awake by Norah in the morning.

Norah was full of questions, of course, and Hilda had to fight the impulse to tell her what was happening. Deciding that a portion of the truth was best, Hilda said only that Patrick had found Erik and that he was safe, but no, they still had not unmasked the villain.

The day was long. Hilda went up to her room to rest after lunch. She knew she had to conserve her energy for the night ahead, but this time her nerves wouldn't let her sleep.

What if something went wrong? What if the man found Erik by himself, before she and Patrick and the others could get there to protect the boy and capture the man? What if the villain managed, despite all the precautions they could take, to harm Erik?

What if nothing happened at all, no one followed Hilda, and they couldn't capture the villain? Would Erik and his family and other boys continue to live in fear?

She went back to her work almost with relief. It was torture to dust and sweep and scrub when she wanted to be with her brother, but it was better than lying on her bed, her head filled with horrific visions.

She hardly knew whether she feared or hoped for evening to come. The clocks in the house seemed now to be creeping, measuring off the time in agonizing inches, now to be leaping forward at a terrifying rate. Tick-tock, tick-tock, closer and closer to joy or doom.

Patrick came at five o'clock. He had changed his work schedule so as to have the night off, and had alerted his family and some of his friends to the plan. All was in readiness.

"I haven't told the police yet. They're just as apt to go lookin' for him themselves and charge in, boots and all, ruinin' everything. But look here, Hilda. It would be better for

me to be the one to lead him, whoever he is, to Erik. I can say
I'm goin' to bring him home to you, or take him to me uncle's
house, or—"

"No, Patrick." Hilda had anticipated this objection, and
was ready to meet it. "That will not work. Then the villain will
wait here, or at your uncle's. And when Erik does not come,
he will know something is wrong, and we will maybe lose our
chance forever. No, you must say that you tell them because
you thought they might be concerned about him, and that I
am of course eager to see him, but that I cannot leave the
house until my work is done for the day. They will understand
that. You will say that you do not know what I will do then,
whether I will bring him here or take him to his home. And
you will say that you cannot tell them where he is, because
you are afraid, still, of the wicked man."

"Which the good Lord knows is nothin' but the truth,"
Patrick interjected. "And that's why I think I—"

"No, Patrick. I know you are afraid for me. That is good. I
am happy that you care for me, and worry. But I will go
tonight. He is my brother."

"And if you aren't the stubbornest mule of a Swede I ever
knew, I'll—I'll call meself an Englishman!"

Short of profane expressions he wouldn't use around
Hilda, it was the worst thing Patrick could say.

"I am stubborn, *ja*. Sometimes it is good to be stubborn.
When will you come for me, Patrick?"

He sighed. "When can you get away?"

"Whenever you say. This is important, Patrick. It is too
important for me to worry about Mr. Williams's rules. I will
not ask him if I may go. If he tries to stop me, I will tell him I
go anyway."

"But aren't you afraid you'll lose your job?"

"There are other jobs. What time?"

"As soon as it's really dark, then. I'll bring a lantern."

"Yes. And come to the porte cochere. I will try to leave
without him knowing, if I can."

"And how do you plan to get back in, when it's all over?"

Hilda stamped her foot. "Patrick! I cannot think about that now! Through a window maybe; I do not know. Now go, and I will wait for you when night has fallen."

Hilda was fortunate that there was no dinner party that night. The servants had their meal, served and cleaned up after the family, and by eight-thirty Hilda was able to escape to her room. She took off her white cap and apron, and reached for her black winter hat, but paused to think. It was necessary that she be visible, without being obvious about it. Recklessly she took up the discarded cap, a starched lace affair, and crushed and folded it into the semblance of a rosette. She pinned it to the side of her hat. It looked peculiar, and the cap was probably ruined, but it was certainly visible.

After a quick but heartfelt prayer, she ran silently down the back stairs to the main floor. A quick glance in either direction, then she let herself out the porte cochere door. Patrick was waiting with a lantern, but it was shuttered. He had no wish to announce himself to those inside the house.

"The police will meet us there?" she asked after a look around. She spoke close to Patrick's ear and he had to strain to hear.

"No," he answered in the same low tone. "I didn't tell them where we're going. I don't trust them not to give the show away. No, a couple of them are to follow us from the corner of Sample and Chapin. I told them to keep themselves well hidden."

"Sergeant Wright?"

"Don't know. He wasn't in the station when I went there."

Hilda nodded. "I think he will come." She hesitated for a moment and then went on in a stage whisper, meant to be heard. "We had best get away quickly. Mr. Williams does not know you are taking me to see Erik."

By the light of the street lamp on the corner Hilda could see Patrick's wink of approval. She clung to his arm. The little gesture helped with the illusion she was trying to create. It also felt extremely comforting.

As soon as they were out of sight of the mansion, Patrick opened the dark slides to let the lantern light shine out. Hilda began to chatter.

"Is he well, Patrick? Does he want to come home?" The questions sounded artificial to her ears. She hoped anyone else listening might think them natural.

"He wouldn't talk much," said Patrick, on the principle of sticking to the truth whenever possible. "I think he's a bit scared."

"Do you think he knows anything about the boy who was killed in Niles?" Hilda's voice wasn't loud, but it was clear.

"I wouldn't know, but it's pretty sure he was there at the time." Patrick, too, spoke clearly, if quietly.

They kept it up, trying not to give away too much, trying to make sure they would be followed, acting the fear they really felt.

Hilda's apprehension grew with every step. This was a stupid, a terrible thing to do. Why had she not sent Erik to safety, somewhere far away? Even if he never saw his family again, it would be better than . . .

She could not finish the idea, even in her mind. She took a tighter grip on Patrick's arm and made another remark designed to lure a killer. They were committed to this course of action now, and they were under a terrible obligation to do it right.

When they reached the hobo camp, no one was in sight. There was no fire. The place seemed utterly deserted.

Even though that was what Hilda had expected, she felt her heart lurch. There was no pretense in her anguished whisper to Patrick: "Where is he?"

"I don't know! There, now, don't cry, darlin'." He pulled Hilda close and breathed into her ear, "He's hidin', don't forget. I'm sure he's fine. I'll pretend to have a look 'round." Aloud, he said, "I'd best look for him."

"No! Don't leave me, Patrick!" That cry was real, too.

"Come with me, then, if you want." He hugged her shoulders and again murmured in her ear, "Be careful not to say anything if you see someone."

Hilda had almost forgotten that a number of stalwart men, including the police, were keeping the watch with them. It made her feel only slightly better.

The windy night was filled with ominous noises. Here a small board was blown with a crack against an abandoned boxcar, there a loose shutter flapped on a roof. Somewhere a door or a gate creaked as it was blown back and forth. Boughs of distant trees moaned, new leaves rustled madly. Hilda couldn't hear the crunch of their own footsteps on the gravel-strewn waste ground.

Nor could she see much. Clouds hid both moon and stars, and the light from their lantern did little to penetrate the gloom. Once she saw a pair of feet, the feet of a large man, and drew in her breath for an involuntary scream, but Patrick's hand clamped down hard on her arm and she released the breath again.

"Well, he's gone again, so far as I can see," said Patrick when he felt the little drama had gone on long enough. "I'd best see you home, darlin', and then I'll come back and look a little more." His arm did a little dance.

Hilda picked up her cue. "Very well, Patrick. If he is just hiding, I will be very angry when we finally find him."

Patrick nodded, just slightly, just once, and he led Hilda away, talking quietly all the while.

When they were well out of sight of the hobo camp, he darkened the lantern once more. "We'll have to feel our way back from here," he said in her ear. "Be careful."

"Yes," Hilda breathed in reply, "but we must be as quick as we can."

They tried to hurry, but the night was so dark they could move only at a pace Hilda found maddeningly slow. There were no sidewalks or paved streets in this part of town.

"I'm going to try to find the tracks," Patrick murmured. "It will be easier to feel our way along there, and we can't get lost so long as we stay between the rails."

"But *hurry!*"

They found the railroad line, or Hilda did, by stumbling over one of the rails. Patrick kept her from falling and stepped over the rail with her.

It was easier, now. The wooden ties came at regular intervals; they soon learned the rhythm and stumbled seldom.

The darkness was so complete it was hard to tell just where they were. Hilda thought they must have gone too far, and was about to tell Patrick so, when the clouds parted for a moment and the moon brightened the scene. They paused to get their bearings, and that was when they heard the scream.

30

It is remarkable that the administration . . . permits the police to rest under the almost universal charge described by the forceful, if not elegant word, "rotten."

— SOUTH BEND *TRIBUNE*, JULY 16, 1903

PATRICK uttered an oath, opened the shutters of the lantern, and ran toward the sound. Hilda screamed and ran, too, heedless of her dress, of her footing, of anything except the sound of Erik in trouble.

She fell, tripping headlong over some obstacle, she never knew what. She heard a seam in her skirt give way as she caught herself on her hands and tried to scramble to her feet.

The silent darkness of a moment before was alive now with sound and light. Shouts, the flare of lanterns from behind sheds and railroad cars, the thud of heavy footfalls.

Patrick, now far ahead of Hilda, disappeared into the fray. Half-limping, half-running, sobbing, she followed. "Patrick! Erik! What is *happening?*"

She ran around a shed and stopped, bewildered.

There seemed to be a lot of people. Lanterns swung, shadows moved crazily, but dark bodies converged on some sort of melee. More shouts, curses. Grunts and panting. Finally a triumphant voice, Patrick's voice: "Got him!"

Hilda pushed her way through the angry crowd. "Please! It is my brother, please let me through!"

The men fell back a little. Hilda reached the center.

There was Erik, standing next to the tall hobo, who clasped him tightly 'round the shoulders. Hilda could see the tears glistening on her brother's cheeks.

A few steps away four men held firmly to a fifth, who, arms and legs pinioned, still struggled and cursed.

The one who held the prisoner the tightest was Patrick, his arms confining the man's neck in a complicated hold.

The prisoner was Sergeant Wright.

He saw Hilda and screamed in a choked sort of voice, "Miss Johansson! Tell these fools to release me! They're allowing Erik's attacker to escape! Damn it, man, let me GO!"

"No!" shouted Erik, at the same moment that Hilda, steel in her voice, said, "Hold him!"

"He is the one!" Erik said desperately. "He said he came here to take me home, but he was the one at the circus, with that boy—the boy who died—I know he is the one—the smell, and—" He made a gesture with his hand and wrist.

The man who was sheltering Erik spoke, and Hilda recognized him as the hobo who had befriended him. "I heard it all, ma'am. When the boy screamed, this feller started cursin' and carryin' on somethin' terrible. He said—well, it's not fit for me to repeat, ma'am, but he's a villain, right enough. Who is he?"

"A policeman. And a killer."

"Ah." There was no surprise in the hobo's voice.

Erik choked on a sob. Hilda fell on her knees before him and clasped him in her arms. "I know, little one," she murmured, again and again, in Swedish. "I know. It's all over now. He'll never hurt anyone again."

* * *

It was a tired, disheveled, and ragged group who assembled, much later, in Sven's front parlor drinking coffee.

Mama sat in the rocking chair in the corner, Erik on the stool next to her. He was nearly asleep. His head rested against her elbow; with her other hand, she caressed his hair.

Sven and four of his sisters sat wherever they could find space. Near Erik, Hilda sat on the red plush divan, Patrick on the end. And ranged uneasily against the walls stood Patrick's three stalwart brothers, making the small room look even smaller.

"Erik!" demanded Freya. "Wake up! I want to know how you knew for sure. I still think the sergeant is too nice a man to do such a thing."

Erik roused for a moment. "I thought he was nice too—at first. Then he started being—funny. I didn't like it." He eyed Hilda, then his younger sisters, and said no more.

Mama glared at Freya and snapped, "Let him sleep. He has been through enough." She spoke in Swedish, but her meaning was plain to everyone in the room.

"Let Hilda tell her part, then," said Freya, refusing to be diverted. "I'll bet she knows most of it."

"If she knew, she had no business to let Erik be put in such danger!" Swedish again.

Hilda rolled her eyes and translated for the benefit of the Irishmen. "Mama thinks we should not have allowed Erik to help us tonight."

Sven frowned. "It is not good that he was frightened, but he was in no real danger, was he? With so many men hidden to watch over him?"

Mama pursed her lips and refused to look at anyone except Erik.

"You see, I did *not* know who the man was, not for sure. I had an idea, but I could not be sure, and I did not dare tell anyone, because I might be wrong.

"I thought, when I was rested enough to think well about anything, that maybe it was a smell Erik recognized, and I remembered that Sergeant Wright always wore toilet water. There was maybe something else, too, on his hand or his arm—"

"He has a scar," Patrick said. "An ugly, puckered one, on his right wrist. I saw it once when he was at a fire, helpin' control the crowd, and he had his cuffs off. It would be covered most of the time, so Erik had probably never seen it before that night after the circus, but if Wright had his shirtsleeves rolled up then, it would have shown, even in a very dim light."

Hilda nodded. "But I did not know about the scar, and a smell—it is nothing to prove a man is a killer! But I know how smart Erik is, and how brave. I was sure he would know the man again, especially if it was night and he was a little frightened again, like before. And then the man would give himself away, and we would know."

Mama frowned fiercely.

"But what about that man Shaw, then?" asked Freya, the irrepressible. "Fritz said it was him."

"Fritz was told what he had to say. He was too afraid of the sergeant to do anything else. And the rest—about the fight in the Shaws' wagon and all—it was the sergeant who told us that. It was all a lie, just like what Wright said at the fire." Hilda raised her eyebrows at Patrick.

Freya looked bewildered, but Patrick nodded thoughtfully. "He was there at the fire," he said. "He could have been the one I heard."

"He kept us busy chasing a lie for several days." Hilda was bitter about that. "Never mind, Freya. I'll tell you later."

"Oh, all right, but I still don't understand about you. I thought Sergeant Wright was courting you."

"Mama thought so, too," said Hilda, looking at her mother, who averted her eyes. "I think now he—um—just wanted to know what I knew." And stay close to Erik, she added mentally, but that thought was not for consumption by Birgit and Elsa. It was one she wished she, herself, could forget.

"Anyway, Erik was very brave to do what he did. And when he screamed, Patrick was there, Patrick and his brothers, to save him and catch that awful man."

"We were almost too late," said Patrick in a near whisper. "I was countin' on whoever it was believin' that we'd left, Hilda and me. But o' course the police knew what the plan was. That meant Wright knew he had only a little time to get Erik away before we got back."

"We'd have got him," said one of Patrick's brothers. Hilda still didn't know which was which. "We were ready. He might have got a block or so away, but we'd have caught up with him."

"He did not dare to move after Patrick took him in that tight hold," said Hilda with some pride. "Patrick might have broken his neck."

"I wish I had," said Patrick. He said it very softly, but with such grim intensity that Sven, across the room, heard.

Sven put his coffee cup on the floor and stood. "Hilda, I want you to tell me something."

His voice was very much that of the older brother, stern and compelling. Hilda looked up at him, full of apprehension.

"Was it your idea, or Mr. Cavanaugh's, to put Erik in this position tonight?"

"We thought of it together," she said defiantly. "But Patrick did not want me to be there. He wanted to deal with it himself."

Sven pursed his lips and then slowly, gravely, took the few steps across the room to where Patrick sat. "Then, Mr. Cavanaugh, I believe I must thank you and your brothers for saving my brother's life. It seems that Hilda has an infinite capacity for becoming involved in trouble, and you, sir, often help get her out. My family and I thank you." He held out his hand.

Patrick stood and clasped the proffered hand. "Hilda has helped our family, too. I was glad to return the favor."

Hilda, who had been holding her breath, let it out in a soundless sigh. Her mother, eyes turned away, said nothing.

Her four sisters dared say nothing, either, but Freya slowly winked, while Elsa and Birgit stared openmouthed.

Hilda stood. "I must go home now. Patrick will see me home."

And no one objected when Patrick offered his arm to her and she firmly took it and walked out the door with him.